Since 2004, internationally bestselling author **Sherrilyn Kenyon** has placed over sixty novels on the *New York Times* bestseller list; in the past three years alone, she has claimed the No.1 spot seventeen times. This extraordinary bestseller continues to top every genre she writes within.

Proclaimed the pre-eminent voice in paranormal fiction by critics, Kenyon has helped pioneer – and define – the current paranormal trend that has captivated the world and continues to blaze new trails that blur traditional genre lines.

With more than 25 million copies of her books in print in over 100 countries, her current series include: The Dark-Hunters, League, Lords of Avalon, Chronicles of Nick, and Belador Code.

Visit Sherrilyn Kenyon online:

www.darkhunter.com
www.sherrilynkenyon.co.uk
www.facebook.com/AuthorSherrilynKenyon
www.twitter.com/KenyonSherrilyn

Praise for Sherrilyn Kenyon:

'A publishing phenomenon ... [Sherrilyn Kenyon] is the reigning queen of the wildly successful paranormal scene'
Publishers Weekly

'Kenyon's writing is brisk, ironic and relentlessly imaginative. These are not your mother's vampire novels'
Boston Globe

'Whether writing as Sherrilyn Kenyon or Kinley MacGregor, this author delivers great romantic fantasy!'
New York .... Lowell

Dragonmark

SHERRILYN KENYON

piatkus

PIATKUS

First published in the US in 2016 by St Martin's Press, New York
First published in Great Britain in 2016 by Piatkus
This paperback edition published in 2017 by Piatkus

1 3 5 7 9 10 8 6 4 2

Copyright © 2017 by Sherrilyn Kenyon

The moral right of the author has been asserted.

A CIP catalogue record for this book
is available from the British Library.

ISBN 978-0-349-41325-9

Printed and bound by CPI Group
(UK) Ltd, Croydon, CR0 4YY

Papers used by Piatkus are from well-managed forests
and other responsible sources.

MIX
Paper from
responsible sources
FSC® C104740

Piatkus
An imprint of
Little, Brown Book Group
Carmelite House
50 Victoria Embankment
London EC4Y 0DZ

An Hachette UK Company
www.hachette.co.uk

www.piatkus.co.uk

To my boys and husband, who are my life and who have seen me through untold heartaches. For my readers, who are family, and to my friends for keeping me sane. Thank you all for being part of my life.

And as always, to Monique, Alex, Robert, John, Eric, Ervin, Mark, Nancy, Angie, Jen, and everyone at St. Martin's and Trident who work so incredibly hard on the books to make them a reality. And The MB Staff: Kim, Paco, Lisa, and Carl, and all the volunteers who keep things running smoothly! You guys are the best!

Dragonmark

PROLOGUE

Samothraki, Greece
9501 BCE

"The bastards cut his throat. Severed his vocal cords entirely."

Materializing from the frigid depths of his lair, Falcyn cursed as he saw his brother, Maxis, dragging Illarion into his dark den behind him. For years they'd been searching for their youngest dragon-brother, who'd been captured by humans for who knew what nightmarish horrors. But no trace had ever been found of the young dragonet.

Until now.

So large that he barely fit through the cave opening, Maxis released his hold on their baby brother and allowed Illarion to sprawl across the floor. Blood seeped over his yellowish-orange scales. Both of his wings lay broken and useless against the cold earthen floor.

His breathing shallow as he struggled desperately to stay conscious, Illarion blinked his serpentine yellow eyes slowly. Painfully.

So much needless misery—it radiated from the child to the core of Falcyn's being. And it made his own eyes turn vibrant red as bloodlust rose within him. Knowing he couldn't tend his brother in his native dragon body, Falcyn shifted into the hated form of a human.

The moment he did so, Illarion let out a gurgling hiss and rolled into an attack position even though it had to be agony for him to move.

"Easy, little brother." Falcyn spoke in their native drakyn—the true language all dragons spoke. One that sounded feral and unintelligible to humans.

He held his hand out toward Illarion as a peace offering. While he might temporarily wear the skin of a man, Falcyn was and would always be a dragon in his heart and soul. "You know me. I need this form to heal you. Now calm yourself before you do more harm."

A single crystalline tear fell from the corner of Illarion's serpentine eye.

In that moment, Falcyn hated humanity more than he ever had—something he wouldn't have thought possible. He reached to stroke Illarion's gray-scaled snout. "Shh . . ."

Illarion backed up, then collapsed.

Maxis gasped as he gently nuzzled the much smaller dragon and tucked his own wings against his body.

Ignoring the fact that Max was a giant beast of a dragon who could swallow him whole in his current incarnation, Falcyn shoved Max's head away. "He's passed out from the pain, Yaya. Now move your hulking arse so I can help him."

Max shuffled back to make more room. "Will he live?"

"I don't know. Where did you find him?"

"I didn't. He found me." Guilt and agony haunted Max's eyes. "He can no longer Bane-Cry. The bastards took his ability to call us when they slit his throat."

Falcyn ground his teeth as even more unmitigated rage tore through him. "Then we will teach him a new way to call for us. One they won't be able to stop."

Max nodded and looked away. "This is my fault."

"Don't!"

"It is and you know it. My mother gave him to the humans to get back at me for what I said to her. Had I cooperated . . . given her what she—"

"She would have screwed over the world, and he still would have paid for her cruelty. The lilitu are without the ability to care for their young. You know this. My own mother watched as they sacrificed me on my birth. All it did was teach me that we're in this life alone, cradle to grave, and make me bitter and disgusted."

Max swallowed before he spoke again. "Is that why you can take human form when no other dragon can?"

Falcyn didn't answer his question. It was the one thing he would never speak of.

To anyone.

No one needed to know anything about him. Not even those he considered his brothers.

Nor was he the only dragon who could shift . . .

But there were many things his brothers and sisters didn't need to know about this world.

"His physical injuries are not so bad," he said, changing the subject. "We should be able to heal him."

"But?"

"He's only a child. I fear for the mental damage they've wrought."

"As do I. They were using him to fight in their wars. Riding him like he was a thoughtless beast."

Falcyn winced. Too bad Illarion hadn't been a full-grown drakomas. That was the fury the humans deserved.

Not the small child who lay helpless at his feet. One who'd been unable to fully fight them and give them the fyrebreath and dragon's fury they deserved.

In that moment, he felt the demon within him rising. It wanted to set fire to the world and watch it burn to cinders. If mankind had any idea how often they tempted him toward destruction they'd never sleep again.

Times like this, it took everything he had not to give in to that darkness that burned inside him, calling for the hearts and souls of all sentient beings.

Even the gods.

That was what made it so hard to relate to Maxis.

Part Arel, he was the direct opposite. He saw only good inside even the most corrupt.

It was sickening, really. The way his brother wanted to help others. That innate need Max had to protect and to serve. It was ever revolting.

Now Illarion had been given his first taste of humanity. And like Falcyn's, it had been a most bitter meal. If the dragonet did survive this, he wouldn't have Max's blood in him that would want to protect the human vermin who'd tortured him.

Illarion's father was the Greek god Ares. A war god. The humans had no idea what they'd been toying with. With the blood Illarion carried, he would become one of the strongest of their kind once he reached his majority.

A dragon of fierce, unmatched powers.

Falcyn's hand lingered at the brand on his brother's back where the humans had marked Illarion like cattle. It festered and bled.

Sadly, it would leave as bad a scar on his body as this entire ordeal had left on his brother's psyche.

May the gods have mercy on them all. . . .

For Illarion would not.

1

St. George's Day, 619

"If you could piss away stupid, I daresay the majority of the candidates today might actually stand a chance against you."

Edilyn ferch Iago bit back a squeak of laughter at Virag's unexpected words. "Shh . . . you get me into enough trouble as it is."

Barely the size of her index finger, he looked up at her with a cocked, innocent brow. "Can't help it if the rest of those wankers are too dim-witted to see your ebullience right before them." Walking along the edge of the shoddy, worn sill, he mocked the village voices they could overhear passing by her open window, making faces and rude gestures to go along with their innocuous conversations. It was all she could do to not burst into laughter.

"Stop it, or I shall force you back into your bottle."

He snorted dismissively. "As if *that's* a threat. I like my bottle. Much better than being out here with all these—" He glanced out the window to the street and wrinkled his nose. "—people." With a fierce shudder, he sat down on the edge to eye her with an expression of even greater distaste. A light breeze fluttered his golden, gossamer wings. "Why are you dressed like that again?"

"St. George's Day."

"Ah." Virag released a long, tired sigh. "This year went fast. So what are your plans for being unacceptable to the dragons this time?"

Biting her lip, she stepped forward and revealed the small vial she'd purchased from the old witch woman who lived on the edge of the forest. She held it out toward him. " 'Tis the scent of rotted bear guts."

He let out a fierce sound of protest before he fell back and kerplunked on the sill. "That would do it," he choked between gasps for air. "Yeah. Please . . . bathe that off your skin before tonight. My eyes are watering. Burning, too." Crossing his eyes, he stuck his tongue out and feigned a dying pose that left one arm and leg dangling off the edge as he continued to sputter and gasp.

Edilyn laughed at her half brother and his antics. It was hard to take him seriously in his natural state of a gold-skinned, golden-haired and -eyed, winged sprite. Like this, he was ethereally beautiful and a far cry from the terrifying dark-shadow beast she knew he could transform into. "What kind of pixie are you?"

"Not a pixie," he snarled indignantly as he kicked his fur-covered legs at her. "Kikimora! Sheez! Inhaling those fumes has already addled your noggin. Any more and you'll be as daft as those lackwits outside."

She snorted at him. "Like you don't smell worse than that on a regular basis."

He laughed. "Only when I'm drunk on elderberries or mulberries . . . or . . ." He paused to consider the truth of her accusation. "Well, you might have a point." Sitting up, he bent his knee and propped his whiskered chin on it to watch her while she finished belting on her mismatched costume. He was devilishly handsome with his short, spiked hair and angular features. But it was his personality and the way he always looked after her that made her love him best.

Since the day he'd magically appeared in her room three days after the death of her father, she'd been hopelessly devoted to her older brother. There was nothing she wouldn't do for him.

Not that he needed her help, given the depths of his godlike powers. Honestly, she had no idea why he'd come to her or why he stayed. She liked to think that he loved her, but the tales said that his kind were incapable of feeling such things. Immortal nightmare spirits were supposed to be devoid of any tender emotions whatsoever.

Rather, they were self-serving, vain creatures who used human weaknesses to prey on others. To manipulate humans for the gods and higher powers they were enslaved to or had bartered with.

Yet in spite of his random, surly threats, he remained by her side. Ever loyal. Ever caring, and even kind to her.

He was just like their mother, who'd been as full-blooded a kikimora as he was. Only her mother had made a pact and given up her immortal life to become human so that she could marry Edilyn's father.

It was something they never spoke of, as it angered Virag to an unholy level.

"How do I look?" Edilyn turned around and held her arms out to show him her outfit for the day.

He burst into raucous laughter that would have offended her had it not been the reaction she wanted. "Ridiculous."

She grinned as she reached for her horned helm. "Good. That's what I was going for."

He made a sound of utter pain-filled disgust. "What in the name of all Samhain is *that* on your head?"

"My battle helm."

He screwed his face into a mask of horror. "What are you? A bull?"

"What?" She feigned innocence. "Dragons have horns. I'm trying to blend."

"You're not a dragon." His tone was flat and dry.

"True."

He let out another pain-filled groan. "Thank the gods your parents are dead. I shudder at what they'd say if they could see you looking like this."

She stuck her tongue out. "Don't you have an old lady to frighten or torment?"

Virag scratched at his chin and lowered his legs to swing them over the sill's edge. "Not really. Rather harass you. It's far more entertaining."

"Great." She sighed wearily.

As she started to smear the gut scent on her skin, Virag stopped her. "Really, precious . . . overkill. Given the heinousness of your ridiculous outfit, you don't need to smell on top of it. No dragon is going to choose *anyone* wearing that *scytel*. You'll be lucky if they don't all flee at your approach. Probably vacate the hall like it's afire. They might even leave the whole of the Ynys Prydein."

She capped the vial and smiled again. "Good." Last thing she wanted was a forced mating with some hybrid creature who'd eaten her father. And probably his own as well. "I don't understand why we need them for our army, anyway. What's wrong with riding horses?"

"For one? They can't fly." He fluttered his wings at her. "Something I'm rather fond of doing myself, and I highly recommend. Poor you, to be so deprived."

"So? There's much to be said for having two feet planted firmly on the ground. I can't break a wing and fall three hundred feet, where I shatter all my bones and land as a big bloody stain to be spooned up later."

"The second reason?" he continued, ignoring her interruption. "Horses tend to burst into flames when dragons attack them and spew their fire all over them. Other dragons don't do that. They fight back."

He had a point. Still, she wasn't willing to give it to him. "Horses take up a lot less room and they don't eat you out of house and home."

"I wouldn't go that far. Horses eat quite a lot, including your shoes."

"Humph." She wrinkled her nose as she belted on her sword. "This is a stupid tradition to hold on the day that celebrates a saint known for slaying dragons, don't you think?"

"Perhaps. But it's more a taming celebration. Man over beast, and all that rot."

"Do you really believe that?"

"You're asking a nightmare demon if I think a dragon can be tamed by a mere mortal? Sure. Why not? I'll go with it. I've seen much stranger things in my day like a kikimora who gives up her immortality to be a dirt farmer in some backwoods village kingdom no one's ever heard of. Penllyn . . . really?"

She rolled her eyes at his sarcasm over their mother's decision that he still held against her. Meanwhile, the dreamer in Edilyn thought it was the most romantic thing she'd ever heard of.

If not the most practical, given what it had ultimately cost her mother.

And father, too.

Sadly, she'd never met a man as honorable as her father. Nor as loving or fierce. If one existed, he definitely didn't live in Penllyn. It was little wonder that her mother had been so reluctant to let go of so rare an individual as her father. Such a unicorn needed to be cherished and kept.

Edilyn cast a wistful smile at Virag. "I just want to be a warrior on my own. Like my father was."

"Then I wish it for you."

"Thank you."

"You're very welcome. May you never live to regret the decisions you make." And with that, he pushed himself to his feet and flew from the sill to the small, dark green bottle that made up his home. In a flash of white light, he vanished inside it.

Edilyn carefully picked the bottle up and secured it to her neck by the thick black leather cord, then settled it in the pocket of her tunic.

"Can't see. Let me out!"

"You sure?"

"Absolutely. I want to witness this coming travesty firsthand."

Laughing at his dry tone, she obliged him and placed the bottle to hang outside her orange tunic so that he'd be able to see as it swung loose about her neck. Then, she grabbed the handcrafted bow her father had made for her so that she could leave for the Great Hall, where the day's celebration should be in full swing.

But as always, her heart wasn't in the coming festivities, and it definitely wasn't light. "Why is it ever the curse of humanity that the most cherished dreams of our lives are oft the hardest to achieve?" Edilyn sighed at the rhetorical question that had haunted her for years. A sane woman would give it up and let go this useless pursuit of her heart.

If only she were sane. . . .

With a deep breath, she glanced about the sparse, unwelcoming room that had served as her dormer since the day her father had died in battle. How she prayed that after today she'd look at it no more. Nor would she be forced to work in the dreadful fields with the other impoverished orphans the church had taken in.

That this year, she'd *finally* succeed in making Brenin Cynfryn realize that she could stand as a warrior without a dragon lord to partner with.

Determined to be steadfast in her goal, she took her weathered war bow into her gloved hand. Yet as she did so, an unbidden memory of the previous eight years of failure and heartache brought a most bitter lump to her throat. *Don't think about it.* The past didn't matter.

Only today did.

Today would be different. She could feel it deep in her bones. Destiny would finally take note of her and reward her diligent persistence.

It would.

Hoping desperately that she wasn't lying to herself—again—Edilyn lifted her chin. She slung her brown leather quiver over her shoulder before making her way from the small hut toward the Great Hall where everyone in her village had gone for the day's celebration and test of arms.

For the last eight years on this very day, she'd won every game she'd participated in. Everyone knew that, like her father before her, she was the best archer among them. Her sword skills were at the top of their clan—while she could be overpowered, she could never be out-skilled. She'd even won the obstacle footrace.

Eight years straight.

And still Brenin Cynfryn refused to grant her freedom.

Stop it! Life's not fair, you know that. It's not supposed to be.

If it were, her parents would still be with her.

She categorically refused to let her negative thoughts impugn her courage or undermine her confidence as she neared the massive building that dominated their small town.

Nothing and no one would get in her way. Not this time. One way or another, she was going to prove to them all that she was worthy of being one of the brenin's marchawgion.

"Get out! You're not welcome here!"

Concerned that angry shout might be directed at her, Edilyn slowed as she neared the oversized oak doors that were marked with ornate iron hinges. Then she realized the two guards shoved at an old man who was dressed in dirty rags and matted furs.

"How many years do we have to throw you out, slagge?"

With an admirable obstinacy, the old man refused to budge. "I was given an invitation, same as the others. Is this not open to all?" The ancient voice was barely a raspy whisper that came from the depths of his filthy hood. Oversized and in the shape of a wolf's head, the cowl revealed no trace of his features.

"Beggars aren't welcome. Now begone with you before I set the dogs on you! Bother us no more!"

This time, they shoved him so forcefully that the one would have fallen had Edilyn not caught him. But that charity cost her, as it was quite painful when his back slammed into her front, proving that he was much heavier and more hale than his shabby, hunched-over appearance gave him credit for.

Stifling her cry of pain, Edilyn helped him regain his balance before she stepped away to address the guards. "He's right. 'Tis St. George's Day. Should we not all be on our best behavior? After all, that blessed saint gave away everything he had before he died to those who were less fortunate. Surely we can find a modicum of charity for those in need?"

The guard sneered at her. "You would break bread with something that reeks like the back end of a horse's arse?"

Rather that than feasting with a dragon.

Wisely, she kept that thought to herself.

Instead, Edilyn cast a kind smile to the old man, who was strangely quiet now. "Better to break bread with someone who smells like an arse than to be one. Stenches can be washed off. But an ass today is an ass tomorrow."

The guard curled his lip as Edilyn boldly took the old man's arm, and in direct defiance of their cruelty, led him inside. However, her victory was short-lived as the guard's parting words struck her like a blow.

"Speaking of asses, you can tell by the ample girth of hers that she's never skimped a meal or been picky over when or where she finds sustenance. Never mind with whom."

The other guard laughed at his snide tone while she ground her teeth, refusing to give them the satisfaction of knowing that those cruel words had struck their mark, and left another bloody wound on her heart.

"Ignore them, my lady. You are by far the most beautiful one here."

She smiled at the old man's kindness and patted his arm. Poor thing must be blind as well as indigent. "Thank you, gentle sir. But I'm no lady. Merely a simple archer's daughter."

"I take it your father is very proud of you."

Those words brought a lump to her throat. "I should like to think he would have been."

"He's passed on?"

"Aye. When I was a girl."

"I'm sorry to hear it."

She offered him a kind smile. "As was I. He was everything to me—a good man with a cheerful disposition, and a wonderful father. He is sorely missed." Her bottle necklace warmed, as it always did whenever Virag wanted to let her know that he was with her and sending her his love and affection.

Edilyn released the old man's arm to show him her most prized possession in all the world—her beloved bow. "But he did give me this, though, before war took him from me." With a bittersweet smile, she ran her hand over the runic engraving her father had placed above the grip while she'd watched him work on it with eager eyes.

"*My precious Edilyn?*"

Nodding, she blinked back a sudden round of tears. How she missed her father. Instead of becoming easier, his loss and absence seemed to sting more with every passing year.

Same for her mother.

She cleared her throat. "He made the bow himself from the strongest yew he could find, and then gave it to me on my birthday. Since it was just the two of us, we would spend hours in practice. Every day. The women of the village used to say that I drew my bow so much I had the arms of a man." A frown creased her brow as she recalled the old wives' tale about how it was bad luck to cut down a yew tree. Supposedly, anyone who dared such would die within the year.

Was it mere coincidence that her father had perished on the thirteenth day of the eleventh month after he'd dared cut the wood for her bow? She'd always wondered about that.

Not wanting to consider something that was forever near her mind whenever she held her bow, she led the old man to a seat. "You rest and I shall get you some nourishment."

Still completely shielded by his filthy, worn cloak, he complied.

And as she made her way across the room, she overheard numerous familiar conversations. . . .

While the seasons and years changed, the people here and their concerns never did. She'd heard their whining gossip so much, she could recite it from memory. And with that sudden thought, she had to bite back a laugh as an image of Virag's earlier play in her room went through her head.

Her brother was ever rotten.

"Think you he'll come this year?"

"The Ancient Drakos? Nay, not likely. He never does. I'm told he cares nothing for pomp and noise."

"I heard the brenin offered the Ancient Drakos the hand of his only daughter in marriage to join our ranks."

Another nobleman scoffed. "I heard he'd give up one of his *sons* to him in marriage to procure him as our guardian. His skills are *that* great. 'Tis said none can defeat him."

"Son, nothing. I heard he'd give up both testicles for it."

They laughed at something that rang with truth, knowing their brenin. And it explained why Morla was dressed in such fine and expensive armor. No doubt she was hoping to do her father's bidding and catch the attention of one of the oldest, most lethal of the dragon clan. The mysterious Illarion Kattalakis who no one had ever seen.

Not even the dragons themselves. They merely whispered tales of him—as if afraid to say his name too loudly lest they somehow offend him with it.

He was more myth than reality. A shadowy sorcerer of unparalleled power and skills who hated humanity with legendary fervor. Older than time itself, he only left his cavernous den to prey on those who angered him. And those fools, he consumed with his incendiary breath.

The circulating tales said that he guarded ancient treasures and weapons forged by the old pagan gods. Some even believed he might be the keeper of the Holy Grail itself. Others speculated he'd been the snake who'd tempted Eve in the Garden of Eden.

Never had she known any creature to hold more outlandish speculations. Many claimed he was the inspiration for the new tale the Geats, Jutes, and Wulfings had been passing around that had recently come to their shores—the tale of the noble Beowulf, who'd been slain after a slave had stolen a golden cup from a mysterious dragon's lair. Furious over the theft, the dragon had razed their settlements, demanding the return of his enchanted cup and the head of its thief.

After all his noble battles and victories that included slaying the infamous Grendel and his mother, Beowulf had finally succumbed to the dragon's fierce prowess.

Some tales claimed Beowulf had slain the dragon before the

Geat had died of his wounds, but others said that was a total fabrication made by Beowulf's clan in order to save face. That the dragon had reclaimed his cup and feasted mightily on the hearts and heads of all those who'd taken part in its theft.

It made her wonder what such a beast might really look like. Not that she cared. She hated all dragons for what they'd done to her father and people. The only good one was a dead one. She was merely curious about the creature that inspired such fanciful legends.

Nothing more.

Daydreaming about the coming day and how she wanted it to end—in her favor, of course—Edilyn prepared a platter for the stranger.

As she reached for a cup of mead, she felt a pair of angry eyes glaring at her. She glanced up to find Morla curling her lip in distaste at Edilyn's mismatched clothes.

Tall, slender, and with hair so golden, it appeared to have been spun by the fey, the noble maid dropped her gaze to the platter. "Don't you have food at home?"

Her dark-haired best friend, Lady Nesta, snorted. "No wonder she's the size of a man. She eats like three of them."

Annoyed by the spoiled women who'd never known a day of starvation or hardship of any kind, never mind the grief that had plagued Edilyn all her life, she didn't bother to correct their misconception. They weren't worth her time. Instead, she took the platter to her guest, who seemed to be watching Morla and Nesta intently. Not that she blamed him. They were two of the richest, most beautiful women in their village, and every man, young and old, would sell his soul for a night with them.

If only they weren't quite so aware of it. And if they hadn't allowed that knowledge to go to their oversized heads. Heads that if they grew any larger, would overfill the hall and cause the two women to be unable to stand upright.

But that was their problem. Not hers.

Grateful she didn't have to live with those massive egos and petulant moods, Edilyn set the platter down next to her new friend. No sooner had she stepped back than the doors opened to admit their long-awaited guests of honor.

The dragon clan.

Her lips involuntarily curled as they entered the hall in all their expensive finery. Their dark leather armor was trimmed in gold and silver that glimmered in the bright sunlight as it spilled in through the windows. More beautiful than any human, they were here for the Winnowing—to choose the best, noblest warriors of her clan to be their partners in war.

And life.

Supposedly, it was the greatest honor to be chosen by them. The men and women of her clan clubbed each other for the chance and spoke of little else the rest of the year. All the eligible youth practiced for this day, hoping to be among the ones taken to live with them.

It was the last thing she wanted.

"Why do you tremble so?"

Rage. But she didn't answer the old man. She couldn't.

"Are you afraid?"

"Nay," she scoffed.

"Not even a little?"

She shook her head. "Not even a little," she repeated his words. "Merely concerned that I *might* make muster."

"What do you mean?"

Pain lacerated her soul at his innocent question that forced her to remember things she wanted to keep buried. But what was the use? And before she could stop it, the truth tumbled out of her lips. "Every year I audition for the brenin with my skills, and I best all my clansmen."

"Then what's the problem? Why aren't you mated to a dragon?"

"Don't want to be. Rather, I want the brenin to choose me as a marchoges."

"But not for the dragons? Why?"

"Because she knows she'd break their backs and cripple them," Gryffyth said as he walked past them.

His friends burst out laughing.

Stifling the urge to toss something at the arrogant prick, Edilyn narrowed her glare at Gryffyth's worthless hide while he and his cronies vanished into the crowd.

But she wasn't so callous.

She turned back toward the old man. "I've no interest in being chosen by the dragons. In fact, I never appear for the Winnowing. Rather, I withdraw before it begins. I want to stand on my own. But the brenin refuses me. Every year. He only wants draiogogion for his army."

And speaking of, the call rang out for the contestants to gather.

She glanced down at her guest. "Do you need anything else before I join them?"

"Nay, my lady. Good luck to you."

"And to you, my lord . . ." Heat crept over her face as she realized how rude she'd been to him. "I'm so sorry that I forgot to ask your name. How thoughtless of me."

"You've been anything but thoughtless, dear Edilyn. Call me Emanon."

"Lord Emanon. It's been my pleasure to assist you." She gave him a slight bow, then ran to join the others.

Emanon sat in silence as he watched Edilyn push her way through the crowd. Taller even than most of the men, she held an exotic kind of beauty that made her stand out from the others. Or maybe it was her zest for life. Her innocent exuberance in the face of their negativity.

She was a beacon through their dull storm.

He'd never seen anyone so determined in the face of adversity. Rising to his feet, he kept to the outer edge of the crowd so that he could watch her compete. Like a free-flowing ebony banner, her long black hair blew behind her as she raced to her place beside the others. Her cheeks were mottled bright red from her exertion while her ample breasts rose and fell with her excitement.

Aye, she had a lush, full body that said her appetite wasn't just for life, but was robust in all things.

Several of the women curled their lips or rolled their eyes at her approach.

She smiled in response and boldly wished them luck. She was such a cheeky, jovial lass, dressed in a garishly orange tunic that fell to her feet. It was interlaced with green and blue that seemed faded or smeared. She'd placed sprigs in her hair and horned helm.

Emanon wasn't sure if she wanted to appear as a drunken sprite, a tousled flower . . .

Or a drunken bull that had rolled around a field for a bit.

And that forced a rare grin from him. If he could appreciate anything in life, it was that degree of defiance in the face of those who wished you ill.

"Did he come with you?"

Emanon narrowed his gaze at the man nearest him as he heard the brenin's gruff voice questioning Tarius Kattalakis. A rare Katagari Drakos, Tarius was the current leader of this group who'd come here to pick mates from the humans. It was a spring ritual they'd been practicing for decades now, and it left Emanon sickened.

Every year, the Drakos came, watched the humans, and opposed the Greek gods' decree for their people by selecting a mate when they all knew that only the Fates themselves were supposed to assign them their life partners. It was this kind of hubris that had caused their race to be first cursed.

Yet the Katagaria Drakos, because their progenitor Illarion was a son of Ares and had been biologically bonded against his will to the Arcadian prince who was a grandson of the goddess Nyx, thought themselves above it.

Dumbasses.

Illarion would never intervene on their behalf to save them from the wrath of the gods. Honestly, he had no greater love for their hybrid species than he did for humanity. If the truth were known, he'd tried his best to get his brother to leave them all to die after their creation. The only reason any Were-Hunter had ever survived was the benevolence of Maxis Drago. He was the one they should be currying favor to.

Not Illarion.

He was the one dragon who would gladly hand-feed them to their enemies, and laugh while they bled out at his feet. The son of Ares cared nothing for these creatures. Nothing for their races or their wars. He felt no obligation to them whatsoever.

And he never would.

Burn in Tartarus, you bastards. . . .

Their treatment of Edilyn was exactly why Illarion had no love of humanity. The whole problem with human beings was that they were so seldom humane. And those whose genetics had been combined with animals were even worse. Instead of being made better, they'd sunk to an all-new level of viciousness.

Emanon ground his teeth as he started to leave so that he wouldn't have to stomach another moment of their vile presence, and yet his gaze went back to Edilyn.

She rubbed at the bottle on a string she wore around her neck, and smiled a smile that enchanted him in a way nothing ever had. Damn. It left him breathless.

Worse? It quickened his blood and fired a need inside him to taste those lips. For the first time in his exceptionally long life, he actually desired a taste of human flesh for something other than a quick, bloody meal.

He hungered for her.

What the Hades?

And still the men in front of him continued to speak. "Nay, he's not here. But fear not. We are more than able to protect your village and people."

"Did he not receive the offer to marry my daughter?"

Tarius sighed. "It's not that. They claim he's sterile."

"I heard he's insane," Bracis added. "As the first of our kind, he couldn't handle the transition from beast to man. While he physically survived, he broke mentally."

"It's a shame." The brenin let out a tired sigh. "Our enemies grow bolder and stronger. We lost half our best warriors in the last battle."

"Well, we're here now and we'll take care of you." Tarius turned his head back toward the contestants. "Who is that tacky brunette who keeps winning?"

"Edilyn?"

"Aye. She's here every year." Scoffing, Tarius passed a smirk to Bracis. "She's a stout one, isn't she?"

The brenin shook his head. "I think she's hoping one of you will take her since no man among mine will have her."

"Why's that?"

"She's an orphan with no property. No dowry. No family. All she has in this world is that old war bow she carries. Pathetic, really."

And yet she who had so little held more kindness than any of the rest. The last thing that made her in Emanon's eyes was pathetic.

As he watched her racing against the others, his respect for her grew. They did everything they could to trip her, knock her from the path, or cause her to veer from the goal.

Edilyn didn't falter or stumble. Steadfast and determined, she ran with her head held high and kept her gaze on the goal, without regard to any of the others or the tricks they used to foil her journey. Nothing and no one could stop her.

In the end, she crossed that finish line first. Way ahead of the others.

It'd been a long, long time since he'd seen such intrepid courage. Instead of congratulating her for the achievement in spite of their ill behavior, they glared. Their hatred increased to such levels, he could feel it as a living creature slithering in the air around them all. It raised the hairs on the back of his neck to see such tangible evil.

Still, she continued on with resolute grace. She even glanced at him, smiled, and waved.

Stunned by that unexpected act, he gaped and felt the most peculiar fluttering inside his stomach. One that only fueled his hunger. He had no idea what it was. Never had he experienced anything like it.

Brushing at the perspiration on her brow, she went to retrieve her bow for the last round of games. He didn't miss the way her exotic features softened ever so slightly the moment her hand touched the wood.

Aye, it was exceptionally dear to her.

With an adorable bite to her lips that betrayed her uncertainty, she brushed her gloved fingers against her father's engraving as if taking comfort from it. Then she moved into place before her target and carefully nocked her arrow. She held the bow and arrow low to her thigh while she waited patiently for her turn.

One by one, the archers released their shots.

When it was her turn, Edilyn lifted her arms with the mastered precision that came from years of practice. "You've got this," she whispered in a tone so low, he was sure that he was the only one who heard it.

But as she pulled back the string for her release, the unthinkable happened.

Her bow snapped in half. The top part, along with the arrow, fell to the ground, while the bottom remained in her firm grip, tethered by the string.

"No!" Tears filled her eyes as she lost the last link with her father.

The immaculately dressed Morla tsked at her. "Shame, that. But it's not like anyone was ever going to choose you anyway. No one was even looking." Then she made her shot.

Emanon took an involuntary step toward Edilyn before he even realized it. Yet he knew there was no comfort anyone could give her for what had just happened.

For what the rich bitch had just rudely and needlessly taken, without regard of consequence or compassion.

Morla had cracked Edilyn's precious bow to remove her from the competition because she knew she lacked the skills to compete. Because she'd been unwilling to spend the years it took to learn the skill. Nor did she care what she robbed from another. All that mattered was that *she* got what she wanted. To hell with the rest.

How could she?

Suddenly, a loud cry rang out. No sooner had it settled than the crowd around them erupted into a vicious attack party. Cloaks

were thrown off soldiers who'd come in under the guise of cele-
brants.

Morla and the rest of the humans who'd been competing to be
mates for the dragons scattered to hide.

So much for being warriors, or for showing any skill. That said
it all about their loyal bravery.

The only one who stood her ground was Edilyn.

Seizing Morla's dropped bow, she slung her quiver over her
back and began aiming for their enemies. Enemies who were quickly
cutting a swathe through the Kattalakis dragons and the brenin's
people.

Awed and impressed, Emanon watched Edilyn fearlessly protect the very assholes who'd been so cruel to her. Why? He couldn't
imagine. Personally, he'd let them all burn. The only ones he'd ever
protected were his brothers and sister.

No one else was worth a single drop of his blood.

That had always been his firm stance and his oath.

Until he saw the killing blow aimed at Edilyn's back. A blow
she couldn't see at all, as she was focused on others. In that one
quick, vital heartbeat he made a decision he'd sworn would never
be his.

Lunging to save a human's life, he transformed into his true
dragon form.

Edilyn froze as a huge, massive dragon circled her. With a giant,
spiny head, he formed a wall of yellow-orange scales that rippled
and shimmered in the daylight. Terrified, she thought he was attacking her at first.

Yet rather than attack, he let loose a stream of fire at those who'd snuck into her village. With a ferocious hiss, he whipped his tail and lowered his black-tinged wing toward her. *Climb aboard, my lady Edilyn.*

Her jaw fell as she recognized the deep voice that no longer held the cadence of an ancient man. "Emanon?"

His yellow serpentine eyes gentled as he gave her a bashful grin. *Illarion, my lady. And it would be my honor to serve you.*

The moment his true name was spoken through telepathy, their enemies ran for the gates in full retreat.

But Illarion wasn't having it. As soon as Edilyn was secured on his back, he ran them down and made sure they never threatened her people again.

Edilyn held tightly to his scales as she felt his muscles rippling beneath her legs and thighs. A saddle and reins appeared magically for her, along with a harness that secured her in a way that guaranteed nothing would separate her from her mount. It felt as if she were fused into place.

Fear and respect for the dragon's immense power mingled inside her as she watched him effortlessly reduce their enemies to ashes. She held her breath in awe, trembling and praying that he never turned that anger loose on her.

You have no need to fear me, Edilyn.

She wasn't so sure about that. And while she'd always scoffed at the stories of the Ancient Drakos's powers and dismissed them as fantasy, she now wondered how many of those tales were actually factual.

Dear heaven, he was exactly as they'd said. His powers greater than any dragon she'd seen or heard of.

Once he'd dispensed of their enemies with virtually no effort on his part, he returned to the archery field and allowed her to dismount from his back. The bodies of the wounded and killed surrounded them. The entire area was still in chaos as people sought to find their loved ones or to render aid.

Though she had often resented how they'd treated her over the years, Edilyn felt no joy at seeing her people like this. How could anyone take pleasure in another's pain? Seek harm when they didn't have to? She'd never understand cruelty for the sake of it.

What was wrong with people?

There in front of her, Illarion shifted from his dragon form into that of a man. Only this time, he wasn't old or hunched over.

He was glorious.

With a gasp, she looked up into a pair of silvery blue eyes that radiated intelligence and heat. Never had she seen eyes that color. And they were set in a face of utter male perfection. Firm, sculpted jaw, high cheeks, and an aquiline nose. Best of all were lips that neither mocked nor sneered at her. His long, dark auburn hair fell free and held a number of small braids laced with feathers.

"Were you injured in the fighting?" she asked.

Never by a human.

A shiver ran up her spine at the realization that his voice didn't come from his lips. Rather, he spoke to her through her thoughts. No wonder he'd kept himself completely covered before. He must have been disguising the fact that the old man wasn't really speaking, rather telegraphing his thoughts to them.

With a tenderness that belied the size and strength of him, he brushed the moisture from her cheeks where she'd cried over her broken bow. His gaze darkened with curiosity as he lingered his thumb over her lips.

"Wait!" The brenin rushed forward. "You've grabbed the wrong woman. She's not my daughter. Morla is beautiful and rich. She's the one you seek."

Illarion cast an irritated glare toward the much smaller man as he dropped his hand from her face. *I didn't come here for a false princess with a withered heart and callous soul who knows the value of nothing, except her own overestimated self-worth.*

Edilyn frowned at the disdain in his voice. "Then what *did* you seek?"

In a very dragonlike manner, he cocked his head to glance at his drakos brethren, then to the brenin. *Nothing. Truly. Every year I come for shits and giggles, expecting the same, and every year I've been turned away by fools who never fail to reaffirm my lowly opinion of humanity. It's always been a game to me to see how far I'd get.*

He curled his lip at Morla. *The promise of a princess definitely didn't lure me here, for they are vain, worthless creatures who are only concerned with their own petty needs. I have no need of such a nuisance.*

Then, Illarion turned back to Edilyn and the corners of his lips lifted ever so slightly. *Instead, I've found the rarest vision of all.* He met her gaze and the sincerity in that cool blue depth sent a chill over her. *I found a most beautiful queen who knows her own mind and isn't afraid to protect those surrounding her. One who sees what's around her and isn't blind to the feelings of others, or their value. For more than ten thousand years I have walked this earth, my lady. Never have I seen your equal, in heart or form. And if you will have me, repugnant and disgusting as I am to you, I swear that I shall ever be your faithful servant.*

With those words spoken, he handed her the bow her father had lovingly made that Morla had tarnished and tried so cruelly to destroy in her vicious vainglory.

Fully restored.

2

Mated to a dragon.

And not just any dragon . . . one of the oldest of the Were-Hunter breeds. Illarion Kattalakis.

This was most definitely not the way Edilyn had seen this day ending. Not in her worst nightmare, and given the fact that her mother had once been a warrior of nightmare demons, that said a lot.

They knew nothing of each other. Not really.

Yet here she was. Feeling stupid and vulnerable. And wishing she'd chosen a better outfit.

At least one that matched.

That sensation wasn't helped as Illarion righted the horned helm on her head and reminded her of her intentionally matted hair and the brambles in it, while he patiently waited for her response. He arched an expectant, teasing brow.

Gracious, he was the handsomest man she'd ever seen.

For a dragon.

"Father!" Morla wailed. " 'Tis unfair! He's supposed to be *my* husband! My dragon! I want it!" She stamped her foot. "I did everything to win him and get rid of her. Do something! Now!"

The expression on Illarion's face said it would be a mistake for the brenin to try.

When he started forward, the other dragons kept him back.

"My lord?" Tarius approached Illarion respectfully. "It's an honor to meet you."

Illarion's features turned to stone and all humor and friendliness fled his eyes as he turned toward his brethren drakos. This was the cold countenance of a killer. A lethal beast who hated them all.

How peculiar that he had no greater fondness for the dragons than she did.

At her delayed answer, sadness darkened those enchanting eyes. *Very well. I shall bother you no more, my lady. Good life to you.* He pulled his hood up to conceal his features again and turned to leave.

"Wait!" Edilyn spoke before she even realized it.

Illarion stopped and turned back toward her.

You hate dragons. You hate them all, she reminded herself.

And yet . . .

She saw in her mind the way he'd rushed to protect her.

Remembered the way he'd teased her and made her feel warm, even while the others mocked her during the trials.

This was all kinds of stupid. She knew it.

Even so, she couldn't stop the words from leaving her lips. "I'll come with you."

With a hesitation that seemed incongruous for such a powerful creature, he held his hand out to her. But he made no move toward her, letting her know that the final decision was entirely up to her and her alone. He would not encroach on her choice in any way.

That made this much easier.

Illarion wasn't like the others. He seemed as uncertain of this as she was.

Her hand shaking, she took his and stepped into a most uncertain future with the last creature she'd ever thought to meet.

The moment she made that tiny physical contact, a bright flash blinded her. Everything spun until she couldn't gather her bearings. She floated in what appeared to be a dream. Or was she falling? She couldn't quite tell what was happening.

Not until she found her feet on solid ground in the center of a huge, dark cave.

A massive cavern, really.

Yet it wasn't cold. Rather it seemed a pleasant temperature. Nor was it overly dark. Especially since torches lit themselves the moment they appeared inside it.

She turned around slowly so that she could examine the glistening black walls. "Where are we?"

My home.

"Which is?"

Where I live. His tone was flat and dry.

As well as irritating.

She gave him a peeved stare. "And that is?"

In a place where no one can find me. He lowered his hood to stare at her. *Are you afraid now?*

Edilyn knew what he wanted and she refused to give him that satisfaction. "Should I be?"

One corner of his mouth lifted. *Most would be terrified.*

"I'm not most."

Nay, you are not, especially for such a tasty little morsel.

For some reason, the note in his voice warmed her, in spite of words that could be construed as a threat. "And I still wish to know where this place is."

Where I cannot be disturbed or attacked.

Or found.

Someone even less trusting than she. Had she not borne witness to it, she wouldn't have believed it possible. Truly, this was amazing.

And that made her curious about another matter where he was concerned. "Are you incapable of speaking?"

I have no vocal cords, if that's what you're asking. They were severed by a cruel hand when I was a small dragonet. He slowly drew near her, stopping just as he reached her back. Yet he didn't touch her. Not that he needed to. His presence was so fierce and intimidating. Overwhelming. The power of him bled and filled the room to capacity.

It electrified her.

And terrified her in spite of her bold words and resolve to not let it. He was a savage beast, even in the guise of a man. No matter how hard she might want to pretend otherwise, she couldn't deny it. There was something innately raw and commanding about him. Something so sinister and cold.

He didn't have to say he held no value for human life, it was as if the very fiber of his being telegraphed it for others.

With a gentleness that belied the bloodthirsty dragon she'd seen rip apart her enemies, he lifted a lock of her hair from her shoulder. A light smile hovered over his lips as he brushed her hair against his skin and inhaled its scent. In that moment, she was grateful she'd listened to her brother, who was being uncommonly quiet through all of this.

Which led her to a much more awkward thought. . . .

"Do you wish to rut with me now?"

He let out a peculiar scoffing sound of air rushing from between his teeth. *Is that what you want?*

She swallowed hard at his question and the fear it wrought. While she knew he would expect it, she had to admit to her reluctance. Not that he was unappealing, but rather . . . "I've never been with a man, my lord."

Illarion froze as those unexpected words slapped him. He would have thought a woman with her zest for living would have tasted many. The fact that she hadn't . . .

He was dumbfounded.

More than that, he was at a sudden loss. There was only one reason he could think for it.

Are you not old enough?

She laughed, then caught herself. "Sorry. I guess compared to someone who's over ten thousand years old that's a legitimate question. And aye, I'm more than old enough. Rather long in the tooth for most human women."

Then why—

"Personal choice. Have you seen the idiot men in my village?"

"As if that!" Virag shouted. "She's a pain in the ass. Men tend to notice."

Edilyn cringed as her brother finally announced his presence in the most rude and annoying way possible.

Illarion arched a brow. *Should I ask?*

Sighing, she shook her head and lifted her bottle up for his gaze. "Nay. But since you have . . . Illarion, meet my brother, Virag."

Virag manifested from the bottle into a full-sized man. Blond and muscular, he stood eye to eye with Illarion. While most were intimidated by Virag's intensity, Illarion merely folded his arms over his chest and postured bored tolerance.

He swept a bemused stare over Virag's body that said he was unimpressed. *Kikimora. Rare to see a male of your kind in the world. You must be highly sought after.*

Now it was Virag's turn to be caught off guard. "You know what I am?"

Illarion nodded. *Been around a long time. Seen many unsavory things.*

Virag laughed at the way he said *unsavory* and the small dig it carried. "I can imagine."

Well, as you are as capable of transporting your sister out as I am, then I shall leave you both to your futures. Good day.

Edilyn passed a scowl to her brother. "Good day or good-bye?"

They are the same, are they not?

"Nay. One is brief. The other quite permanent. Are you saying you bid me adieu?"

You're the one who said you've no wish to be mated to a dragon. Nor have you been with a man. I've only one use for a woman and it's a very brief biological exchange. He glanced to Virag. *And I've no use whatsoever for a male kikimora. So I see no reason for us to remain together. Better we part cordially than wait for ill feelings to kick in and the roasting to begin.*

More hurt than she should be, she forced herself to remain as callous about it as he was. "I see. Very well, then. Virag?"

Her brother shook his head. "Nay. I won't do it."

Illarion turned a harsh stare toward him. *Pardon?*

"I concur," she growled, wanting to kick him for not getting her out of here before she betrayed the pain that was so hard to swallow and not show.

Virag stubbornly crossed his arms over his chest and took up a defiant stance. "You've no idea how they treat her at Penllyn. I won't take her back there to their cruelty. Not after the spectacle you made in claiming her and snubbing the princess. They'd be merciless to her now. Much worse than before. She doesn't deserve that. Better you should have let her die than save her life for such a fate."

When she started to protest, he held his hand up to silence her. "Don't you dare argue with me, Eddie. There's plenty of room in this hole for the three of us. I take up a thimble's space. Your human's life span is but a blink to his. He won't even remember it in time. He can suffer you a few decades to live out your life here in peace while he mopes about in silence. He can ignore us. We'll ignore him. Everyone will be happy."

Maybe not *every*one.

Something proven as Illarion rumbled a sound that didn't come from his throat. She wasn't sure exactly what the source of it was. But it was terrifying.

Do not mistake your powers, kikimora. I've picked my teeth with the bones of far greater creatures than you. I've devoured gods.

"Yet it was a god who turned you into your hybrid existence, was it not?"

This time, there was no mistaking the hiss Illarion let out. *You go too far! And you know nothing of what you speak!* He moved to attack her brother.

Without thinking, Edilyn stepped between them.

Illarion collided with her.

She wasn't sure which of them was the most stunned by the unexpected contact. Or why it left her so breathless.

Illarion put his arms around her to steady her. *Are you all right?*

She nodded. "You didn't hurt me."

Relief lightened his features, but there was an unmistakable heat in his eyes. Along with a pain so profound that it made her ache deep in her stomach. She had no idea the source of her feeling or his look. But something haunted him.

Stepping back, he let go. *There's a bedchamber above. It's yours. There are also chests of silks and jewels. Use whatever you wish for your comfort. But nothing is to leave this cavern.*

And with that, he transformed back into a dragon and lumbered off into a dark recess where he vanished from her sight. An unbelievable feat, she would have thought, given the vibrancy of his colors and size. Yet he made it appear easy and effortless.

Stunned and angry, she scowled at Virag.

He was completely unrepentant over his actions. "Don't give me that pout."

"I'm not pouting."

"Aye, you are. And you should be thanking me and celebrating."

"For what? That you've imposed on a poor soul who doesn't want us here?"

"That you're not returning to the hovel your parents damned you to by their thoughtlessness. Besides, your dragon could use some company. This is a dismal existence. Just look at it." He gestured around the stark cave. "It actually makes your crappy place look like a castle in comparison. And it takes creepy to a whole new extremity."

She hated to admit he was right. Still . . .

Was this all there was to Illarion's existence? To his life? It was so . . . so . . .

Bleak.

Barren. A thousand adjectives went through her mind. But the ones that haunted her were the last two.

Sad and lonely.

Feeling bad for the dragon, she pulled her helm off her head and handed it to her brother. "Wait here."

"Why?"

She let out a long-suffering sigh. "Because I asked it and you're an ass."

"Fine." He propped her helm on his head and went to sit on a nearby stalagmite.

With one last glare at Virag to make sure he was staying put, she headed after Illarion.

The walkway he'd ventured down was long and winding. Terribly narrow. How he'd stayed on it given his great size, she had no idea. Maybe he'd flown over it. It certainly seemed more likely than his walking down without slipping and falling.

Biting her lip, she tried to settle her nerves over the danger of the path. She'd never liked heights. She liked darkness even less.

It was also a lot colder down here. Frigid, really. Why would he want to stay here when he could be in the warmer, brighter part?

What are you doing?

She let out a brittle shriek at his unexpected voice that intruded on her thoughts. "Where are you?"

A subtle sigh filled her head. *In my bed.*

She heard a deep shuffling before the torches lit the darkness around her. Her jaw dropped as she realized that the walls weren't black, after all. Rather it was a deep, sparkled green that shimmered with the light. And as much treasure as there had been above, it was nothing compared to what filled the chambers here. Everything glimmered and shimmered with gold, silver, and jewels. Treasure even littered the floor. She could practically swim in a sea of it.

On his side, Illarion took up most of the room. He apparently made his bed on straw scattered over a river of gold coins. That did not seem to her as if it would be particularly comfortable. But who was she to judge? Her straw tick mattress wasn't what she'd call luxurious, either.

Lifting his head, he was so large that he met her on the ledge without moving any other part of his body. *Did you need something?*

She ignored his question as she stared aghast at the supreme wealth surrounding her. "May I ask why, with this"—she gestured at the treasure—"fortune around you, you sleep on a floor and hide in a cave? I don't understand. You could live like a king in a palace."

I'm not a man, Edilyn. I am drakomai. Do you know this word?

She shook her head.

We are born the cursed children of demon mothers. Abandoned at birth and left to die, only a handful of us survive. Because of what we are, we are extremely solitary and territorial. I am not like those hybrid creatures who come to your Winnowing to pick mates. I'm much older and much more feral.

"Is that why you can't talk?"

Nay. That is a result of your kind and it's why I hate your race so vehemently. What was done to me was done quite intentionally and with enough venomous vim that it is all I can do to restrain myself from becoming the very monster they think I am.

Those words and the brutal torment they betrayed brought tears to her eyes. "I'm sorry." And before she could stop herself, she reached out to lay her hand against his leathery snout.

Illarion froze at the unexpected kindness. No human had ever laid a gentle hand to him while he'd been in his natural form. For that matter, they'd seldom done so in his human one.

While it was true that women were initially drawn to his prince's body, their ardor was often cooled the moment they realized he couldn't speak. More times than not, they assumed him addled as well as mute. Especially since he seldom spoke to them with his telepathy as that would betray his preternatural powers.

But Edilyn didn't hesitate or withhold her kindness. It was as innate to her as breathing. She couldn't seem to help herself.

Closing his eyes, he savored the warmth of her hand as she rubbed his scales.

"If it's any consolation, dragons ate my father."

He grimaced at her. *How could that ever be consolation for me?*

"It's not. I just wanted you to know that I understand your hatred. That it's hard for me to be with you whenever I think of it."

Yet here you are. He opened his eyes to find her staring at him with a peculiar expression he didn't quite understand.

"Why did you protect me?"

You gave me kindness first.

"And that's all it took?"

Sadly, when you've been given as little of it as I have in my life, aye. I fear I'm a cheap whore whose affections are easily bought.

She laughed out loud at his unexpected comment. "It's a good thing the brenin didn't know that, then. He could have bought you from me."

Indeed. Illarion sucked his breath in sharply as she moved her hand to rub him beneath his chin. It sent shivers the length of his body and fire through his veins. A part of him wanted to purr in response to it.

"You still haven't answered my question about all the treasure."

He sighed contentedly and wagged his tail. *It's not mine.*

"What do you mean?"

Others bring it to me for safekeeping. Gods and heroes. Those who want it protected from the ones who would misuse it in your world. Unfortunately, many of them die before they reclaim it and so it accumulates over time.

"You never get rid of it?"

Too dangerous. While I may hate dragons and mankind, I share this world with you. Last thing I want to see is one of the others use it to rise up and take over. I shudder at the thought of paying homage to a gallu or Charonte or one of the other billions of possibilities— such as your brother.

Laughing again, she nodded. "I can see your point. He would let such go to his head and be even more impossible to suffer." Much to Illarion's chagrin, she let her hand fall away as she glanced about his chamber. "And this is enough for you?"

How do you mean?

"This life? You're content to live here among your treasure and do . . . what is it dragons do?"

We exist.

"And?"

He shrugged. *And what? There's nothing more for my kind. Anytime we leave, we're hunted. We're so large, we cannot hide. Every species born, including the gods, wants to enslave us for our powers or slay us to use our parts in their potions or to mount as trophies. We dare not gather. So we exist in our dens and wait for the day when death finally spares us from our loneliness.*

Edilyn swallowed hard as his words brought a lump to her throat. Strange how she'd never given thought before to what a dragon might actually feel. 'Course, she'd never really cared. Never really thought about them being sentient creatures. "But you don't have to be a dragon."

The look he gave her then terrified her. His breathing turned to ragged, angry gasps. The serpentine pupils of his yellow eyes narrowed in warning of his fury. *Think you I wanted this done to me? To become a weak, pathetic, helpless man?*

Those words struck her like a blow. "We're not *that* weak and we're certainly not pathetic. We at least live. And we fight. We don't hide like cowards in dark caves, feeling sorry for ourselves." And with that, she got up and left him to wallow in his self-pity.

Illarion drew back in shock as he watched her storm away. No one other than Max, Xyn, or Falcyn had ever spoken to him in such a manner.

Fear? Yes. Even when the humans had held him for torture when he'd been a child, they'd been terrified of him.

No one, especially not a human, had ever told him off before. Not when he wore his dragonskin. Even his younger mandrake brother, Blaise, backed down from him.

I don't feel sorry for myself.

He was quite happy being a dragon. Happy with his solitude and his cave. He had no other needs whatsoever.

Except a suddenly incessant one to set the record straight with an irritating woman who thought she knew things she didn't. . . .

3

"I take it it didn't go well?"

"Shut up," Edilyn snapped at her brother. "Go scare an old man."

Virag tsked at her. "You are in a foul mood."

"Why shouldn't I be? I've had one dream the whole of my life and no matter how hard I try, I can't seem to make it real. Have you any idea how frustrating that is? Nay, you do not. You snap your fingers, use your magic, and everything you want is done." Edilyn clenched her eyes shut to hold back her tears of frustration.

She'd worked so hard. . . .

And for what? To be hidden in this cave until she died?

The dragon might covet that existence, but she didn't.

With a ragged breath, she glanced around the elaborate bedchambers. They were actually quite luxurious. Still, that didn't make her feel better.

A gilded cage was a cage nonetheless!

"What is this place?"

Virag laughed. "I'm thinking our little dragon wears the guise of a man more than he lets on." He lifted a corner of the bedcovers, that were made of some fabric the likes of which she'd never seen before. Much like the walls of the room where Illarion slept, it shimmered in the light. "This is silk from a future time period. The sheets? Egyptian cotton."

"Beg pardon?"

He nodded. "Aye, love. Come feel it. The mattress is *memory foam*."

"What language are you speaking?"

Virag laughed. "Oh the things you miss being a mortal bound to one time period." He tsked at her.

Wrinkling her nose at him, she stepped around his surly form to inspect the bed. He was right. It was like touching a cloud. "What is *memory foam*? How does it remember things? Does it have its own brain?"

Virag laughed even harder. "You wouldn't believe me if I told you. Suffice it to say, it's something future man will thank modern science for. There's also a toilet in the bathroom."

"A what in the who?"

"Exactly. You are going to die when I show *that* to you."

She scowled at him. "How do you know of such things?"

"Unlike you, sweet sister, I'm not locked into this time and place. I don't have to live linearly. Just like I don't have to keep this body or size. I choose to be here because I want to stay with you, and I'm forbidden to take you from here."

"Forbidden by whom?"

"The law of my people."

Strange that he'd never mentioned that to her before. While she knew he had great powers and the ability to shapeshift, he'd never mentioned that he could travel through time.

Suddenly, a loud rumbling sounded. The walls around them shook.

Gasping in alarm, Edilyn caught herself against the bedpost as some of the ceiling fell in.

Were they being attacked? Terrified of the answer, she rushed from the chambers, down the narrow corridor to the main cavern where she found Illarion.

"What was that sound?"

Illarion used his massive head to indicate a passage on his left. *I made an opening for you to the world outside. You are no longer trapped here. Now you can come and go as you please.*

Her jaw went slack at his kindness. Especially after his earlier words. "Isn't that dangerous for you?"

He didn't answer. Rather, he headed back for his inner den.

Edilyn exchanged a perplexed frown with Virag. Why would Illarion expose himself so needlessly?

Curious, she went after him.

"Illarion?"

He expelled an exasperated breath as he settled back down to rest on his straw. *Aye?*

She moved to stand in front of his giant head. "Why did you make a doorway into your cave? What if someone finds your lair?"

Let them come. I could use the protein. He closed his eyes.

She snorted at his dry response. Then she popped him on his nose.

Startled, Illarion opened his eyes to stare at her in complete disbelief. *Did you just hit me?*

"Playfully so. Aye." She wrinkled her nose at him. "You deserved it for that nonchalant comment. It wasn't amusing."

He pulled his head back to stare down at her with the most adorable grimace. *I can't decide if you're the bravest woman ever born or the most foolish.*

"My father always said it was a very fine line between the two. And one I walk constantly."

He made a peculiar sound.

"Was that a laugh?"

I think it might have been.

"You think?"

Illarion had to pause to consider it. *Laughter is a rather foreign concept for me.*

And that broke her heart for him. Laughter shouldn't be foreign to anyone. Not even a surly dragon.

In that moment, she made a decision that she would probably regret one day. "Get up, Lord Dragon."

Pardon?

"You heard me. Rise and make my saddle for me."

Why?

"Because I wish to ride."

His pupils narrowed to threatening slits as smoke billowed out from his nostrils. *I'm not your beast of burden to heel at your command,* he growled in a low, deadly tone, letting her know she'd touched a nerve with him.

But she refused to be intimidated when she'd meant nothing by it. "Didn't say you were. I'm talking to you as I would a friend or my brother. You're moping about and I'm dragging you out the door for fresh air. Now get your lumbering arse off the floor, saddle up, and let's get out of this depressing place for a while. It'll do you good, I think."

And you wish to ride me? He quirked a brow at her.

She tucked her chin to her chest and gave him an evil grimace. "Get that look off your face. I'm afraid of flying. Terrified of dragons. It's time I buried both those fears. Let's do this."

Do you always face your fears?

"Of course. Don't you?"

Don't know. Never really had any.

"Well, I guess when you're the size of a castle, 'tis a luxury you can afford." She watched as the saddle appeared, along with the reins. "Thank you."

He inclined his head to her, then lowered his wing so that she could climb into place.

With a deep breath, she slowly began ascending his large body.

Illarion closed his eyes at the warmth of her supple skin sliding over his scales. Earlier, he hadn't noticed just how soft a caress it was. Mostly because they'd been under attack and he'd been more focused on other things.

Now . . .

The feather-light weight of her body against his left him breathless and he was well aware of every feminine curve. In particular, her large breasts as she scooted up over his back and struggled to get into the saddle.

And when she finally straddled his spine, it was all he could do not to roll over and strip her bare.

"Are you all right?"

His breathing ragged, he fought for control. *Aye. Why do you ask?*

"You seem really tense and stiff."

She had no idea. Especially when her hands swept against him to gather the reins. Damn, it'd been far too long since he'd been inside a woman. This was sheer torture. The last time a human had ridden on his back, it'd been under duress. They'd forced him to it and he'd been hell-bent to get away from his *master*.

Now, her touch soothed him in a way nothing ever had before. There was a calm peacefulness he couldn't quite explain. And at the same time, every nerve in his body was fired and alert. Acutely attuned to her.

He felt every breath she took as if it were his own. Every heartbeat. For the first time in his life, he wasn't defiant or angry. He actually wanted to please her. To make her laugh and see her smile.

What is your choice, my lady?

"No idea. Where would you like to go?"

There's a waterfall in the valley nearby.

"Really? I've never seen a waterfall. Is it pretty?"

I'll let you judge for yourself. Hold tight.

Edilyn had no idea what to expect as Illarion carefully picked his way through the cave and out through the opening he'd made. But the moment she saw exactly where his home was, she gasped and latched onto his neck as utter terror claimed her. His cave was high atop a mountain with a narrow pass leading to it. From her vantage point, she looked down on the clouds. "Where are we?"

Hybrasil.

"Hybrasil? I've never heard of such a place."

It's an island, off the coast of your homeland. One that can only be seen when I allow it. Or I'm too wounded to hold my shields in place.

"No wonder the others fear you so. You *are* the most powerful of your kind."

She felt him scoff under her.

Nay, my lady. My powers pale to those of my older brothers. Either of them could spank me with little effort.

"You have family?"

You are surprised that I have brothers?

"A little bit."

Well, don't be. I have many. And sisters, too.

"Really? How many?"

SHERRILYN KENYON

More than I can count. Even more who have died. But of the hundreds over the centuries, I've only been close to a few.

"Their names?"

Maxis, Falcyn, Sarraxyn, Hadyn, and Blaise.

"Do you ever see them?"

Rarely. We don't congregate like humans. It tends to scare the natives and cause them to do stupid things. He flexed his wings and turned his head to look back at her. *Are you ready to fly now?*

Cringing, she glanced down at the clouds and felt her stomach lurch at the thought. "This is much higher than we went before."

It is, indeed.

And as he'd done for the fight, he used his powers to make the saddle straps rise up to wrap around her body and secure her in place. The fact that he took such care caused a wave of warmth to surge through her. It also made her feel a bit better about this perilous venture. "I'm ready when you are."

I won't let you fall, Edilyn. Remember that I've done this for thousands of years. For me, flying is as natural as breathing. Do you trust me?

Edilyn hesitated at the sight of the clouds that obscured the ground so far below. Always terrified of heights, she'd never dreamt that she'd ever be this high above anything. "I trust you. But if I scream, don't take it personally."

With a soundless laugh, he spread his wings wide and fell forward into the sky.

Her stomach sank like a stone as her breath caught in her throat and strangled her with absolute terror. The winds whipped against her skin and hair, more akin to talons than some unseen natural force. It was actually quite painful. Her heartbeat pounded in her ears. Yet for all that, it was exhilarating.

Spectacularly beautiful.

The sky was far bluer up here than when she was in the fields where she worked. The sun brighter. Below her, everything was a mesh of unidentifiable greens and browns. She couldn't tell what was what. Nor could she see any people or animals. The world looked nothing like she was used to.

Are you all right?

"I am. But how do you know where you are? Everything's indistinguishable."

I have magnetoreception that allows me to see the earth's magnetic fields and magnetoreceptors in my ears and snout for contour and altimeter tracking.

That made as much sense to her as memory foam and the other nonsensical terms her brother had used. "What language are you speaking?"

He laughed under her. *My drakomai vision is different from that of a human. I can see shadows rising from the earth that allow me to know and determine cardinal directions. They guide me like phantom spirits, pointing me to the right path. Likewise, I have different nerves and senses in my ears and nose that tell me how high I'm flying and what is below me even when I can't see the ground. So even on the darkest night, during storms or fog, I know exactly where I am and what's around me. Ergo, I shouldn't accidentally fly us into the side of a mountain . . . at least I hope not.*

She let out a squeak over something she hadn't considered. "Is that truly a possibility?"

It only happened once. Most of the scarring healed . . . after a few centuries.

Her breathing turned ragged as total fear claimed her.

Illarion laughed even harder. *Relax, Edilyn. I'm jesting with you. I've never hit the side of a mountain. And while I have crashed into a few trees, it was only because I was wounded in battle and brought down from it.*

That made her feel better. At least that he'd crashed from the fight, not that he'd been injured. "Have you seen many battles?"

Not by choice, and I've no wish to speak of it. Such discussions turn my mood sour.

And with that, he began to lower them through the clouds toward the ground at a speed that left her gasping.

Only this time from joy and not fear.

True to his word, the waterfall was gorgeous. It fell like a majestic veil in the sunlight to splash down into a tranquil oasis. She'd never seen anything more beautiful. The air around her was scented with the most delicate fragrance. It reminded her of the stories her brother had told her of his fey homeland that could only be reached by his people.

He unwrapped the leather from her body and knelt so that she could dismount.

Impishly, she slid down his wing like a slide, to land on her feet.

Illarion arched a brow in stunned surprise at her actions as she gave him a proud smile. No one had ever been so playful around him. *At least you've conquered your fear of me.*

"Not entirely." She flounced away, toward the pond where he sometimes went to bathe.

Beguiled by her, he followed and watched as she explored his favorite place. He still wasn't sure why he'd brought her here to share it. Not even his brothers knew about his private spot. It was his own haven that he'd reserved from everyone.

Edilyn went to sit on a rock that jutted out over the crystal-blue water and pulled off her worn shoes. Wiggling her toes, she plunged them in, then leaned back on her arms to sun herself.

Would you like to swim?

She tilted her head to cast him a wistful pout. "I don't know how."

It's not deep.

Her look turned doubtful. "For you, the man? Or you, the dragon?"

Point taken. He moved closer to her. *I could teach you to swim. It's not hard.*

She wrinkled her nose at him. "Should I wet these, I've no other clothes to wear."

One corner of his lips curled up into a roguish grin as he considered that. *You could swim naked.*

She tsked at him. "Ah, the truth of you, now."

Her words rang with a veracity he wanted to deny. If only he could. But he wouldn't mind watching her frolic naked in the water.

Instead, he changed forms before he'd even realized what he'd done so that he could join her on her rock. He wanted to be close beside her and he could only do that in a human body. Otherwise, he might inadvertently harm her.

If you wish to swim, I'll get you more clothes.

Edilyn didn't miss the way his voice in her head had dropped an octave. Nor the light in his blue eyes as he watched her. "Why do your eyes change color when you become a man?"

Sadness replaced the heat. When he started away, she reached out and stopped him. "I'm sorry if that hurt you. I was only curious. You really do hate your human form, don't you?"

He nodded.

She couldn't fathom why. He was unbelievably handsome. Far more so than any man she'd ever seen in her life. His features were perfectly sculpted. His brownish-red hair unlike anyone else's. Up close, she could see that it wasn't a single hair color. Rather it was made up of all of them. Even random strands of blond were laced through it.

And though she'd never kissed a man before and she knew deep inside that they were supposed to be enemies, she couldn't help wondering what it would be like to taste his lips. While she'd never coveted the thought of being with a dragon before, she didn't mind being with him.

"Teach me to swim, my dragon lord."

He gave her an adorable grin as her clothes turned into the strangest outfit she'd ever beheld. Gasping, she tried to cover herself with her hands.

"What is this you've done to me?"

Put you in a wetsuit. It'll keep you warm and dry in the water.

"It's so tight!"

True, and it sadly covers you from head to toe.

"But leaves no mystery!"

I beg to differ. Should we peel it off and compare?

"Nay!"

Shaking his head, he redressed himself in something a lot more scandalous. While her black *suit* as he called it did cover her neck to wrist and ankle, his was barely more than a scandalous breechcloth.

They're called board shorts.

"I only understand half of what you say to me."

With that adorable grin in place, he took her hand and led her to the water.

She bit her lip and hesitated. "Is it cold?"

He shook his head before he released her hand and dove beneath the small waves to swim with an ease she envied. True to his word, he was quite accomplished. That gave her more confidence to wade into the sparkling depths, which were incredibly warm. There must be a spring here to keep it heated that much.

When the depth reached her waist, she paused to look around. Illarion had been under for quite some time. *Much* longer than he should have been.

Had he drowned?

The thought terrified her. "Illarion?"

He rose out of the water to stand in front of her. His eyes twinkled with merriment. *I can breathe underwater.*

"I cannot."

Smiling, he brushed a strand of hair from her cheek, then gently kissed it. *I know. Have no fear. I won't let anything happen to you. Now lie back in the water and I'll keep you afloat.*

Not quite trusting him, she reluctantly obeyed.

Illarion bit back his amusement at how tense she was—as if she expected him to let go of her at any moment. *Relax, my lady. Feel the water's movement. Let it carry you.*

She slowly began to trust him. "It's very soothing, isn't it?"

Normally, he'd agree. But right now . . .

All he could focus on were the parts of her body that protruded from the water. He should have put her in a bikini. Had he not feared sending her into a screaming fit of protest, he would have.

And before he could stop himself, he placed his cheek against hers, pulled her back to his chest, and lifted his legs so that he could cradle her with his full body.

Edilyn gasped at the sensation of Illarion pressed against her as he swam in the water for the two of them. "How are you doing this?"

Most true drakomai are amphibious. We're even stronger in the water than we are in the air or on land.

There was a little-known fact about his race. And as she felt his muscles rippling, she realized just how powerful and strong he was in both incarnations.

How lethal.

She lost track of time as he gently taught her how to swim, and while she lacked his abilities, she was rather proud when she was able to stay afloat and make progress on her own. Best of all, Illarion stayed right beside her, ensuring her safety as he'd promised.

As the sun moved lower in the sky, they left the water. On shore, he conjured a blanket to wrap her in. *Are you hungry?*

"A little. You?"

He cast a bashful, longing look at her. *Not for food.*

When he started away, she caught his hand and pulled him back toward her.

He arched a questioning brow.

Edilyn bit her lip as she debated the sanity of what she was about to do. It was all kinds of stupid. She knew that. And once done, there would be no going back.

This was a major decision that would forever alter her life and she knew it. All she'd ever wanted was to be a member of the brenin's army, and she'd been thwarted at every attempt.

The last thing she'd desired was to be bound to a dragon.

Now . . .

It didn't seem as horrible as she'd imagined. And before she could allow her common sense to take root, she rose on her tiptoes and captured his lips with hers.

"Where did you get this?"

Virag glanced around the drab gray Adoni court where no color was allowed except for the vibrantly red gown that adorned the great queen bitch of the fey—Morgen. He'd always hated the duplicitous role he was forced to play. But if he didn't, both he and Edilyn would fall to their mother's stupidity. Damn her for the bargain she'd made with Morgen that had cost them all so much.

"That I can't tell you. But if it's not enough, there's more treasure. Chambers and chambers filled to overflowing."

Morgen le Fey, the queen of all evil, the bitchtress who'd brought down the legendary King Arthur himself, sat on her ebony throne eyeing him like her next meal. Dressed in a gown that seemed to bleed, she passed the ornate peach stone in her hand off to her most trusted servant—Narishka duFey. Every bit as beautiful as the demon she served, Narishka was blond and dressed in black—like all the other Adoni members of Morgen's Circle. "It was a dragon's lair you found, you say?" Morgen asked.

"Aye."

"And this island?"

"Hybrasil, I think."

That set off a round of gasps through the Adoni around him. A beautiful race of fey, they were lethal and cruel to an unholy level. None of them could be trusted, except to betray and to lie.

And kill without mercy or compassion.

It also got Morgen's full attention and brought her to her feet. "You found the hidden lair of the son of Ares? Plundered there and lived to tell it?"

Virag's stomach shrank at the way she asked that question. "Aye?"

She let out an evil laugh as a slow, insidious smile spread over her breathtaking face. "Oh, I'm impressed with you, little sprite. That took great balls." Crooking her finger at him, she motioned for Virag to approach her. It seemed like a profoundly bad idea, but not approaching seemed like an even worse one.

So he took a deep breath and obeyed.

"You and I need to speak in private," she whispered. "There is something else of his I want. You do this and I'll give you what *you* want."

Virag knew this was going to be bad, especially since Morgen and Narishka led him from the hall, down a dark, cold, eerie hallway that was lit with the glowing guts of disemboweled fey creatures.

Something he really hoped his own internal organs didn't do.

Morgen led him into her room, then closed the door with an

ominous thud. "This dragon will have a mark on his hide. I want you to bring it to me."

"The dragon? The mark, or his hide?"

Morgen grimaced as if he were daft. "Kill him, you fool, and carve the mark from his body. Bring me the skin of the mark. More than that, if he's who and what I think he is . . . he will be the guardian for the Halter of Epona. Find it! You bring me that, and I will grant the freedom you ask. You fail and I will feed your heart to my demons."

Virag winced at her harsh words. Illarion had done them a favor. And how was he to repay it?

With treachery.

It figured.

But what choice did he have? It was either the dragon's heart, or their heads on a pike.

Or the worst of all . . .

Eternal slavery to this wretched bitch.

4

Breathless, Illarion pulled back to stare down at Edilyn in utter disbelief of her innocently sweet kiss. One so inept that it drove home just how inexperienced she was. More touched than he wanted to admit, he smiled at her. He placed a tender kiss to her forehead, then started away.

Once again, she stopped him.

What are you doing?

Biting her lip, she placed her hand on his chest. "I know what it means to be chosen by a dragon. I'm ready."

He ground his teeth. *You keep offering yourself to me like this, Edilyn, and one day I won't say no.*

"Illarion." She caught him about the waist.

He drew his breath in sharply at the sensation of her hands on his skin. The fact that she ran her right hand up his abdomen to his neck, where the wretched scar of his captivity remained, didn't help his mood.

"Do you really want me to leave?"

No, he didn't. It was the first time he could remember that he craved the presence of another.

Do not play with me, Edilyn. Dragons are fierce, unforgiving creatures. Passionate in all things. We are not like your people. If I claim you, it is eternal. I won't ever let you go. You need to understand that and be willing to accept the fact that I can't mingle with mankind. While I can agree to bring you and your brother into my world, I refuse to widen my tolerance further. This would be your life. Lonely and secluded. Forevermore.

Edilyn brushed her hand through his damp hair as she considered his earnest words. The fact he was being patient and selflessly explaining it to her made her decision just that much easier. "I've been among my people the whole of my life and I've been lonely most every day of it. You say that I'll be giving up something I never had. If you can promise me more days like this, I swear there is nothing I'll ever miss about my village or people."

This time, *he* lowered his lips to capture her mouth in the most passionate kiss imaginable.

Edilyn sighed as his tongue swept against hers and her blood ran thick through her veins.

With a frightening ease, he scooped her up in his arms as if she weighed nothing and carried her to a shaded spot that was softly cushioned by moss and grass. He manifested a fur blanket before he lowered her down on top of it.

Closing her eyes, she savored the way his muscles flexed and moved beneath her hands. His skin was so soft, yet beneath that his muscles were rock hard. It was so different from her body. Especially his whiskers that scraped against her lips and cheeks, and left them tingling.

Playfully, he nipped at her chin before he opened the front of her strange suit to expose her body. His gaze locked with hers and he watched her carefully as if waiting for any sign that she'd reconsidered. With an agonizing slowness, he slid his hand inside to gently cup her breast.

Edilyn hissed at the warmth of his hand that sent a strange heat through her entire being.

A slow smile spread over Illarion's handsome face as he lowered his head to taste her. She buried her hands in his hair as he moved back and forth between her breasts, carefully laving each one until she was writhing from his exquisite torture.

She didn't think anything could feel better. Not until he used his powers to remove her suit and kissed his way over her belly, down to the part of her that ached the most.

Edilyn cried out loud as he began to gently tongue and tease her down *there*. "Illarion?"

Mmm?

"Are you supposed to be doing *that*?"

He used his fingers to stroke her in time with his tongue. *Are you enjoying it?*

She answered with a loud, soul-wrenching moan of pleasure.

Do you want me to stop?

"Nay!"

Illarion laughed at the desperation in her tone as she clutched at his hair. His little morsel was every bit as passionate as he'd predicted. She gave herself to him fully. It was the first time he'd ever taken a woman who knew who and what he really was.

For some reason, that made her all the more dear to him. Made this more tender and intense. They weren't merely *rutting* as she'd called it. She was sleeping with the real him—with the full knowledge of his broken heritage and curse. And he was the first one to touch her. She'd never allowed any other this right.

She was his alone.

And when she came a few minutes later, he realized that that too was a brand-new experience for her.

In fact, she pulled away from him and stared at him in utter terror. "What did you do to me?"

That was an orgasm, my lady. It's the ultimate goal for coupling.

Edilyn tried to catch her breath, but it was difficult. Her body was still pulsing inside. "Is it supposed to feel like that?"

Illarion grinned at her. *Aye.*

"Did you feel it, too?"

Not yet. I wanted you to have your pleasure first, as I'm told it's often painful for a woman her first time. I was trying not to frighten you. But that plan went to hell.

His dry tone amused her. "Sorry. I've ruined the mood, haven't I?"

He ran his gaze over her naked body. *Not for me.*

Snorting, she scooted back toward him. "I won't be afraid."

With a doubtful grimace, he slowly peeled off his breechcloth.

Edilyn regretted her statement as she took in the size of him and his earlier words about pain made total sense now.

Illarion held his hand out to her. *Are you ready for how my species bond?*

She had no idea what he meant until she slowly closed the distance between them. Illarion had her kneel in front of him with her back to his front. He rose up on his knees and pulled her against his chest so that he supported both their body weights.

Nuzzling her neck, he breathed softly in her ear as he ran his hands over her skin. They stroked and teased until she was molten in his arms.

That's it, my precious. Just relax and enjoy it.

Illarion sank his fingers inside her to make sure she was ready to receive him. Arching her back, she reached over her head to bury her hand in his hair again.

More hungry than he'd ever been, he used his knees to open her thighs wider before he slid himself deep inside her body. She cried out instantly.

Worried, he froze. *Are you all right?*

Edilyn bit her lip at the strange fullness of him buried deep within her body. "I'm fine. It was just a bit startling."

But as he teased her ear with his tongue and his hand returned to stroke her, she began to relax again. After a few minutes, he slowly began thrusting against her.

Edilyn couldn't believe how quickly the pain fled and gave way to more pleasure. Now she understood why so many sought this. She felt so incredibly close to him right now. And when she felt him tense and release himself inside her, she smiled.

"You are mine, Lord Dragon."

His breathing ragged, he kept himself buried deep within her as he covered them both with another blanket. *I will always be yours, Edilyn.* Lifting her hand, he pressed it to his lips so that he could nibble her fingertips. Then he gently kissed her. *And here the last thing you wanted was a dragon.*

"True, but you're nothing like I thought you'd be."

He made a strange noise before he manifested something in his hand. When he opened it, she saw a peculiar gold whistle.

"What is this?"

Brushing her hair aside, he placed it around her neck. *So that you can call me should you ever need me and I'm not near you. Or if something happens to me, it will summon my brothers to protect you. It's called a Bane-Cry. Once sounded, all dracokyn are honor-bound to answer.*

She glanced up at him. "Thank you."

He inclined his head, then kissed her. *I told you, I voraciously protect everything that is entrusted to me. That now includes you.*

"Should I be afraid?"

Nay. As my dragonswan you, alone, will never have cause to fear me.

"Your what?"

Dragonswan.

Biting her lip, she smiled up at him. "I like that. So that makes you my what?"

Dragonswain.

Leaning back against his shoulder, she fingered his stubbly chin. "My dragonswain."

Illarion closed his eyes and savored those words, along with her gentle caress and the scent of her skin. Honestly, he never wanted to bathe the scent of her off him. But sadly, he would have to eventually.

A light frown creased her brow.

Is something amiss?

"Nay. I was just trying to imagine what kind of children we'll have. Will they be dragons or human? Do you know?"

Now was the time to find out exactly how she truly felt about him and his kind. *Unless the gods decide to bind us at their own discretion, whims, and time, I will never be able to impregnate you. As with all Were-Hunters, I'm sterile, Edilyn. The Greek Fates took that from me after they cursed our newly made kind.*

Sadness darkened her eyes. "Nay! That's not fair for you!"

Happiness flooded him at her honest sincerity. She was truly upset and indignant on his behalf. *I would have thought you'd be relieved.*

Tears glistened in her beautiful eyes. "Then you would be wrong. Nothing would have pleased me more than to have borne your children for you. But you said that there is a chance it could happen?"

There is.

"Then I shall hope for that day."

Something inside him shattered at those words. *And if I said they'd be dragons?*

"You would have to show me how to care for them. I have no idea what they'd need. But I'd learn."

He brushed his fingers along her cheek. *Could you love such creatures?*

"They wouldn't be creatures, Illarion. They'd be my children. Just as my brother isn't human and I love him no less for it. I'm told my mother had quite a bit of a surprise when I was born and my father had to teach her how to care for a human baby. Apparently, we're very difficult compared to the Kikimory. Yet it didn't stop her from loving me. Nor did I love her any less when I found out she was a nightmare demon. Rather, I found it strangely comforting as I never had to worry over my dreams so long as she was alive."

Illarion couldn't fathom the miracle that had sent her careening into his world. Honestly, he'd never thought to mate at all. Never thought to find anyone who could make him feel the way he felt in this moment.

Like he was human, while she knew for a fact that he wasn't. Neither man nor beast scared her. She saw both sides of him and faulted him for none.

It was perfect.

At least until he felt her stomach rumble from hunger. Sighing, he knew he needed to find her food. While he could go days without nourishment, humans were different. They didn't store meals the way dragons did. Her body required constant maintenance.

I shall have to rearrange things for you in my cave.

"What do you mean?"

Just thinking out loud of what you'll need to live there. I have no kitchen. Not even a pot for you to make the most basic of meals. I'll need to make you a place to store and prepare food. And you'll need more clothes. What else do humans require for sustenance and happiness?

She lifted her head to scowl at him. "Do you eat your food raw?"

He grinned and shook his head. *I can cook it instantly. Benefits of breathing fire. And once I eat, it takes days for it to digest. A single meal can sustain me for almost a week—longer if need be, and depending on the size of it.*

"That must be nice."

He rolled over with her and gave her a light kiss. *But you are not a dragon, my rose. And you, I need to feed. Come, let us bathe and I'll see you fed.*

Edilyn felt the strangest wave of weakness sweep through her at his endearment. She couldn't believe how tender her dragon was. How kind.

Or playful, she realized as he swept her into the water to frolic more than bathe.

This time when he conjured clothing for her, it was the finest shimmering dark green samite she'd ever seen. Truly, it was fit for royalty.

"It's beautiful," she breathed as she ran her hand over it.

His eyes darkened. *Nowhere near as beautiful as the one who wears it. Personally, I'd rather keep you naked. But I know you would protest such extremes ... so this shall have to suffice to please us both.*

Heat rushed into her face at his words. "You're the only one who's ever thought that of me, I assure you." Most men had turned their noses up at her approach, preferring women like Morla and Nesta.

Only a fool would not think you beautiful.

Edilyn smiled as she quickly dressed. The moment she was finished, Illarion returned to his dragon's body and flew them back to his cave to retrieve her brother.

They had no sooner landed inside than she felt the sudden tenseness of his body. "Is something wrong?"

Illarion didn't respond. Rather, he shifted from dragon to man with an alarming swiftness, and without warning. He did it so quickly that he almost caused her to fall. But he caught her and set her on her feet, then rushed through his cave.

"My lord?"

Still, he didn't respond. Instead, he began searching through his chests and chambers.

"Illarion?"

Finally, he turned on her with rage blazing in his eyes. He pinned her with a murderous glare. *Was this your ruse?*

She stepped back from the hatred he pinned her with. "What ruse? What are you talking about?"

Where's your brother, Edilyn?

"He should be where we left him." She headed for the stone steps that led up to the bedchambers. "Virag!"

When her brother didn't answer, a bad feeling went through her. One that wasn't helped by the accusatory suspicion in Illarion's eyes.

You betrayed me!

"What? No! Why would you think that?"

I think nothing. I know it for a fact. You had no interest in taking me out of here except to give your brother time to pilfer through my chambers and take from them!

Those words slapped her. "That is wholly untrue! Virag would never do such a thing and I damn sure didn't!"

Don't lie to me! Think you I don't know every single item I keep? That I can't smell every place your brother snooped in my absence? My whole cave reeks of his stench. Illarion raked her with a cold, lethal stare that would have infuriated her in turn had she not seen the tormented pain behind it. *I commend your acting abilities. You took me for a fool entirely.*

"Illarion . . ." She reached to touch him.

He pulled back sharply. *I hope whatever he took was worth the price of turning his sister into a whore for it.*

All sympathy for him fled at the harshness of those words. "How dare you!"

How dare you! he snarled in return. *Get out! Never let me catch either of you here again or so help me, I will be the beast you fear most.*

He'd barely finished speaking before she found herself standing out in the middle of her village—still dressed in the samite and with her bow and quiver resting at her feet. Everyone there turned to stare at her.

Including Brenin Cynfryn and Morla. Their amused, judging gazes all said they knew that her dragon had repudiated her. A few, including Nesta and Morla, even went so far as to snicker and smile in smug satisfaction.

Too horrified and humiliated to speak, she retrieved her bow and quiver with as much dignity as she could muster, and headed back to her hovel, all the while choking back her tears.

Nay, this day had not turned out the way she'd planned at all.

As bad as she'd thought it *could* be, this was so much worse. Where was Virag? Could he have really pilfered from Illarion's treasure? Why would he have done such a thing?

She didn't want to believe her brother capable of such a dastardly deed and yet . . .

Everything had been like a dream with Illarion until then. His anger had been too real to be feigned. His wrath too absolute. For whatever reason, her brother had betrayed them both and abandoned her to Illarion's fury. He knew the one rule her dragon had made for them—they could use any item there, but were to leave with nothing.

Why, Virag? Why? Why would you have done this to me?

Heartbroken, she sat on her bed and cried.

Illarion cursed at the absence of his dragonstone. Without it, he lacked the ability to heal himself. And it wasn't like he could get another. Between mankind and other fey creatures, they'd stolen them, down to only a tiny handful. Slaughtered his brethren for them until the world was all but devoid of what had once been in abundant supply.

He'd been one of the very last drakomai to possess one, and only because Max had given his to him out of guilt over what had happened to him as a dragonet.

Dammit! He knew better than to trust anyone, especially a human and a sneaky kikimora. Was he really so desperate for kindness that he'd be such an easy fool for her?

The answer was obvious. He was all kinds of stupid. Max would be the first to beat him over this.

And he deserved it.

Sick to his stomach, he wished he could still roar. Anything to vent the fury inside him that craved blood.

Trying to calm himself, he focused on the one bright spot of the day. At least the kikimora hadn't stolen . . .

Shit!

Complete and utter horror went through him as he realized that for all he knew, Virag had taken *it*. The worst *it* imaginable.

Please be here. Please be here. Please be here. . . . That frenzied litany raced through his head as his heart pounded and his breathing turned ragged with panic.

If that bastard had taken *that*, all manner of hell would be unleashed.

And his father would mount his worthless and stupid ass to the walls of Olympus.

Illarion teleported into his chambers and ran to the guarded wall where he kept the most sacred possession in his collection. It was so rare and dangerous, not even his brothers had been trusted with the knowledge that he kept it.

No one knew about this.

His hands shaking with trepidation, he slowly opened the ancient carved oaken chest and held his breath.

He didn't release it again until he saw the enormous white teeth that lay on a bed of red satin. If one didn't know what they were, they could appear to be insignificant pieces of smooth tusks or innocuous bits of ivory.

But they were not innocuous and definitely *not* insignificant.

With this handful of teeth, any creature could destroy or subjugate the world. Conquer any nation.

Unravel the fabric of the very universe.

Thank you, gods, they're safe. . . .

Sitting back on his heels, Illarion was giddy with relief. No one had disturbed the Spartoi. All twenty were here and accounted for. Grateful beyond description, he secured and locked the chest, then hid it again in his chambers. That was the one thing he could *never* allow anyone to find.

Originally, there had been three sets of teeth. One set had been used in ancient times by Kadmos to found the city of Thebes. The second, Jason and his Argonauts had sown in the fields of Colchis when he'd sought the Golden Fleece.

Both times, the invincible army that had risen up from the drakomas's planted teeth had almost destroyed the world. After Jason's experience with the second set of warriors, who'd only been defeated when they'd turned on each other, Ares had brought the remainders to Illarion and bid him keep them far from the world of man. Since he was the war god's son and unable to speak—and took antisocial to a radical level—Ares had thought Illarion would be the safest guardian for them.

So far, his father had been right.

Yet this had been too close a call.

Let no one close to you. How many times had Falcyn told him that? He'd always agreed with his brother. Unlike Max, Illarion didn't believe in the good of others. Nor was he under the delusion that man or anyone else deserved to be protected or saved.

Honestly? He didn't give a shit. Let them all burn.

He was done with this world. Never again would he concern himself with the matters of other species. Today had taught him a vital lesson. Every time he left his home and dared mingle with them, it ended badly for him.

And as he settled himself down to rest, he tried not to notice the lingering scent of a woman in his cavern. Nor remember the gentle caress of a hand on his skin or scales.

He was drakomai. Solitary. Since the dawn of time, his kind had been bred to live alone. To die alone.

They needed nothing. They wanted nothing.

Ever fierce.

And ever protective of what fell under their protection . . .

Most of all, they were devoutly loyal and once their word was given, they would die before they broke their oaths.

5

"Are you ever going to speak to me again?"

Huffing and puffing as she carried her heavy water bucket, Edilyn ignored her brother. Just as she'd done for the last three days. She was still so mad at Virag she could stab him through his heart.

Or groin. Aye, definitely the groin.

After all, that was where he lived and breathed. And apparently it was also where he stored his brains. It was all he really valued. Because he apparently had no love of her whatsoever or he'd have never done what he did.

"Say *something*!"

"Sod off!" she snarled as she struggled to get her bucket from the well to the field where she was having to tend that damnable wheat she hated with every piece of her being. But thanks to Virag, this would be the rest of her miserable life. She would live and die in this wretched field, tending those disgusting vegetables and plants, and plowing and tilling the earth until she went mad from the boredom of it.

No man would have her now. They all knew she'd been rejected by Illarion and sent home in disgrace. As horrible as the mockery had been before, it was thrice as bad now.

Only since her return, every man thought her to be a whore atop it all.

Thanks to Virag.

"She speaks!" Virag shouted. "Granted, not what I was expecting. But finally, I got something out of you."

Edilyn slammed the bucket down, spilling half its contents. That made her hate her brother even more since she'd have to go back all the sooner to collect another round. She glared at the insufferable beast. "Go to hell and rot!"

His eyes glowing with sincerity, he winced. "How many times do I have to apologize?"

She scoffed at his useless words. "There will never be enough. For what your actions did rend, mere words will *never* mend."

A tic started in his jaw. "Do you want me to leave?"

Honestly? She wanted him to die. But having lost the rest of her family, she choked on those words, because she knew the true finality of them. Just as she knew the finality of losing Illarion.

What she couldn't understand was why this hurt so much. She'd only known Illarion a few hours. Virag, however, she'd known so much longer. He'd been with her, her faithful guardian, since her childhood. She didn't really want to lose her brother.

But her anger at him over what he'd done was an unreasoning beast. It wanted to lash out and cut him to the bone. To make him feel just a pittance of the pain he'd caused her.

Thoughtless bastard! How could he think only of himself? Unlike her, he had magic aplenty to get whatever he wanted, whenever he wanted it. To do whatever he wanted. He'd lived a long life, and he would continue to live on, centuries after she was dead and buried.

His actions in this against her made no sense. It was the epitome of selfish.

"Why did you do this to me? You knew how much I wanted to get away from this life. Yet you refuse to take me from here because you say that you can't, for stupid reasons, and the one time I found my own way out, you forced me back. Why would you damn me to this? What were you thinking?"

"I didn't think he'd notice, to be honest. Damn, Eddie. Did you see that cavern? How the hell did he miss one little stone?"

"Ugh!" She threw a muddy dirt clod at him. "You're such a horse's arse!"

Disgusted, she wiped at the perspiration on her forehead as more rolled down between her breasts where it itched to an unbearable level, and fought the urge to strangle him. If she gave in to that need, he'd just overpower her and make her angrier, anyway. And what really didn't help her foul mood was the fact he used his powers to clean off the mud and be impeccably dressed again. Meanwhile, she was covered in filth and sweat. Her arms coated to her elbows in mud, her dress, and in particular its hem, mired with muck from her chores. She smelled so bad, even she was offended by her stench. Every strand of her hair was caked and plastered with field dirt and sweat.

She didn't want to think about what was stuck on the bottom of her worn leather shoes. That pungent odor choked her every time it wafted up on the scarce, stifling breeze.

Damn oxen.

And damn her for not paying closer attention to where she put her feet.

"I can see that you're upset—"

She cut his words off with a murderous are-you-kidding-me glare.

"We'll discuss this later."

"Aye, preferably while I'm armed with something sharper to throw at you!" she called after him. Grumbling, she returned to watering the shoots that were just beginning to jut up from the soil. But in all honesty, she wanted to stomp on them until her anger was spent.

Actually that wasn't true. She wanted to stomp her brother's head. They would just make a nice, non-sentient substitution.

Sighing, Edilyn blinked as her tears returned, and she hated those even more than her anger. Fury sustained her. She could work with that. It was this unrelenting pain, the desolation that came with the knowledge she'd lost her dream and future that hurt so much.

The hopelessness that there was nothing more for her. She'd had her one chance.

Now it was gone.

For such a needless reason. Such a selfish reason.

Heartbroken, she picked up her empty bucket and headed back to the well at the same time she saw a rider approaching.

Shouting and screaming, the other workers fearfully rushed to the village walls. Edilyn didn't bother. She knew from experience that they'd lock her out. They always had. There was no need in giving them the amusement of watching her run for it anymore.

So she walked casually toward the well while the rider approached her.

To her surprise, it was a woman on the horse. Normally women didn't travel alone. For that matter, men didn't normally travel alone, either. Too many wars had broken out over these last few years, leaving behind enemies who wanted the throats of their rivals, and displaced bandits who would prey on anyone they could find.

The woman slung one long, graceful leg over her mount and slid to the ground beside Edilyn. Dressed in black ring armor and clothes that said she was a hooded Saxon, she was a woman of exquisite beauty. Surely she had to be a princess or queen, if not a goddess. Her olive skin was flawless and contrasted sharply with vibrant green eyes that were sharp with her intelligence. As she approached Edilyn, she lowered her hood to expose a wealth of flamered hair she'd intricately braided and coiled around her head. "Is the water fresh?"

"It is."

"May I have some?"

Edilyn drew it up and offered her a cup, then she took her field bucket to the horse for his refreshment.

The woman quirked a brow at her actions. "That was kind of you."

Disregarding the praise, Edilyn stroked the horse's black mane as he drank. "He's beautiful. What's his name?"

"Samson."

She smiled as she admired the great warhorse. "A fitting name for one so handsome." She gave him a gentle hug, then returned to pull up more water. "Would you like another drink?"

"I'm good, thank you." When the lady warrior went for her small leather purse, Edilyn stopped her.

"There's no payment necessary." She retrieved the bucket so that she could fill it and return to work.

The lady cocked her head to watch her while she labored. "You've been crying."

It was a statement, not a question. Edilyn cleared her throat. "'Tis the sweat rolling into my eyes. Nothing more."

"So I see."

Edilyn scowled at the way she said that. There was a peculiar note in her voice. "See what?"

"Why Illarion chose you. You *were* innocent in the deed, weren't you?"

"Pardon?"

A gentle smile spread across the woman's face as she tucked her hair back behind her left ear to show that it was quite pointed. "I'm Xyn. Illarion's older sister."

She sucked her breath in sharply. "He didn't tell me you were Arcadian."

Xyn let out a sinister laugh. "Not Arcadian, love. Something far, far worse. And much older than their breed."

Suddenly frightened, Edilyn stepped back from her. "What do you want from me?"

Before she could blink, thick storm clouds rolled over the sun, darkening the sky to pitch. The color faded from Xyn's eyes, turning the green to a ghostly white that shimmered and glowed. Her skin faded as strange markings appeared to bisect her cheeks from hairline to jaw. Spiny and jagged, they reminded Edilyn of bleeding thorns, or claws. Morbidly pretty and absolutely terrifying. A set of black wings sprang from her back as she closed the distance between them.

"Innocent or not, makes no never mind. For what you've done to my brother, little human . . . you will die."

6

Unwilling to lie down and die without a fight, Edilyn ducked as Xyn flew toward her. She ran for the closest thing she had to use for a weapon—an old hoe someone had cast aside before they'd fled for shelter at Xyn's earlier approach.

Aye, it was only slightly better than throwing her dung-encrusted shoe at the demon, but it was better than nothing. She broke the end of it off over her knee to use the handle as a fighting staff, and stood her ground, prepared to battle to the end.

Granted, she'd most likely only be able to soil her opponent's clothes with her own blood. But by the saints, she'd ruin Xyn's wardrobe if nothing else!

Yet as Xyn flew in for her, something snatched Edilyn off her feet and cradled her against a solid leathery wall. Her attacker jerked the staff from her hands and cast it to the ground.

Edilyn started to fight until she realized it was Illarion in his dragon's body, holding her. Stunned, she froze as he carefully landed a few feet away and set her down with a startling gentleness.

Transforming into his male personification, he turned to face his sister with a mask of fury that should have sent Xyn fleeing in terror.

What are you doing? he growled at Xyn.

"Protecting you."

From what? She's a harmless human.

Brazen and foolish, his sister laughed out loud. "Bullshit. So long as she lives, she's a weakness . . . as I just proved. Now, man up, dumbass. Either let me kill her or you two make nice, and you take her back home and stop your infernal moping."

I can't do that.

Xyn snorted dismissively as she closed the distance between them. "Then you have a big-ass problem, don't you? Yes, yes, you do. 'Cause you can't leave her out here where your enemies can use her to lure you to her defense any time they want, can you? No, moron, you *can't*." She poked her finger into his chest to emphasize her angry words. "You're so lucky *I'm* the one who stumbled upon her when I wasn't even looking. Because I thought she was *you*. I mean, hey, I thought it weird you were out and about after I left you curled up and pouting in your cave yesterday, but hey . . . possible. You could have come to your senses or gotten hungry. Then, lo and behold, the scent I caught a whiff of wasn't you. Damned if it wasn't the little sweet-cheeks you were pining for, out on her own, who *reeks* of you and your unique powers. *Voila!*" She gestured at Edilyn. "And *that* has disaster written all over it."

I hate you. His tone was every bit as sullen as his sister had said.

Xyn reached up and pinched his cheeks together like a mother might do her toddler child. "Hate me all you want, punkin', just don't make me have to spank you. I'm getting too old for this shit. And so are you."

Tilting her head, she met Edilyn's gaze over Illarion's shoulder. "Sorry I had to scare you. It was the only way to get Sour Sally out of his hole and show him what an idiot he was being. I swear. Take my word on this. Wise up. Get a girlfriend. Men are so not worth the effort, most days."

And still Illarion glared at both of them, refusing to reverse his opinion. *I can't trust her.*

"Yet you still knew when she was under attack from another dragon and came rushing in to protect her . . . 'cause what? You don't care at all? Yeah, bud, your actions belie those words." Xyn rolled her eyes and pressed the palms of her hands to her temples as if she had a massive headache from dealing with him. Honestly, Edilyn knew the feeling.

Though to be fair, it was her own brother who most often gave her that particular look of frustrated agony.

"And you can't live without her . . . at least not happily. You're so screwed, baby. Whatever are you going to do now?" She gestured at Edilyn. "Now turn around and apologize to her. Grovel if you have to. Tell her you're an ass and take her home where she belongs."

Edilyn was so confused about their peculiar exchange. And even more perplexed by her own conflicted emotions where Illarion was concerned. While she understood his feelings, she wasn't too sure she wanted to go back with him.

Not after all this.

She, too, was still angry over what he'd done.

Xyn let out an exasperated breath. "Tell me the truth, Illy. Do you want to be like Max? He's miserable. He's *celibate*," she said in an evil, demonic tone. "Cranky bastard. Really, is he better off?"

His dragonswan almost killed him.

"Aye, she did. However, your dragonswan is innocent in this, and you know it. She didn't do anything. Her douche of a brother did it. We all have assholes for relatives. . . . I'm yours."

He snorted.

Laughing, Xyn cuffed him on the arm. "You know it's true. Falcyn's even worse. One day, you'll have to introduce them—shudder the horror of *that* nightmare. He might actually eat her whole." She playfully wagged her hand between them. "You come into this with a lot more baggage than she does. She only has the one dickhead you've already met. You got a whole herd of us. I don't have a clue how you're going to explain our mother or Blaise to her. Never mind that thing you call a father. Good luck with that."

Grinding his teeth, he met Edilyn's gaze over his shoulder.

Her breath caught at the accusation in his steely gaze.

"I didn't know Virag was going to do that, Illarion. I would have stopped him from it, had I known."

At first, he didn't seem to care. Not until his gaze went to her cheek. Then he moved to stand in front of her. With a feather-light caress, he brushed his fingers against her skin. His eyes darkened to a furious glower.

Who struck you? That calm, deadly tone was even more terrifying than his sister's earlier attack.

So much so, that she hesitated to answer.

Edilyn? he demanded emphatically. *Who dared to lay a hand on you?*

Xyn answered for her. "One of the townsmen. He wanted to sample a piece of dragon ass, even if it was cast off."

He made a sound the likes of which Edilyn had never heard, an instant before he stormed toward the village.

When she started after him, Xyn caught her arm and stopped her. "Let him go. This is a matter of honor."

"I already took care of it."

Xyn grinned. "I know. But Illarion is about to take better care of it and ensure that no one ever disrespects you again. Contrary to what you're thinking, this isn't about him and his male ego. It's about your safety and making sure they understand you are never to be threatened or harmed. He's doing this for you, Edilyn. It's to ensure that they give you the respect you're entitled to."

She turned toward Edilyn and let out a long breath. "My word of advice to you? Think of him from this day forward as a vicious guardian who's barely restrained. You have at your command your personal house dragon, Lady Edilyn. Not a man. Never lose sight of that. He isn't human. Never fool yourself into thinking that. That is not *his* body you see. It was one forced on him by an ancient god and he resents *every*thing about it. The fact that he wears human flesh around you is a miracle and should be cherished for the rarity that it is. I assure you, he doesn't do it lightly."

Suddenly, Edilyn heard screams and shouts from the village. Then the sound of large, flapping wings filled the air an instant before Illarion rose up into the sky to return to them.

Xyn let out an irritated laugh and shook her head. "Point made with a flourish. . . . My brothers are never subtle. But then, neither am I." She clapped Edilyn on her arm. "By the way, your brother stole Illarion's dragonstone. It's what heals him whenever he's wounded. We need that back. Get it and I won't cut off your brother's head. Fail to do so and I'll send my older brother after him . . . you don't want to know what Falcyn will do to retrieve it. He is indeed a bitter, nasty bastard."

She didn't have time to comment as Illarion swooped down to pick her up and cradle her in his talons. Edilyn closed her eyes and held her breath so that she couldn't see how quickly the ground receded under her. Still, she felt it as her stomach sank and heaved. Along with the wind that rushed against her while Illarion climbed higher and higher into the sky.

Her breathing labored, she knew he wouldn't drop her, but it didn't stop the overwhelming panic that seared her, through and through. She was not acclimating to this flying business at all.

By the time he returned to his home, she was no happier about it. She was, however, relieved to be back on solid ground. Panting and weak, she stumbled against the wall while he lumbered away.

"Don't!" she snapped in a sharper tone than she'd meant.

Still in his dragon form, he turned back toward her. Though it was hard to say for certain, she swore he cocked a disbelieving brow at her command. *Pardon?* There definitely was no mistaking the incredulity of that tone.

Steadying her breath, she straightened. "What did you do in my village? Did you kill him?"

Not sure you want me to answer that. Suffice it to say, they will treat you with the utmost respect should you ever venture there again. . . .

Or run screaming to the hills.

She let out a pain-filled groan. "Very well. I can't go home."

You are home.

No sooner had he spoken than her bow and quiver appeared at her feet, along with the small chest of her clothing that she'd kept in her room.

Her jaw fell open, not just that he'd known they were hers, but that he'd fetched them for her.

Your brother is not welcome here. Nor are you to leave.

"I'm a prisoner?"

I prefer the term protected guest.

"You've got to be kidding me!"

Indeed, I am not. Seems you are the nightmare fairy tale of the brave damsel carried off to the dragon's lair—there to be kept among his treasure and never seen again.

She didn't appreciate his dry recitation of her situation. Rather, it made her want to kick him. "Is that all I am to you?"

Aye. Another burden I'm charged with caring for and protecting.

Those words stung a painful blow to her heart. "Well then, can I at least have a bath?" She gestured at her filthy clothes.

He jerked his spiny dragon's chin toward the stairs. *Bathroom's above. Good luck with it.*

And with that, he left her alone.

Illarion did his best to pretend he was still alone in his cave. That there wasn't a bit of feminine fluff naked upstairs in his shower. But he could hear the water running.

Worse, he could imagine it sliding over her voluptuous body and dripping down her breasts. Pooling in the dark hairs at the juncture of her thighs . . .

Supple thighs that had cradled him. Succored his entire being.

In agony, he rolled to his side and cursed.

Surely, she was doing this to torture him. She had to know he could hear her. That he knew she was naked underneath her clothing and that it drove him mad with lust.

Yes, he was being unreasonable and his random stupidity made no logical sense whatsoever. The truth was, he was too horny to have enough blood left in his brain to think with. And it was all *her* fault.

Dammit! The scent of her was back and it was worse than before. It permeated his cave. Without the opening he'd made, there was no ventilation whatsoever.

No escape.

She was everywhere!

And before he even realized what he was doing, he'd transformed back into his man's body and was standing outside the shower where she leaned with her head underneath the flowing water. She was even more beautiful than he'd remembered. Her delectable curves far more lush and inviting.

With a contented sigh, she lifted her head, opened her eyes, and screamed.

Loudly.

Illarion jumped back, but didn't retreat as she glared at him in fury.

Turning the water off, she grabbed for a towel and covered herself. "What are you doing?"

He backed up as she came out of the water in a soggy huff. *Staring.*

Her eyes blazing, she tucked the towel in between her breasts. "Well at least you're honest. Do I want to know *why*?"

If he'd thought his body was hard before, it was nothing compared with now. Now, he could practically taste her.

It was all he could do not to jerk that towel off and pin her to the wall behind her until he was sated. Only the knowledge that she'd never forgive him for it kept his feet planted and his manners in place.

His breathing ragged, he ran his gaze slowly over the length of her. *I think you know the answer to that.*

"After the way you insulted me, forget it. Lucifer will sit on icicles before I do *that* with you again."

Even if I grovel?

She snorted at his offer. "Do you know how?"

No. He'd never begged for anything. But his sister had been right about how he felt toward his dragonswan. She was a bit different. *I might be willing to learn.*

Edilyn growled at Illarion's playful tone. In spite of her anger, he was charming her, especially with that boyish expression. It was hard to remember why it was important to stand her ground. "I'm not the forgiving sort. I can hold grudges for a very long time."

Good thing I'm immortal, then.

She frowned at something she hadn't known. "Are you?"

Barring a grisly death. Aye.

"That makes *no* sense."

He quirked a beguiling grin. *There are a few beings and things that can kill me. But save for those handful of catastrophes, I'm immortal.*

"Is that what you meant when you said that dragons wait for their deaths?"

He nodded.

Sad, but at the same time . . . "That is incredible that you can live for so long."

Not really. Rather boring after a few thousand years.

"You sound like my brother."

Is that why he stole my stone? Was he hoping I'd kill him and end his suffering?

"Nay, that's mostly because he's an idiot."

Finally, we agree on something.

She laughed before she could stop herself. "So . . . are you really going to keep me as a prisoner?"

I don't know yet. The risk has to be weighed. I have much here that I can't afford to have stolen.

"Would it make you feel better if I told you there's only one thing in this entire cavern that I have any interest in stealing?"

Depends on what it is.

She moved to stand in front of him, where she placed her hand against the center of his chest. Then, she looked up at him from beneath her lashes. "Your heart, my lord dragon. There's nothing else here that holds any interest for me. Though at present, when you treat me with such disregard, I'd much rather carve it out and eat it. But in time, I'm sure my anger will subside and again I will find you the sweet dragon I thought you were. That is the one whose heart I crave to hold and keep safe."

His breathing turned ragged. *When you say such things, I want to believe you.*

"You can. I promise. After all, you are a huge, giant beast of a dragon and I'm one unarmed woman. What could I ever do to harm you?"

He laughed bitterly. *Your actions have already cut me deeper than any blade. Others left scars on my body. But when I thought you'd helped your brother against me . . . it scarred my soul. Cut me deeper than any battle wound or insult. After all, the deadliest wounds aren't the wounds you see, Edilyn. They're the ones that bleed internally. And yours was damn near fatal.*

Those words brought tears to her eyes as she fisted her hand in his tunic. "Then you should know that I could never be such a duplicitous creature. I don't work in secret. That's not my nature. When I'm angry, you will have no doubt of it. For like you, I rain down my wrath for all to see. And I can hide it from none." She leaned toward him and impishly wrinkled her nose. "Just ask my brother. He still limps from it."

Illarion let out a silent laugh as her words finally set his pain to rest. *I've missed you.*

She wrapped her arms around his waist and laid her head against his chest as she hugged him. "Missed you, too."

Closing his eyes, he rested his cheek against the top of her head and inhaled the precious scent of her hair. His rose was ever the sweetest thing he'd ever known. Honestly, he never wanted to let go of her. This was all he ever needed. To be with her and feel like this.

If the price for it was his dragonstone, then he could live with it. He would have made the bargain with her brother. He just wished the kikimora bastard had asked and not taken. It was the theft that set so ill with him.

There was nothing in life he wanted so badly that he'd let it make a thief of him to possess it. Such treachery was beyond his comprehension.

Sadly for his kind, the rest of the world didn't feel that way. It was why the gods had been forced to use his brethren as guardians throughout the centuries to protect and oversee their sacred objects and ensure their safety. But he didn't want to think about that right now.

He only wanted to lose himself inside his dragonswan. . . .

More than that, he wanted to bind himself to her.

Edilyn gasped as Illarion pulled the towel from her body, exposing her to his gaze. There was a light in his eyes that was so ferocious it actually scared her. This was definitely the feral dragon part of him. He literally stalked her and pinned her back against the wall. The kiss he gave her this time was unlike all his previous ones. It was intense and demanding, and it left her breathless—gasping for breath.

More than that, it made the blood rush through her body. He dipped his head to gently tease her breasts, then he was inside her so fast that it stunned her.

He lifted his head to capture her lips as he made love to her furiously. It was raw and consuming. And when he pulled back to meet her gaze she saw the true depth of his emotions.

She lost herself to the vulnerable pain she saw there. Hissing as he thrust against her, she smiled up at him. "Did you really mope in my absence?"

He ground his teeth before he drove himself deep inside her. *I grieved every second I was forced to endure without you.*

Those words brought tears to her eyes. "You will grieve no more."

Illarion tightened his grip around her as he buried his face in the crook of her neck and inhaled the scent of her skin. He let it fill his head until he was drunk with it. Her nails dug into the flesh of his back and sent chills over him. She was his sustenance.

Damn, he owed his sister a debt that could never be repaid. Xyn *had* saved him from his own stupidity. She'd been right. He couldn't live without his human. Edilyn was his Achilles' heel.

She, alone, left him vulnerable.

And when Edilyn came a moment later, calling his name, he

found a special level of paradise he'd never known existed. Smiling, he kissed her as he found his own release.

Breathless and weak, he picked her up and carried her back to the shower so that they could rinse off.

Edilyn paused as she caught the peculiar expression on Illarion's face. "What's on your mind?"

Pardon?

"You look worried?"

Not worried . . . I was considering something.

She waited for him to elaborate while he gently bathed her. When it didn't appear he was going to, she prompted him. "And that was . . . ?"

Foolish. Suicidal. All kinds of stupid. Would you be interested?

She laughed, until she realized he was quite serious. "What are you proposing?"

Something forbidden. Something I know I shouldn't do. It's an act in the face of the gods that will defy them and piss them off to no uncertain end. And yet I don't give a shit. It would ensure that I never lose you. That we are forever bound together. It would make you forever my dragonswan.

"I thought you said only the gods could bind us."

There is another who can do it. If he can be persuaded, and he does owe me a favor. But I won't ask it unless you're in full accord. Because once this is done, there's no way to undo it. We would be forever linked. My life force to yours. A single strand of life.

"I'd be able to have your children?"

He nodded.

"No one could divide us?"

Not even death. But my enemies could use that bond to track you down and use you against me, as you would become the deepest part of me. Indistinguishable from my soul.

She reached up to cup his cheek. "Don't look so fretful, my dragonswain. The irony is that I may not have been dreaming of this, but you are everything I wanted for my future. You will bring me into your world and I will show you mine. Humans aren't as bad as you think us."

You're sure?

"Absolutely."

Then I will go to Savitar alone and ask.

Edilyn frowned at that as trepidation filled her. "Alone? Why? Should I not be with you?"

Definitely not. He set fire to the last beast who asked this of him. In the event he has another similar hissy fit, I'd rather be the only one he comes after. I'm harder to set ablaze than you are.

7

Much like Hybrasil, Neratiti was an island that couldn't be found unless the one who called it home allowed it to be seen. It was kept shrouded and sacrosanct from the world because he who reigned here had even less tolerance for mankind and fey and gods than Illarion.

In fact, Savitar made Illarion appear downright extroverted in comparison. But Illarion was a little different from most, and the blood flowing through his veins could find the elusive island even through Savitar's powerful shields.

It was something that seriously pissed off the ancient being who was lying adrift on a surfboard not that far from the island's shore.

With one leg bent and resting on the board while the other dangled into the water, Savitar groaned out loud the moment he saw Illarion in the sky above him.

"You better be doing a flyby, dragon, and not planning to drop in and destroy my zen."

Illarion disregarded the warning and lightly skimmed the water so as not to make large waves until he came to a gentle rest beside the cranky Chthonian. Floating on top of the surface, he remained in his full dragon form and tucked his wings in at his side. He towered over Savitar, and while that might intimidate someone else, it didn't do anything other than annoy the former protector for Atlantis.

Just think of me as your personal giant rubber duckie.

"Heh." With his entire muscular body covered in colorful tattoos, Savitar was a complete enigma. No one knew where he'd been born or when—he refused to comment on it. His lyrical accent was so old that no one could identify it. But there were times when Illarion thought he detected a hint of Lemurian.

All Illarion knew for certain was that Savitar predated him, and that over thirty-six hundred years ago when the Were-Hunter race had been created after the god Dagon had fused Illarion's life force with that of an Arcadian prince, and Illarion's brother Max's with the prince's half brother who'd been born of a slave, Savitar, alone, had run interference with the gods to spare them all a death sentence for Dagon's hubris. A hubris borne from Dagon's defiant need to spare the king's children from a spiteful curse that had been unjustly levelled against their mother's entire race by the Greek god Apollo centuries before their births, after a handful of Apollites had murdered his mistress and son out of jealousy.

Only a Chthonian had the powers and authority to make the gods back down. And for reasons only Savitar knew, he more than any other Chthonian in history seemed to enjoy exercising that ability—especially against the three Greek Fates. There was no denying or ignoring the fact that he had a hard-on for them that no one understood.

It was that grudge Illarion was hoping to exploit today.

You told me once that I could ask a favor.

Savitar growled low in his throat. "As I recall, that was directed more toward your brother than you, as you weren't particularly cooperative that day when the offer was made. If memory serves, and it does, *you* wanted the Arcadians and Katagaria put down."

Well . . . not all.

Snorting, Savitar passed an irritated grimace at him with those eerie lavender eyes. "True. You did want yourself and Max spared. The rest . . . not so much."

Do you blame me?

"Not really. And you're lucky I share your feelings toward most of the world. Now what brings you to these treacherous waters, my little rubber dragon?"

I found a woman.

Savitar cocked a brow at that. "What? None of your brothers ever had a sex talk with you? Well . . . it's not a hard concept to master. Simply put, tab A goes into slot B."

Illarion rolled his eyes and shook his head. *You enjoy playing the asshole, don't you?*

"One of the few pleasures left in my long, insufferable life. I hear from Max that you partake of it quite a bit yourself."

He couldn't really deny that in good faith. *Anyway, back to the topic at hand . . . I want to bond with her.*

Savitar went stock-still. He didn't even breathe. In fact, he held it for so long that Illarion began to fear the bastard was dead.

Finally, he blinked slowly. Then let out an elongated sigh. "Do you understand what you're asking me to do?"

Illarion nodded.

"I don't think you do, dragonet. You think you know, but you really have no clue." He turned his head to pin him with a hostile glare. "The madness we, the damned, find when we seek salvation. We're so desperate for some semblance of sanity that we will take whatever shred of it we can find—to hell with the consequences. Even if I were to tell you the price you would ultimately pay for it, you'd still tell me it doesn't matter. For you can only see the angel in her eyes today. The succor you currently hold. Maybe the price for it will be worth it in the end. I certainly hope for your sake that's true."

Illarion went cold at those dire words of warning that sent an icy dagger skimming up his spine. *What do you see?*

"You know I can only see what currently is, and all what could be. I won't see the absolute, final path until after I bind you. Then it'll be too late to undo it. But given the myriad of possibilities of what I see . . . not sure *I'd* chance it."

Which was why Savitar stayed secluded here where he could impact no one's future and see nothing of the world around him or his part in anyone's life. His curse that immobilized him was to be damned to see every single outcome. To know everything, except the one final truth.

That he could only see once it was too late to stop it. Once the inevitable course was laid and irreversible.

Yeah, Savitar must have really pissed off the wrong god at some point in his life for *that* to be his fate.

Savitar sat up. "So . . . how suicidal are you?"

She makes me laugh.

"Suicide for the win. You poor bastard."

Illarion gave him a dry stare. *Have you never had a woman you would do anything for?*

"Oh yeah. Got the scars to prove it. Inside and out. I'd tell you to get out before it's too late, but I can see that you're already drowning in that stupidity. Damn, Dragon . . . damn." A deep, dark sadness descended over Savitar's features.

At least you get to piss off the Greek Fates.

A slow, insidious smile curved Savitar's lips before he laughed deep in his belly. "True. How many times do I have to tell you and your brother that you should lead with that whenever you want a favor from me, as it's one of the few things I truly find motivational?" Savitar slid off his board, to float in the water. "I will do this for you. But remember, little dragon, from a thorn comes a rose, and from a rose comes a thorn."

Meaning?

"With all good comes an equal share of bad. Savor your happiness while you have it. Let her be your balm and beware those who seek to divide you."

Another chill of foreboding went down his spine at those words. Aye, there was something the Chthonian was withholding. A dark harbinger was stalking them.

But Illarion refused to let fear rule him. He'd never been a coward in any matter. And while he knew that an iron rod bent while hot, he wasn't rushing into this. He'd been alone his entire life.

Thousands of years.

No woman had ever touched him like this. Edilyn was like no other. And he would never feel this way again. As Savitar had said, all things ended.

If he had to die, he wanted it to be for his rose.

She was his heart. If need be, he'd carve it from his own chest and hand it to her.

"Edilyn?"

With a curse under her breath, Edilyn froze as she heard Virag's voice in her head. She started to ignore him, but she knew she couldn't just vanish and not tell him what had happened to her. She wasn't quite the jerk he was. "What?"

"Where are you?"

She glanced around the walls of her bedroom, where she sat alone. "At Illarion's."

He paused for a long time before he spoke again. "Why can't I visit?"

She scoffed at his ridiculous question. "Why do you think? You're forbidden to come here."

"You're serious?"

"Aye! Now, go away before he returns and hears you."

"He left you alone?"

By the saints, why had she told him that? She could kick her own posterior for being so foolish.

"Virag! Go away! He'll be back any moment and he'll be furious. You've done enough harm."

"I'm your brother!"

She hugged her pillow against her as guilt rose up. But she refused to let it overwhelm her. *She* had nothing to be remorseful over. "You stole from him!"

"I had no choice!"

She scoffed at his sorry excuse for an apology. "We all have choices. You made a bad one."

"So that's it then? After all these years of protecting you, caring for you, you throw me out?"

"Nay!" How dare he put that off on her. "You did this yourself! Don't you even attempt to blame me! Not when you're the thief and caused this!"

"Then you choose his life over mine? Really?"

Edilyn froze. "What are you talking about?"

"If I don't hand over your dragon, Edilyn, the fey queen will kill me."

"You're still lying!"

"Nay, I am not. And you need to decide, little girl, whose life you value most—the dragon you just met, or the brother who has spent these past years giving up everything to keep you safe. It's me or him. You have to choose, because only one of us can survive this."

8

Edilyn drew up short at the sight of the giant man who stood beside Illarion. While her dragon was no small beast in human form, he was several inches shorter than the one now vising them in their cave. Truly, she'd never seen anyone so tall. She barely reached the middle of his chest.

The stranger cracked an amused grin. "You should meet the Dark-Hunter Acheron. He stands eye level to me, and some think he's even scarier."

"Dark-Hunter? Acheron?"

"A good friend of ours. And Illarion can explain Dark-Hunters to you later."

Holding his hand out for her, Illarion closed the distance between them. *Have no fear, Edilyn. This is Savitar.*

His skin was darkly tanned as if he spent a great deal of time in the sun. Windblown dark hair hung to his shoulders and framed perfectly sculpted cheeks that were dusted by whiskers he hadn't groomed in days. He was incredibly handsome, except for the aura of intolerant homicide that clung to him and warned everyone to keep their distance. Like Illarion, he was a feral beast who valued his solitude, and it bled out from every part of his being.

Worse, she had a feeling that he could see her innermost thoughts. That somehow he was crawling through her mind to spy on her deepest secrets.

Unsettled, she took Illarion's hand and let him tuck her in next to his side. She'd never been more grateful for his protection than right now.

"Will this hurt?"

"A small burn, and you will be mates." Savitar raised his gaze to meet Illarion's. "Then later, if you two decide, Illarion will lead you through the rest of the bonding."

"I thought this was the bonding."

"In part. The second step will combine your two life forces so that your life span will match his. If one of you dies . . ." He paused ominously and returned to stare at her as if he knew what Virag had said. "The other will die instantly. But fear not, Edilyn. Illarion can't force you to take that step. The woman must make the choice of her own accord and be willing to accept the bond or it won't work."

Sweat beaded on her forehead as her heartbeat sped up. Savitar knew! He had to know! There was no other explanation for the way he looked at her. Stark cold terror flooded her and made her heart pound. It was all she could do not to turn and flee.

But if she betrayed herself, Illarion might kill her. Her hands turned icy.

Illarion frowned at her. *Are you all right?*

"Fine," she said, quicker than was natural.

Unlike Savitar, Illarion didn't catch on.

And still Savitar stared at her with that gimlet intensity that said he could see straight through her soul, into her heart. With a deep breath, he arched a brow. "So we're doing this?"

Illarion deferred to her one last time.

Terrified, she nodded.

Savitar held his hands out. Illarion placed his palm to Savitar's. Praying that this wasn't a mistake, she did likewise.

At first, nothing happened. But after a few seconds, warmth rose from his hand to engulf hers.

Savitar moved their hands so that he could lay their opposite palms against each other and they could lace their fingers. The heat of Illarion's hand spread to hers, then up her arm.

He leaned forward to kiss her. And as he deepened the kiss, she closed her eyes and inhaled the sweetness of his breath and savored how tender her dragon was. Then she felt the slight sting. With a hiss, she pulled back and shook her hand in an effort to alleviate it.

The moment she did, she saw the elaborate dragon scrollwork on her palm that was a mirror image to his.

They were mates.

Forever.

Or until her brother killed him. . . .

What have I done?

As of yet? Nothing. It was what she *might* do that scared her. The fear of what her brother could talk her into to protect him that terrified her most. He could be terribly persuasive when he tried. And he'd already taken Illarion's stone.

She was sure that wouldn't be the end of it.

Savitar stepped back. "There, all done. Feel like I should say something profound. But why bother? All great advice is left unheeded, then looked back upon with great regret. So let's not be pithy, shall we?" And with that, he vanished.

Illarion tightened his hands on hers. *You're shaking.*

She practically jumped at his observation. "It's a big step."

Do you regret it?

"Nay."

He cupped her face in his hands. *You are now officially my dragonswan. Strah Draga.* He placed a gentle kiss to her lips.

She sank her hand in his soft auburn hair and savored the taste of him. But still she couldn't get his sister's words out of her mind. Pulling back, she bit her lip. "Is it true that without your dragonstone you can't heal?"

He scowled at her. *What do you mean?*

"Xyn told me that it was crucial to your survival."

Illarion made a face that alarmed her. *Aye and nay. I will heal from most things . . . eventually. But in some cases, failure to have one could prove fatal.*

She didn't care for the sound of that at all. "Then we must get it back!"

The thought has crossed my mind.

His dry tone made her smile. "So what's to become of us?"

A strange light came into his eyes. *I know it was your dream to be a marchoges—*

"You want me to give up all thoughts of it," she whispered past the sudden lump in her throat, interrupting him. After all, it was what everyone had always said to her.

I didn't say that. However, I wouldn't be as comfortable with you as a marchoges as I would a draigoges. I will still train you for war. The only thing to change is what you ride into battle. He wagged his eyebrows playfully at her.

She laughed, unable to believe that he was in accord to her wishes. "You would indulge me?"

I don't want you to rue your decision, my lady. Or give up your dreams. Nor do I want you to regret being with me. If this is what you want most, then I will be there, by your side, for every battle. I would trust no one else to carry you.

For the first time, she truly understood what Xyn had been trying to tell her about Illarion and his protectiveness and loyalty.

He wasn't like the *men* she was used to.

Illarion was her dragon.

Smiling, she walked into his arms and held him close. Burying her face in his neck, she inhaled the scent of his skin and let it soothe her. How she wished it could stay like this—just the two of them.

Forever.

But nothing ever lasted—she knew that better than anyone.

Virag had drawn her into a nightmare. One where evil schemed against them and wanted to take the very thing that had finally brought her happiness. He wanted her to make a decision between them and that was the last thing she could do.

With that thought, though, came another. . . . "Have you ever fought against the fey?"

Few times. Why?

"Could you teach me to do it?"

Again, I ask why?

"Should I ever have to fight for or against my brother, I would like to stand a chance."

Illarion grinned. *Sure.*

Maybe that was the answer. If she could learn how to fight Morgen and the others, maybe then she could save her brother and not sacrifice her happiness.

Surely, there had to be some way out of this other than offering Illarion's life?

9

Six months later

Edilyn was stunned by how much had changed in such a short amount of time. True to his word, Illarion had taught her every skill she needed to ride a dragon for battle.

Are you ready?

Dressed in the Greek armor Illarion had given her that had been forged by Hephaestus, she'd been dreaming of this moment when she could take her place with the others.

Now . . .

Edilyn looked up at her dragon mount and made a startling realization.

She couldn't do it.

With a smile, she hooked her hand in the reins and tugged until his head was level with hers. Her smile widened an instant before she placed a kiss on his scaly cheek. "Not worth the risk to my dragon."

Illarion frowned as he watched Edilyn remove her helm. *What?*

"As much as I'd love to do this . . . I don't like the possible outcome of you being harmed because I'm an idiot."

Peeling off pieces of her armor, she headed for the stairs.

Edilyn?

She paused halfway up to bite her lip and wrinkle her nose in a way she knew made him crazy and fired his blood. With an impish grin, she crooked her finger for him. "If you'd care to join me for another matter, my lord dragon. . . ."

He shed his dragon's body so fast it made her laugh. Even more that he rushed up the stairs two at a time to scoop her up in his arms and then teleport them to her room. Though to be honest, she hadn't slept in here since their mating. Rather, she curled up with him on his straw pallet, to sleep with her hand touching his chin.

At first, Illarion had been terrified of accidentally harming her.

Until she pointed out that he couldn't really roll or move in his cramped space. Her dragon was far too large for such things.

Now, they only used her bed for trysts.

Laughing, she nipped his whiskered chin with her teeth. "Eager much, my dragon?"

You think? He tugged at the laces of her armor until he had her bared before his hungry gaze. Though to be honest, he could have simply used his powers to strip it from her. She found it precious that he often refrained from their use as if he feared that it might offend her, or worse, remind her that he was a dragon and cause her to hold it against him.

As if she'd be so petty at this point.

She deepened her kiss. "Bind with me this time."

Illarion hesitated, as he had every time she'd made this request. While he wanted to keep her with him forever, it terrified him that she might one day regret a rash decision. *Edilyn—*

She stopped his protest with another kiss. "I know what you're going to say. But I want this, Illarion. One life. Together. The two of us as one." She reached down to gently cup and stroke him through his breeches.

Sucking his breath in sharply, he found it hard to remember his reasons for not doing this with her. But he wasn't a coward.

He held his marked palm up for her so that she could place hers against it. *Very well, my lady rose. I am yours.*

"Forever."

And always. He pulled her to the bed so that he could lie back on it. *It's all up to you, my lady. You are the one who has to accept me.*

"How?"

Just like our mating ritual. You take me into your body and when the thirio comes, I will lead you through the next steps.

Edilyn pulled back with a frown. "What aren't you telling me?"

Nothing.

She scoffed. "Don't give me that tone. I know *that* tone. You're holding something back. What is it?"

He fingered her lips as he stared up at her. *To bond, I will have to drink from you and you'll have to drink from me.*

"Drink what?"

It's a sanguine ritual, my lady. To bind our lives, we must combine our blood. An adorable grin lit his face. *You still want to do this?*

She slid herself onto him and watched as he arched his back. The sight of his pleasure made him all the more handsome. His breathing ragged, he stared up at her from beneath his thick lashes. Leaning forward as she slowly rode him, she smiled. "Positive."

Illarion felt his powers surge as they always did whenever he was inside her. Most of all, he felt the need he had to bind their lives together. In the past, he'd stamped it down and pushed it aside.

Today, he embraced it.

While other groups and Were-Hunter species had their own ceremonies and words they spoke for this, he didn't want to cheapen it with something so insignificant. The words weren't important.

Their commitment was all that mattered.

Keeping her hand in his, he felt his teeth elongate. Before this, he'd always taken care to hide that from her lest it terrify her. For the first time, he opened his lips so that she could see his fangs.

Her eyes widened. But she didn't pull away.

Unable to believe her courage, he pushed himself up so that he was cradling her while she continued to ride him with slow and easy strokes.

He brushed the black hair back from her neck and gently nuzzled the supple skin there. His heart pounding, he nibbled her flesh.

Edilyn trembled at the heat of his breath on her skin. She had no idea what to expect. Not until he sank his teeth into her flesh.

The moment he did, she felt her own teeth elongate as an unknown fire coiled in her stomach. Breathless and weak, she cradled his head in her palm until he lifted up to meet her gaze.

Your turn, my lady rose. He tilted his head to give her better access.

Wrinkling her nose, she took the invitation and did her best not to think about what she was doing.

Honestly? She expected it to make her sick. Yet it wasn't like that. There was something warm and fulfilling. Something that made this seem right. Made her crave this incredible closeness with him.

And when she felt his release, it set off hers. His arms tightened around her until he was completely sated. With the tenderest of expressions, he led her marked palm to his lips so that he could kiss it.

I love you, my rose.

Those unexpected words shocked her. Unable to believe them, she stared, aghast. Then she smiled at the warmth that flooded through her. "Love you, too, my dragon lord."

A deep sadness replaced the light in his eyes.

"Are you all right?"

He nodded. *I have been cursed by the gods from the moment I drew my first breath. So I cannot help but wonder how they're going to use this against me, too.*

"Illarion—"

He cut her words off with a kiss. *You don't understand, Addy-Rose.* His special nickname made her even more tender toward him. *There's so much I haven't told you. Just promise me that no matter what comes at us, you will never doubt my loyalty to you.*

"I would never."

Good.

And yet his doubts caused hers to rise up and terrify her with their merciless cruelty. What if he was right?

Fate had been no kinder to her. She'd lost both parents within a handful of years. Humiliation had been her steady diet, always.

Why should she think this would ever change? Her heart pounding in fear, she buried her hand in his long auburn hair and prayed she was only being paranoid.

But like him, she didn't really believe that. . . .

How could she? There was something inside her that told her the darkness was coming for them. An inner sense that gave her no peace and left her completely unsettled and cold.

Edilyn finished her dinner while Illarion was off doing his dragon business, which meant finding his own meal. Something he emphatically refused to let her see him do. And that always made her wonder one thing whenever he left her behind . . .

How bad could it be?

But then, there were some things she did she didn't want him to see her do either. So she tried to be understanding and respectful.

And hoped he wasn't out eating people.

Although . . .

There were a few she wouldn't mind adding to his menu.

Some days, that list was much longer than others.

"Edilyn?"

And there was one for the top of said list. She groaned out loud as she heard her brother's voice in her head. For weeks, she'd ignored him.

He'd become progressively more whiny with every brush-off. At this point, she was about ready to tie a bib around his neck and burp him.

"Eddie! I need you to answer me!"

Normally, that wouldn't move her, but there was an odd note in his voice. One that actually concerned her. "Are you all right?"

Virag hesitated before he answered. "I need your help, little sister."

She glared up at the ceiling, knowing he couldn't see her, but feeling the need to do so anyway. "What are you asking me for, this time?"

"You have to help me deliver up your dragon. I can't delay it any longer. There's no choice in the matter."

"There's always a choice, Virag. You made yours. I won't—"

"Eddie . . . it's not that simple. Our mother isn't dead."

She froze as that news slammed into her and stole her breath.

Was he being honest? Or was it another lie?

"What?"

"It's true. The bargain she made? It was with Morgen le Fey and it was only for ten years and a day. At the end of which, she was to return to Landvætyria and enslave herself to Morgen and her Circle. Forever. Your father knew this. He died trying to free her from Morgen. What I stole? I took it in an effort to free our mother from that bitch."

"You're lying!"

"Nay. I swear it's the truth. On my life and blackened soul. Your father was never supposed to die. That wasn't part of the bargain. When he was killed, our mother begged me to come to Myddangeard and watch over you to make sure that no one from our side found you and harmed you, in an effort to get to her or steal her powers. It's why I've always been so protective of you— you know in your heart it's true. Think about it. Now I need you. You've got to help me get what I need or Morgen will kill all three of us. You, me, and our mother." His voice broke on that last word. "Please, Edilyn. I beg you. Never have I asked anything of you, but I need you now, baby sister. Please!"

Anguish brought tears to her eyes. He was right. In all these years, he'd never once made any request of her.

She heard Illarion returning.

So did Virag. "You have to decide," he whispered in her ear. "The family that has watched over you and loved you, or the dragon you barely know. We won't all survive. Who will sacrifice?"

10

Illarion knew the moment he returned to his den that something bad had happened. It wasn't just that he could smell Edilyn's fear, but she wasn't waiting on him, as was her custom.

Strange that he'd never realized how much he looked forward to her greeting. Even more peculiar was how quickly he'd acclimated to her presence in his life. It wasn't just that they were bonded. . . .

She had become a vital part of his existence. The best part, really.

Addie?

She finally came out of the shadows near where they slept. Clearing her throat, she offered him a trembling smile. "Sorry. I didn't hear your return."

Hmm . . . he had no idea how she could miss it. He wasn't exactly quiet.

Still in his true form, he approached her. *Is something wrong?*

"It's all good."

Shifting into his human body, he closed the distance between them and moved to kiss her. Her lips lacked their usual passion. She was cool and distracted. He pulled back to grimace down at her suspiciously. *What is going on with you? I can feel your restraint.*

Edilyn closed her eyes as she struggled with what to do. She couldn't make this decision. It wasn't in her to play God. Not with anyone, and especially not with her dragon.

No matter how much Virag might beg, she couldn't do what her brother asked. She couldn't. "I don't know what to do," she whispered.

About what?

"My brother said that he took your stone to barter with the queen of the fey to free my mother from her."

He scowled. *You said your mother was dead.*

" 'Tis what I was told. Three days after my seventh birthday, she went to gather berries in the forest, and never returned. They said an animal attacked her. I wasn't allowed to see her body. My father said it would be too disturbing for me." A tear slid down her cheek. "I never got to say good-bye. All my life, I've regretted all the things I didn't say to her that I should have. Now . . . to be told that she's been alive and held? I'm furious! And hurt! Virag said that my father died trying to free her. Now . . ."

Illarion kissed the tear from her face. *Shh, my rose. Don't weep.*

She buried her hand in his hair and laid her cheek to his chest. "You haven't heard the worst. Virag told me that if I don't hand you over, they'll kill her and him." Closing her eyes, she ground her teeth as pain poured through her. "I don't know who to believe or to trust. If what he says is true, then he's lied to me my whole life . . . all of them did. So how can I trust this isn't a lie, too?"

Illarion gave her credit for that wisdom. Most wouldn't be so prudent, especially given her emotional state. *And you barely know me, so how can you trust me when the ones you've put faith in for so long have played you so falsely?*

"Exactly!" She blushed as she realized that she'd inadvertently insulted him. With an adorable grimace, she wiped at her cheeks. "You see my dilemma?"

Yet you trusted me with the truth.

"It's not in my nature to lie. I don't like pretense. It's an ugly thing that leads to the worst in man and beast."

Aye, it is. He brushed her hair back to offer her what comfort he could. *You say she's held? Do you know where?*

"Nay. All I know is she made her bargain with Morgen le Fey." Illarion laughed bitterly at the name.

"You know her?"

Aye, bitch that she is. But more to the point, I know someone quite intimate with her.

Edilyn widened her eyes as hope finally began to lift up inside her again. "Who?"

My brother Blaise. If your mother made any bargain with Morgen, my brother will know of it. There's nothing that happens in her court he doesn't know all about.

"You think he can help?"

There's only one way to find out. Come, my precious, and meet my craziest brother.

Edilyn wasn't sure what to expect as she took Illarion's hand. She assumed he'd fly her to wherever they needed to go, as a dragon.

He didn't. The moment she took his hand, he flashed her from his cave out into a bright, vibrant meadow the likes of which she'd never seen. Everything here was surreal and glowing. Or radiating with a strange hum to it. It was hard to even focus or look at.

"What is this place?"

Avalon.

She scowled at the unfamiliar name. "You say that as if I should know it."

One day, there will scarce be a human who doesn't. But for now, this is where I need to be to summon my brother. With a wink at her, he made a peculiar whistling noise.

But it wasn't his brother who answered. An incredibly beautiful blonde woman appeared in the garden not far from them. With skin so perfect that she seemed more fey than human, she pursed her lips. "Illarion? It's been a long time since we had the pleasure of your company. Are you seeking your brother?"

Hi, Merlin. I am. Is he about?

"Not per se. He's off on errands for me." She cocked a curious brow at Edilyn.

My dragonswan. Edilyn, meet Aquila Penmerlin. She's the keeper of the land here, and a great lady.

Merlin waved his words away with a humble blush. "He flatters me, truly. It's an honor to meet you, Edilyn."

"And you, my lady."

Illarion cocked his head as he studied the powerful sorceress. *Is something wrong, Merlin?*

She kept staring at Edilyn. "You remind me of someone I knew a long time ago. An old friend. Sorry to stare. Sevira was just very dear to me."

Edilyn felt the blood drain from her face. "Sevira ferch Vyggo?"

Now it was Merlin's turn to appear stunned. "She was a daughter of Vyggo, but that wasn't the name I knew her by."

What name then?

"Sevira Feythhed. She was the fers of the Kikimory—essentially their queen."

Stunned to the core of her being, Edilyn gasped. "Then it's true. Virag didn't lie."

Morgen hesitated before she spoke the obvious. "You're her daughter?"

By a human father. It's why we're here. Morgen found out and is after Edilyn ... and me.

Merlin cursed. She scowled at Illarion. "Does Morgen know what you guard?"

I will hazard a guess that she does, given her actions and ultimatums.

"Then you need to leave here. Now!"

Edilyn refused to go or be intimidated. "Not without my mother!"

Merlin cupped her chin and gave her a harsh, yet sympathetic grimace. "I loved Sevira, too, but this is much larger than love and friendship. And even the love of a mother. You cannot let Morgen lay hands to what Illarion has. *Any* of it."

Edilyn bit back a curse. This wasn't what she wanted to hear. Aye, it might be childish and selfish, but she wanted to see her mother again.

If there was any chance whatsoever . . .

"Illarion?"

Merlin's right, Edilyn. We can't do this.

"Take her and go," Merlin urged as she gently pushed Edilyn toward Illarion. "I'm banishing you both from here."

"Nay!" She tried to step away.

But it was too late. Merlin sent them out before she'd even finished the word. Tears welled in Edilyn's eyes as she saw Illarion's cave, which she was beginning to despise. "Is this where I'm always going to end up?"

Edilyn—

She shook her head, cutting off his words. She didn't want to hear reason right now. All she wanted was to give in to that part of her that had felt abandoned and orphaned for so long.

"You don't understand, Illarion. You never loved your mother the way I loved mine. You can't even comprehend it. And she was ripped so suddenly from my life. I awoke one morning and everything was like it was supposed to be . . . just another day. I thought nothing of it. Just playing in the yard as I'd done a million times. And then it dawned on me that the sun was setting and my mother hadn't returned to make dinner. I went into the cottage to find her. But she wasn't there, either. Instead, it was my father at the table . . . his head hung in his hands while he wept. I hadn't even known that he could cry. Not my fierce father. He was a giant beast of a man, too powerful to be human. Yet there he sat . . . shattered. And in that one moment so was I. My entire world came crumbling down around me and there was nothing I could do to stop it or fight against it. I was rendered powerless in a single heartbeat."

Edilyn broke off on a sob. "To learn that she's alive and that I could see her again? How could you agree to this!"

Illarion watched as she ran up the stairs to her room. He stayed behind, unsure of what to do. She was right. A mother's love was incomprehensible to him. He barely knew his mother.

All he knew of any kind of a motherly bond came from Maxis and Falcyn. . . .

Neither of whom were particularly maternal. Though they would eat whoever threatened him. There was much to be said for *that*. Still . . .

He went after her and found her lying on the bed, sobbing. The sound wrought strange, foreign emotions inside him that he'd never felt before. He had no idea what to call them.

Edilyn? What can I do to make this better?

"I . . . want . . . t-t-to . . . see my . . . mother!"

He pulled her against him and rocked her gently against his chest while he held her. *That I can't do. I'm sorry.*

She cried even harder.

He winced at her heartfelt pain. *You were right in what you said. I don't understand this grief you feel. I've never really had a tender touch until I met you.*

Edilyn choked on a sob at those words. Stunned and hiccuping, she lifted her head to meet his gaze. "What?"

There was no denying the sincerity in his gaze. *But if it means this much to you, I will find a way to get her out.*

"How?"

No idea. But I am drakomas . . . son of Ares, who's mated to the daughter of a kikimora. Apparently, impossible is what we both specialize in. We will do this!

Laughing, she kissed his cheek and held him close. "Thank you."

Don't thank me. Pretty sure before all is said and done, we're both going to be damned by this. But you never know where the journey will take you until you leave your cave and scale back the jungle vines to find your way through the brambles. Even if they shred us to the bone.

11

"You're not doing this."

Illarion glared at his brother Falcyn, who lay curled in all his red dragon glory around a massive boulder. Unlike Illarion, he had a coating on his scales that caused them to shimmer with every breath, as if they'd been bronzed or were bleeding. *Hold my shields. That's all I'm asking.*

"No. You're asking me to support your stupidity. And you know how I feel about fools. I ate all the dumb ones in every litter . . . or so I thought. Apparently, I somehow missed *you*."

Illarion rolled his eyes. *I promised Edilyn.*

"Your mistake. And I don't give a shit, which, considering the size of what we leave behind, actually means something when it comes out of the mouth of a dragon."

Falcyn!

He let out a long, exasperated breath. "Sarraxyn has already told me what your swan has gotten you into. See, this is what happens when you spend so much time around Max. I keep telling you bastards *dumbass* is contagious. Why don't you listen to me?"

What do you expect from an idiot?

"Don't backtalk me, Illy. Not in the mood I'm in. I might forget how much I like you and decide you'd make a good and hearty lunch."

Just guard my island.

Falcyn growled. "Fine, but you'll never get in."

How do you know?

"How do you not? The only thing you could trade her for is to find the merlin of the Halter. That *might* placate Morgen and get her off your back. At least for a bit."

How?

"She doesn't know what the Halter is, or what it looks like. Find its merlin. Hand him or her over, and then tell her that once she sets loose Edilyn's mother, you'll surrender the Halter."

Illarion's jaw dropped at his suggestion. Had Falcyn lost his dragon-mind? *In what world would that be helpful? Then, she'd have the power to actually use it!*

Falcyn let out another long, pain-filled groan. "No! Follow me, here, cupcake. You surrender a fake Halter because she don't know what it is. By the time she learns she's been duped, you're out of there, with your human, and are home free."

Oh . . . That *could* work.

I like your plan.

Falcyn shrugged. "I know. I'm brilliant."

But if you're wrong . . .

"I'll be scooping your entrails up for soup. Never said it wasn't a gamble. Never really said you *should* do it. What is it Acheron's always droning on about? Just because you can and all that."

They both had a point. Still . . .

You should come meet my Edilyn.

Falcyn snorted disdainfully. "No, thanks. I do that, I might actually like her. For all I know, she alone could alter my outlook on humanity." He shuddered. "Last thing I want is to start liking my favorite snack food. Then where would I be?"

You don't eat people, Illarion said drily.

"True. They're gamey bastards. Stick in the teeth and leave a foul aftertaste." He let out one last aggravated breath. "Go on, little brother. I've got your cave for you, even if you are an idiot. You know I'll always be here for *you* . . . Max can burn in hell for all I care."

I wish you two would make amends.

"Tell that to Hadyn, who should have called *me*. I would have died before I let them harm him."

It wasn't Max's fault.

Falcyn lifted his spiny head to glare at Illarion. "Are you trying to make me reconsider your favor?"

He held his talons up in surrender. *I bow before your greatness.*

"Damn right, you do. Cower, too, if you know what's good for you. Now get out of here."

Illarion inclined his head to his older brother.

To his shock, Falcyn hooked one large talon against his snout and held him there a moment longer. "Don't get killed, Illy. Bane-Cry if you run into any trouble."

Those words touched him more than he could ever verbally express. Because he knew what Falcyn was really saying. What his brother really thought of him and meant by them. They weren't spoken lightly by the brash beast who prided himself on caring about no one and nothing. Nor were they trivial. Unlike Max, Falcyn only answered the Bane-Cry of very few of their kindred. He bled for even fewer. While Max would protect anyone he could, Falcyn flew for next to none.

I will.

Falcyn shoved him away, then ambled off. The surly bastard hated good-byes. More times than not for their kind, they were all too permanent.

Illarion watched him a moment longer as brotherly affection warmed him. The Fates hadn't been kind to any of them, but Falcyn . . .

His heart ached for his brother and his past.

But unfortunately, there was nothing he could do to ease the pain or make Falcyn's burdens easier to carry. And right now, he had his own future to secure.

Determined, he took flight and headed back to his den.

Edilyn finished packing her gear while she waited on Illarion to return. A smile hovered at the edges of her lips when she touched the sword he'd given her.

Closing her eyes, she could still see him in all his shyness. She'd been washing her clothes in the small oasis at the base of the waterfall.

In human form, Illarion had watched her for quite a bit with that adorable grimace he had anytime he didn't understand her human ways. *What is it that you do?*

"I'm doing laundry. Don't you ever wash . . ." She'd let her voice trail off as she realized that no, Illarion never did laundry. Like Virag, whenever he wanted something he thought about it and—poof! It was there. "Never mind. Is there something you need?"

Even more bashful, he'd approached her so that he could sit by her side. *You're almost finished with your war training.*

His serious tone sent trepidation through her. "Are you telling me to leave?"

What?! Why?! Where did that thought come from?

Putting her laundry aside, she sat back on her heels to eye him. "Well, the strange way you're acting. It's obvious that something is bothering you. That seemed the most likely source."

He snorted. *Nay, love. Rather you never react to things quite the way that I think you will. So I know not how you're going to receive this news when I give it.*

That was true, she supposed. "You've eaten my brother, haven't you?"

He laughed. *Nay, but the thought is tempting. And since you're not going to calm until I explain, let me put you out of your agony. . . .*

I have a present for you.

"A present?"

Nodding, he'd kissed her forehead. Then, when he pulled away, an entire set of armor had been on the ground beside them. Complete with a sword and shield.

Her jaw had gone slack. "What is this?"

For your protection. You can't very well go to war with just your bare hands.

Touched by that memory, Edilyn sniffed back her tears as she picked up and caressed the sword. Beside it on the bed lay Illarion's dragon's claw—the weapon his brother Falcyn had fashioned in order to protect him whenever he was in his human form. Because of what had happened to Illarion when he'd been a dragonet, and then after the god Dagon had captured Illarion and made him a shapeshifter, Falcyn was hyperprotective of him. He wanted to make sure that Illarion was never helpless again.

And Illarion, because of his past, was every bit as paranoid and insistent with her safety as his family was with his. So Falcyn made the claw for Illarion and Illarion insisted that *she* carry it now in his stead.

There were so many reasons she'd learned to love her dragon.

Right down to his indulgence of her once she'd learned that he could time travel.

"Prove it!" she'd challenged, expecting it to be utter fabrication.

A heartbeat later, they'd been hundreds of years in the future. In a country she barely recognized as Prydain. But there, she'd fallen under the spell of minstrels singing incredible tales of love and sacrifice. And she'd learned of the King Arthur Illarion had spoken about.

What has brought such an incredible smile to your face, love?

Dragging her thoughts from her memories, she looked up to see Illarion had returned. "I was thinking of the times you've taken me into the future. What was the name of that poet again I love?"

Cercamon.

That was it. She didn't know why she had such a hard time remembering his name when she could always recall his words. "I am pleased when she maddens me . . . when she makes me stand with open mouth, staring."

He closed the distance between them and wrapped his arms around her, then completed the rest of the poem. *And I am pleased when she laughs at me, or makes a fool of me to my face, or my back. . . . For after this bad, the good will come very quickly, if such is her pleasure.* He pressed his cheek to hers.

Reaching up, she placed her hand to his strong jaw and sighed. "You are far too gentle to be such a fierce, terrifying beast."

Only because I like you. The rest of the world . . . they are forever on my menu.

As he started away, she caught his hand and pulled him to a stop.

"What's on your mind?"

He cocked a brow at her.

She tsked in response. "You know I can read your moods. You say more with your silence than most who use thousands of words."

His features gentled. *My brother gave me an idea that I'm toying with.*

"And that would be?"

He didn't answer. Rather, he left her side and headed for the stairs.

Curious and confused, Edilyn followed after him.

Without a word, he continued on to his chambers until he reached a chest that she'd never paid particular attention to before. He opened it and pulled out an incredibly ornate gold necklace. Fashioned in the image of a stag, it was designed to hang low and held teardrop-shaped diamonds that shimmered and reflected prisms all through their cave.

"It's beautiful," she breathed, reaching out to touch it.

Illarion laid it across her palm. *It looks so innocuous.*

"Nay, it's glorious!"

He scoffed. *More than you know.*

"How do you mean?"

He inclined his head toward it, then ran one finger over the gems. *This is what your brother seeks, Addie. It's the Halter of the goddess Epona.*

Her jaw went slack as she studied it with new eyes. Delicate and fragile, she couldn't imagine using this to control a horse. "I don't understand."

He picked it up and hung it over her brow like a diadem. *It's an equestrian browband that hangs on a halter.*

In that moment, she realized what he was doing. "You're trusting me with this?"

He nodded.

"Why?"

Lifting his hand from the browband to her cheek, he softened his stern frown. *In the event I fail, I want you to have your mother.*

"Illy—"

Shh, my Addie-Rose. He pressed a kiss to her lips. *Our lives are a finite path on an intricate tapestry. One thread that is woven through thousands of others to form an elaborate pattern that up close loses all meaning. It's only when we stand back at a distance that we can see the details of it all, and how the threads work together to make us whole. I don't know how things will unravel, in the end. I only know that before I allow you to die because you've tied your life to mine, I will place myself into the dragon's torpor.*

She scowled at the unfamiliar term. "The what?"

It's a form of sleep, so deep that I cannot awaken. At least not without my dragonstone. For all intents and purposes, I'll be as the dead. A stone dragon awaiting the day when someone or something revives me.

Shaking her head, she didn't like the sound of this at all. "You can't do that."

I can and I will. I won't risk you. Should I be forced to it, I want you to free your mother and save yourself.

"And you?"

He took her hand and placed a kiss on her knuckles. *Don't worry about me. Just see it done.*

She tightened her grip around his. "I'm getting your stone back. If I have to face down Morgen myself, I will do it."

Smiling, he rubbed the pad of her forefinger against his whiskered jawline. *I wish you luck with it. Now, we need to see if we can locate the merlin of this device.*

"How do we do that?"

With luck, it'll lead us to its guardian.

"Without luck?"

It'll lead us to our graves.

12

"What are we doing here?" Edilyn watched as Il-larion knelt to pull back the weeds from an old grave that rested near the crumbling remains of a forgotten abbey. The sun was quickly fading over his shoulders.

There was something eerie and solitary about this place. Not just that it was so remote, but the way that it was situated on a hilltop, overlooking the sea. Like his island, there was an almost fey quality to this hallowed place.

This is where Kynon ap Clydno is buried, along with his wife, Morvyth. I'm trying to pick up their scents so that we can track their descendent.

"I don't follow."

Glancing up at her, he gestured at the ground, where a broken Celtic cross capstone marked the gravesite. Worn down by unforgiving time and unrelenting weather, only a few runic letters remained to betray who occupied it. *Kynon was one of Arthur's knights.* With a jerk of his chin, he indicated the grave beside it. *Morvyth, the daughter of Arthur's brother-in-law, Urien. Poor bastard actually made the mistake of marrying Morgen, and breeding with her.*

She choked on what he was saying. "Morgen? As in *le Fey*?"

He nodded. *So you can imagine Urien didn't come to a happy ending.* Sighing, he brushed his hand over the hallowed ground where the couple slept in eternal repose. *Sadly, none of them did. At any rate, it was Kynon who first brought the Halter to me for safekeeping, after Merlin entrusted it to his care.*

Edilyn was aghast at what he was telling her. It didn't make sense. "Wait! Merlin entrusted one of the sacred objects that Morgen can use to take over the world to Morgen's son-in-law? Seriously?"

Hence the reason he gave it over to me. While Kynon loved his wife, he didn't trust her to not surrender the Halter to her mother.

"I'm still having trouble understanding why on earth Merlin put it in his hands to begin with."

He let out a silent laugh. *The legend claims that Epona first fashioned her Halter for Kynon's father, Clydno Eiddin, when he and his army rode out from his kingdom to Gwynedd to avenge the fallen prince, Elidir. When such sacred items are created, only a member of the direct bloodline can access their power. Others might have some success with it, but more likely than not, it backfires and they or others are harmed—usually fatally. So when Camelot fell, the Halter had to go to Kynon. No one else could wield it.*

Rubbing her temples, she scowled even more. "That still makes even less sense. How could Arthur use the items, then, to rule his people?"

Illarion gave her a knowing smile. *Before Uther became pendragon, he was known as Uther ap Modron.*

A chill went down her spine at a name she knew all too well. It was one every child knew the legend of, even though the priests did their best to purge it from them. "Modron? The mother goddess?"

Aye, and no one knows who Uther's father was. But given the powers of Arthur and the fact that he was able to access all the objects and use them . . .

"He had to have been directly connected to the powers that created them."

Exactly. Either way, we know for a fact that Uther's mother was. And if both were . . . It would definitely explain why Arthur was such a formidable king and why he was able to unite the land. Why Emrys Penmerlin was so enamored of the boy and his powers, and went to such lengths to hide and protect him.

Illarion rose to his feet. There was a peculiar light in his eyes. One that never failed to make her scared and nervous.

"What is it?"

He transformed into his dragon's body. *Mount up. Someone comes.*

DRAGONMARK

Her heart pounded as more fear rose and she hastened to obey. No sooner had he secured her to her saddle than she saw what had concerned him.

It was an army of dragons. But they weren't like the Were-Hunters who'd been attacking her village. These were larger. Spinier. They appeared more like hell-beasts bent on absolute destruction.

"What are those?"

Something that shouldn't be here.

"What do you mean?"

Mandrakes. They're part of Morgen's forces.

She scowled at the way he said that. "Are they different from drakomai?"

Aye, very much so. They're the children of dragons who were seduced by the Adoni. Hybrids of the two species, they are evil incarnate, hand-raised to be Morgen's lapdogs.

"How are they here?"

I don't know. They shouldn't be able to cross Merlin's Veil. Ever. Somehow, they found a way—Illarion's words broke off as he flew into something hard and solid.

Something unseen.

Like the hand of an angry god, it swatted him from the sky and drove him to the ground faster than he could recover. His only thought to protect Edilyn, he teleported her off his back and into a small copse of trees.

An instant later, he slammed into the ground so hard that it felt as if he'd broken every bone in his giant body. His breathing ragged, he struggled to stay conscious. More to the point, he struggled to rise to his feet.

What the hell?

But with that came another fear. . . .

Addie? Don't call out to me. They're looking for us. Stay hidden and silent.

Still, he could feel her fear and concern. It reached out to him, making him wish he dared go to her and make sure that she was all right. The best he could do was try to stir up his scent to keep them distracted and away from her location.

Terrified for her and shaking from his pain, he limped through the trees to draw them away.

"Well . . . well . . . if it isn't the lost son of Ares?"

Illarion froze at the familiar voice. Even more furious, he turned to glare at Gale, who *definitely* shouldn't be here. A minor Greek goddess and sorceress, the petite blonde was a handmaiden of Hekate.

That was enough to anger him on his best day. But given the fact that Hekate was the mother of Dagon . . .

He was in the mood for a Greek meal today. With Gale being the main entree.

What are you doing here?

She cracked a smile that made him want to crack her skull. "You know what I want. Hand it over and no one dies."

I'm not about to surrender the Halter.

Gale laughed out loud. "You're not that stupid, Illarion. That's not what Morgen's really after, or Cynfryn. It's child play for our intentions. A trifle. We merely used that to flush you out. I told her that if she pressed Virag to get the Halter, you'd come to the graves to pick up their scents for its cymerlin, thus exposing yourself to our army. And once we had you . . . then we could work on getting what we're really after."

And that is?

"Your father's teeth. What else? Have you any idea what I can bargain those for? Split them between Morgen and Cynfryn. I will be richer than Midas."

He went cold at those words. Shit! He should have known!

But he wasn't about to betray that to her, or to anyone. Instead, he blinked slowly and acted nonchalant. *I don't know what you're talking about.*

"Of course you do, Illy. Now give me the Spartoi. Or I'll feast on the heart of your woman."

You can't threaten me.

She let out an evil laugh. "Oh, but I can. See, I know something you don't. A secret Brenin Cynfryn told me about. I can break your life bond with Edilyn."

Impossible!

"Nay, it is not. Give me what I want. Or I'll undo Savitar's bond and watch you lose everything!"

With a calmness he definitely didn't feel, he moved away from where he'd put Edilyn, trying to pull them in the opposite direction.

Just when he thought it was working, Edilyn cried out as the mandrakes found her. It was her battle cry. God love her, she was fighting them with everything she had.

Determined to help, Illarion rushed at Gale, intending to tear her apart. But no sooner did he reach her than everything spun. It was so foul and violent, he looked around for a tornado.

Yet that wasn't what caused this sensation.

This was Gale. The handmaiden was sucking them from this realm into another. Damn her for it!

Illarion fought her as best he could. But Hekate was the goddess of crossroads and gateways. As her servant, Gale could access those powers.

There was nothing he could do.

Nothing except run to Edilyn, who didn't stop fighting until she saw him. "Illarion?"

Without a word, he wrapped himself around her. He didn't have the heart to tell her what was about to be done to them.

Not until they were both sucked into the vortex and slammed into the ground with such force that for a full minute, he couldn't move or even breathe. But once he was able to catch his bearings and see where they were . . .

Honestly, it was no better.

While it wasn't the real hell, it might as well be.

"Where are we?" Edilyn asked.

Illarion let out a long, slow breath as he saw the drab, colorless sky over them. This was the realm where everything had been forgotten. A realm where time stood still and all things damned here became twisted and preyed upon.

We're in the Tor.

"I don't understand."

Forget the world you knew, Edilyn. The old rules of the human realm don't apply here.

As if some divine being was listening and keeping score, his marked palm began to burn. Scowling, Illarion cursed and shook it, then looked down.

In that moment, his world truly came undone.

Edilyn scowled at her own hand, which was now as unblemished as his. "What's this mean?"

Absolute horror went through him as that significance hit him like a hammer to his stones. The bitch had told the truth . . . it wasn't a lie, after all.

Savitar's spell has been undone by the magick here.

Locking gazes with her, he swallowed hard as his emotions choked him. *We're mates no more.*

13

"How can this be? How can we no longer be mates? We're bonded!"

Illarion shrugged at Edilyn's question. *I have no idea. I didn't know anything could undo it. Never have I heard of a mating being undone, never mind a life bond.*

If that wasn't bad enough, he heard a deep, fierce growling.

Edilyn's eyes widened. "What's that sound?"

You don't want to know. We have to find shelter.

"Better yet, let's find an exit!"

He laughed at her naiveté. *If there was one, my lady, I'd already have us out. You don't just walk out of here. This isn't like Avalon where I have the ability to come and go. This is the Tor. We're locked here. Without a key, we're screwed.*

"How do we get a key?"

Morgen has one, but I doubt she'll share.

Suddenly, out of the darkness around them, an army began to appear.

Edilyn gasped at the terrifying sight. Holy saints! That was more than they could handle alone. "Illarion? What do we do?"

He shifted his forms. *We fight.*

"So glad your sense of humor hasn't fled. But . . ."

He dipped his wing so that she could scramble up his back. *No humor, Addie. We fight. I've trained you. Trust in me and we will beat them back.*

With a shaky breath, she took her seat. Illarion manifested her weapons for her. And as soon as he had her secured, he flew toward their enemies.

Aye, she was petrified, but what stunned her was the fact that her training kicked in and drove out her fear. Once the fighting began, they ceased to be an overwhelming horde. They were merely targets.

By the time the battle was over, they were both coated in blood. Her body throbbed from her wounds and the stress of the hours of fighting. Yet that didn't concern her.

"Illy?" She slid from his back to inspect him. "Are you all right?"

He nodded, but by the way he moved, she knew he was in pain, too.

"Is there anything I can do?"

In spite of his injuries, he shifted forms. Only then did she see the gash he'd taken to his abdomen.

Gasping, she reached to touch it, but he stopped her. *I'm fine. We must find you shelter.*

She ground her teeth as unreasoning fury took over and drove out her pain. "I'm going to kill my brother!"

Illarion knew the feeling.

But before he could speak another word, he felt a shift in the air behind him. Turning, he saw the shimmer there that could only mean one thing.

Gale.

Fury exploded inside him as he seized Edilyn's sword from her hip. With a blind rage, he summoned his powers and rushed the goddess.

She'd barely manifested in front of them before he ran her through.

Just as she started to laugh, she realized that she wasn't immune to the blade. It wasn't a mere mortal weapon.

It'd been forged by the gods.

"What have you done?"

Not I, bitch! You started this fight. You and Morgen and Hekate and Dagon. I'm only finishing it. He kicked her back. *And I will die before I see my father's army in your hands or Morgen's.*

Edilyn moved to stand behind as the goddess staggered back and fell.

She glared at the two of them. "You'll never escape from here. Neither of you!"

Illarion sneered at her. *Neither will you.*

She died a moment later.

Normally, that might have been concerning without a Chthonian to absorb her powers, but because they were locked in this realm and her powers weren't that significant, Illarion wasn't worried about it.

Edilyn clutched at his tunic. "What's to become of us here?"

We will endure. And we will find a way out of here. I promise you.

She grimaced at his wound. "Just swear to me that you won't die and leave me alone in this horrible place."

I swear it to you.

It was an oath Illarion made sure to uphold. For the next ten years, he kept himself and Edilyn safe from every twisted form of shadow fey, every piece of Morgen's army, and every halfling that came for them.

But on the fifth day of the tenth year, Morgen's Stone Legion of gargoyles and her mandrakes hit them with a surprise attack at dawn.

One moment, Edilyn had been on his back, and in the next, Maddor, Morgen's commander, had torn her from her saddle and sent her plummeting to the ground.

Horrified, Illarion had done his best to catch her or use his powers to cushion her fall, but he'd been overwhelmed by their forces.

Edilyn!

By the time he reached her, she'd been barely alive and in more pain than he could imagine. Unmitigated rage and agony had torn him apart.

Her eyes glazing, she'd reached for him.

He'd clasped her hand and watched the light fade from her beautiful blue eyes. In one dreadful moment before any words could be spoken, they'd turned dull, and in a single gasp, she was gone.

An instant later, his enemies had seized her lifeless body and ripped her from his arms.

They'd sent his beloved back to him in pieces.

The irony was that if Morgen had tried to bargain with him before they'd harmed her, he'd have given her the Spartoi. For Edilyn alone, he'd have sold out the entire world.

Morgen hadn't given him the choice. Her cruelty was such that she'd been bent only on his punishment.

Now . . .

He lived only to see her and her mandrakes burn. There was no other purpose.

For the dragon lived on without his heart.

14

Illarion froze as he heard the voices that drew near his cave. Normally, they'd be dead already, but there was something highly unusual about these two.

Something that kept him from eating them.

They were nothing like the ones of the past.

"So there be dragons in these woods?" a woman asked.

"Just one." The man's voice was thick with a Welsh accent that rendered his words barely intelligible. "Well . . . there are many mandrakes, but only one true dragon that I know of. And Gwyn said dragon claw, not mandrake claw. So I'm assuming he wants a claw from the one, true dragon what lives here."

"What's the difference between a dragon and a mandrake?"

"Mandrakes are fey-born creatures. They be shapeshifting bastards who can take the form of either man or draig."

"Draig?"

"Dragon, me love. And they're all currently enslaved to Morgen and live in and around Camelot. But the one . . . he's the last of his breed here. And he slumbers in yon den."

Illarion quirked a brow at those words. So, they were after him, but they weren't an army, nor were they necessarily malicious.

"Cool. I'll distract him. You knock him on the head and we'll be right out. Did you bring a pair of giant dragon-sized nail clippers?"

What the hell?

Even her companion gave her a baffled scowl. "Sarcasm?"

She laughed at his question. "What was your first clue? The words or the tone of my voice?"

The man was dressed as a medieval knight, complete with chainmail and a crusader's surcoat and cape. She, on the other hand, was dressed in clothes that came from far in the future.

At least the twentieth or twenty-first century, if Illarion remembered correctly. Though to be honest, it'd been a while since he'd ventured there.

That was his brother's time period. Not his.

The knight smirked at the woman as he surveyed the area, and carefully led them forward without making a comment on her additional playful barb.

As they drew closer to Illarion's lair, the woman took cautious note of the human bones littering the ground. Something Illarion had done as a warning to others, and as a happy poster for himself. While it couldn't bring Edilyn back, it made him feel better that he'd made those who'd harmed her pay dearly for her life.

And these were the strangest two Illarion had ever seen. He watched as they drew closer and closer to him.

"Um, Cade?"

"Aye, lass."

"How big is this dragon, anyway?"

He paused to consider it. "I've only seen him from a distance. When he's flying in the sky, hunting for prey. But from nip to tail, I'd say about twenty-five to thirty feet."

"Nip?"

"Mouth."

"That's a big-ass dragon. Does he breathe fire?"

"I know naught, but would assume it."

Her eyes widened as she reached out quietly and put her hand on her companion's arm. "What would his range be on that fire, do you think?"

"No idea, lass, why?"

She held him by her side. "Because I'm looking at him and he doesn't appear happy that he has guests."

The knight she called Cade froze as her words hit him. The blood drained from his face as he turned to see Illarion crouched low, watching them to see if he needed to add them to his menu.

"Nice draggy, draggy," the woman breathed in a singsongy

tone. "You don't want to eat the nice people. Do you?" She shook her head. "No, you don't. We're not even snack size."

That woman was definitely crazy. Perhaps he should eat her just as a matter of saving the human gene pool.

Cade's jaw dropped. "What are you doing, lass?"

"Shh," she snapped. "I'm being a dragon whisperer."

Illarion scowled at her. What the hell was a dragon whisperer? The man was even more aghast at her words. "A what?"

"Dragon whisperer." She slid her gaze to Cade. "I'm assuming that if you fight him, it's going to be a bloody mess. Right?"

"Probably."

"Could result in both our guts and entrails flying?"

"Most likely."

Definitely.

She patted his arm kindly. "Then let's try this my way first. Shall we?"

He snorted at her offer. As did Illarion. "I'm not sure I like your way, Josette. It seems even more dangerous than mine."

She winked at him. "Not sure I like my way, either. Just promise me that if he starts to eat me, you'll flash us out of here."

"I shall do me best."

Illarion cocked his head as he took note to watch Cadegan a bit more cautiously, since he knew he was a sorcerer.

"Cool, now shush and let me do something galactically stupid."

This Illarion wanted to see since he couldn't imagine anything dumber than the two of them waltzing into his domain.

With an amused and horrified expression, Cadegan watched her bravely and slowly make her way toward Illarion.

Illarion narrowed his eyes on the dark-haired woman. She was a fascinating creature. While not as beautiful to him as his Edilyn, she was certainly brave. He'd credit her for that.

If not completely stupid to approach him, especially given how much pain he was in.

Biting her lip, she stopped as she reached his nose. "Hi, Mr. Dragon. How are you today? Feeling in a good mood, aren't you? Yes. Yes, you are. You don't want to eat people, do you? No. No, people taste icky. They're sinew and gross. No eat people." She shook her head to emphasize her words. "You're gonna be a sweetie, aren't you?" This time she nodded.

Yeah, she'd been inhaling some of Morgen's better fumes. She must have gotten lost in the Valley of No Return and found all kinds of interesting places before she came here.

She took a step forward.

Illarion inched back, not quite ready to kill her. She seemed more a harmless moron than a serious threat. He made a low growl of warning.

"Shh, it's okay, Mr. Dragon. We're not going to hurt you. No. We like dragons. I used to draw you all the time when I was a kid. I did. I had a whole collection of dragon toys. 'Cause you're a cutie, you are."

Woman, you are effing crazy. . . .

But he kept that thought to himself as he continued to watch her.

She drew up short as she realized one of his wings was on the ground, where it lay broken from his last fight. "You got a boo-boo, Mr. Dragon?"

You think? But again, he didn't share that thought.

Cadegan drew closer to her. "Its wing's broken." He started to unsheathe his sword.

Illarion hissed in warning. This bastard he wouldn't hesitate to eat. Chainmail and all.

"No!" she said to both of them. "Cade, keep your sword down."

"Why? Now's the time to strike."

She shook her head. "I think he understands me. . . . You do, don't you?"

Making sure to keep his gaze on her sneaky, armed companion, Illarion nodded.

She inched closer, until she was able to reach out and touch the gray scales around his nose. Treating him like a dog which he really didn't appreciate, she held her hand out to him for him to smell her skin. As if he needed that to smell her presence . . . or to determine her emotions or mood. "See, I mean you no harm, little big dragon."

Yeah, she was nuts. And he didn't move as he eyed her warily, still unsure of their ultimate intent where he was concerned.

She moved her hand slowly to pet his head, near his ear. Something only Edilyn had ever done. "It's okay." She cradled his ear against her chest and stroked his skin. Then she looked over at Cadegan. "See? He's harmless."

"I wouldn't go that far. But I can understand his motivation. I'd be quiet too for a chance to rest me head on your breasts."

She blushed.

Illarion growled at him.

"Now, boys," she teased. "Play nice."

Illarion didn't care for her tone, but it was nice to feel a kind touch again. Even from a stranger. For a moment, he pretended it was Edilyn who held him.

That weakened him a lot more than it should. And it brought a painful lump to his throat as he missed his wife more than he could stand. Time was forever a merciless bitch who tormented him more with every passing day. Instead of getting easier, it was harder and harder to live without his heart.

Jo placed a kiss to his ear. "We just need a claw from the dragon, right? We don't have to hurt him for that, do we?"

"Depends on how fiercely he fights us for it."

Illarion hissed and growled at the bastard who was about to become his next meal.

Josette stroked his ear. "Can you heal him?"

Cadegan hesitated. "I can, but am thinking a healed dragon might eat us."

If you heal me, I won't hurt you.

"Was that you?" she asked Cadegan in a fear-filled whisper.

He shook his head slowly before he eyed Illarion with murderous suspicion. "That *you*?"

Illarion, and yes.

Still, Cadegan wasn't sold on it. "Can we trust you?"

Illarion glared at him. Really? The *sneaky* bastard was questioning *him*? Sure, that made sense. And this close, he finally could see the truth of what Cadegan actually was. *If I wanted to harm you, demon, you'd both be in flames right now.*

"All right, then." Cadegan moved to Illarion's broken wing. "Stand back, lass. This might hurt him and I don't want him to harm you in turn."

Cadegan was right about that. While he'd never harm her intentionally, he could accidentally twitch in reaction and damage her.

You'd best do as he says. Stand near the cave.

She tapped him on his snout in a way that only his Addie had ever done. "Don't hurt Cadegan, either. I'll be very put out with you."

"And I won't be fond of you, either," Cadegan groused.

Illarion snorted as Cadegan moved to his injured wing and Jo sought cover.

As she started away, Cadegan stopped her. He pulled a medallion over his head and kissed it as a monk would a holy relic, before he placed it around her neck. "Never take it off and it will protect you always."

"Thank you, sweetie." She kissed his cheek and wished him luck.

Illarion choked back his own pain as their actions made him long for what he'd lost. As hard as it'd been all these centuries, their obvious affection for one another, made it even more difficult.

Damn. How he missed his wife.

If only he could have her back for one more day. . . .

Once Josette was out of the line of fire, literally, Cadegan touched the wing.

Illarion grimaced in pain as he debated barbecuing him for the affront.

"What did you do to break this?" Cadegan asked him.

Fell. Now are you fixing it, or am I having Welsh Rarebit for dinner?

"Ooo, you're a bit bold, aren't you?" Cadegan summoned his powers. "Brace yourself. This will burn."

Do it.

Finally, he felt the demon begin to repair his wing. But it was excruciating. And it didn't help his temperament at all.

Once Cadegan had finished, Illarion flapped his wing to test its movement. Something that forced Cadegan to brace himself against the stiff breeze it caused.

"Can I come out?" Josette called.

"Aye, love. He's all better now."

Satisfied that he could suffer them to live, Illarion lifted himself up and sat back on his haunches to watch them. *Thank you.*

Cadegan inclined his head to him. "No worries."

Illarion started to remain in his real body, but there was no need to keep scaring them. Especially the woman, whose fear had yet to lessen. So he flashed himself into his hated human form.

Eyes wide, she jumped to stand behind Cadegan, who didn't react to it at all, except to put his hand on the hilt of his sword.

"Why's he in color when nothing else here is?" she whispered to Cadegan.

"Not really sure," he responded over his shoulder as he kept his eyes locked on Illarion.

Neither Morgen's nor Merlin's magick works on me. For reasons Illarion still didn't understand, this zone negated all their magick, as well as Savitar's mating.

And that continued to burn like the mighty Phlegethon in his gut. It was so unfair that he was left here to live on without Edilyn.

Cadegan arched a brow. "Really?"

Illarion nodded as he tested his arm to make sure it was fully healed.

"I'm confused." Jo kept herself behind Cadegan. "I thought mandrakes were the shapeshifters and not the real dragons?"

Cadegan shrugged.

Illarion offered her a patient smile. *In my true and natural form, I'm a dragon—born from an egg, as all my kith before me. But, because of the magick of a Greek king and his bastard god brother-in-law centuries ago, my kith have the ability to turn themselves into humans.*

"Did you know that?" Jo asked Cadegan.

He shook his head before Illarion continued. *At one time, there were many races and species of dragons. We walked the human realm, and fought untold battles against each other. But between our wars, and the hatred of both your species, all dracokyn have been pushed to extinction, or the brink of it.*

What few of us remain are either enslaved, such as the mandrakes, or, like me, they're in hiding.

Cadegan narrowed his gaze on Illarion. "What is your species?"

I'm a Katagari Drakos. As far as I know, I'm the last of my breed. At least I am here in this realm.

"And you can't speak, even in human form?" Jo asked.

He pointed to the vicious scar on his neck. *While I was enslaved as a hatchling, humans tried to remove my ability to make fire. But the flames don't come from my throat, only through it.*

She cringed at the horrible scar. "I'm so sorry, Illarion."

Placing his hand over his heart, he bowed kindly to her. *Now what is this about a dragon's claw that you need?*

"It's needed for a sharoc potion."

Illarion scowled at Cadegan. *Since when do they make potions?*

"I'm hoping now."

"Hang on," Jo interrupted them. "If the magick here doesn't work on you, Illarion, can you leave this realm?"

His eyes dark with sadness, he shook his head. *As a dragon, I'm too large for the portals, and whenever I attempt to go through as a man, I'm transformed back to a dragon and am stuck. It's humiliating. I once spent two days with my ass hanging out while I tried to get my head back through the portal.* How he wished he'd thought of that *before* he killed Gale.

Jo pressed her lips together to keep from laughing at the image in her head.

"Then how did you get here?" Cadegan asked.

I was brought here by a Greek sorceress who'd been bribed by Morgen. He jerked his head to a stack of bones that he'd pinned to the side of his cave in an artistic display that at least helped to lighten his mood whenever he looked at them and remembered that while he was trapped here, he'd at least had the satisfaction of taking Gale's life. *Needless to say, I wasn't very happy about it. Neither was she, in the end.*

"I'm surprised you didn't befriend the mandrakes."

He snorted at Jo's innocent comment. *Dracokyn are very territorial, my lady. We don't play well with others. 'Tis why there are so few of us left. I'd rather die alone than den down with my enemies.*

"You remind me of someone else I know." She glanced pointedly to Cadegan, then, impulsively, she hugged Illarion. "Again, I'm very sorry for what they did to you."

He passed an uncomfortable glance toward Cadegan, who didn't appear pleased that she was hugging another male. Not that he blamed him. He would have skewered anyone who touched his Edilyn.

Seeing that look, Jo moved to kiss Cadegan's cheek. "Don't look like that, sweetie. We don't need to find out if dragon meat tastes like chicken."

Illarion scowled at her. *What?*

Cadegan snorted. "She does that a lot. I only understand about half of what she says. It's part of her charm." He looked up at the sky. "And we be needing a claw quick. We're almost out of time."

You trust the sharoc?

"Not really."

Smart man. And when they said claw, *what exact words did they use?*

Cadegan paused to think. "A dragon's claw. A stone from Emrys Merlin. The lion's heart. A bit of hair from the White Stag. Arthur's blood, and the blood and sweat of a waremerlin."

Illarion let out a silent whistle. *Quite a list you have there.*

"Aye, believe me, I know."

And it's not a list so much as it is a riddle.

Cadegan arched his brow. "How so?"

A stone from Emrys Merlin would be a goylestone, not a rock. Arthur's blood is a flower that blooms on the other side of the Tor, and a dragon's claw isn't a fingernail.

Cadegan growled low in his throat. "That dodgy bastard. I should have known it was a trick."

Aye. I'm sure the others are every bit the riddle. But I don't know them. I only know those three because the goylestones are what the mandrakes feed on. It's easy to set a trap for them when they go to eat. The Adoni use Arthur's blood for healing, and I know exactly what my claw is.

"And that is?"

One of the most sacred of objects to a dragon. It's almost the same as asking you for a testicle.

Cadegan actually blushed. "Watch your language before me lady!"

Unabashed, Illarion smiled at her. *Forgive me, my lady.* He turned toward Cadegan. *Why do you need this potion?*

"Me lady can't get through the portal without a key. Gwyn ap Nudd says he can make one for her."

At what cost?

"It's for me to pay. Later."

Illarion winced as he understood exactly how harsh the payment would be. As a fey king, Gwyn was indeed a dodgy bastard who screwed everyone over in the end. *For what you've done for me this day, I will loan my claw to you, but you have to take me with you and return it once this is done. Understood?*

"You have me word."

Word of a demon. Illarion shook his head. He was being a complete and utter dumbass. Again. And he knew it. But what choice did he have?

In all these centuries, this was the closest thing to a way out of this hell realm that he'd found.

"He's good for it," Jo said without hesitation. "You won't regret trusting him."

Not so sure about all that, Illarion hesitated before he unlaced the leather cuff from his arm. There was only one person he'd ever entrusted with his claw before.

That thought brought another painful lump to his chest and tears to his eyes. There wasn't a day that went by where he didn't feel her loss like a stab in his heart. He'd give anything to have one more hour with her.

And if she were here, Edilyn would be the first to tell him to help Cadegan and Josette. It was what the romantic in her would demand. Even now, he could hear her voice and see her beautiful face as she ordered him to do something for them.

So he exposed Falcyn's gift—a weapon fashioned to appear as a metal baby dragon sitting over the cuff. It was the very image of what Illarion had looked like as a dragonet—a loving homage from his brother who claimed to care for no one.

He handed it reverently to Cadegan.

"How's that a claw?" Jo asked.

Illarion pulled the bar the dragon was holding on to, until it locked into place. When it did, two sharp spikes shot out and a third shot from the dragon's head.

"Holy crap! What is *that*?"

Illarion smiled at her shocked question. *A dragon's claw. They are given to each Katagari Drakos once he or she comes of age, to protect us should we ever be locked by magick into a human's form.*

"Your weaker state."

He inclined his head to Cadegan. A custom started by Falcyn and one Maxis taught to the rest of the Were-Hunters. *As I said, my people were hunted to the brink of extinction.*

Respecting its sacredness, Cadegan held it with the same reverence. "I shall guard it with me life, and make sure it's returned to you as pristine as it's been received."

Jo frowned while Cadegan wrapped it in a cloth to protect it. "I have a weird question. Why would the sharoc need that? What purpose could it serve for a potion?"

She's right. They had no way of knowing I would simply give it to you when normally I'd kill before allowing another to take custody of it.

Cadegan sighed as he stored the claw. "Believe me, I've already thought of that. The purpose, obviously, was to get one of us killed. Maybe both."

And to have you fail your quest.

"Aye, to be sure. There is no other reason for this assignment." Cadegan winked at them. "Now, what say we go and ruin Gwyn's day?"

15

Not that Cadegan had any doubt that Gwyn had wanted him dead, but the look of shock on his face as they walked through the portcullis of the king's floating castle, Galar, confirmed it for sure.

The fey king stared at him in utter disbelief. "You barely made it back here in time."

"I would say that I'm sorry to disappoint. But I'm not."

Ignoring the sarcasm, the king narrowed his eyes on Cadegan. "So where's the claw?"

Cadegan pulled it out and carefully unwrapped it. When Gwyn reached to take it, he moved back and shook his head. "This be only a loan." He indicated Illarion, who was in human form, with a jerk of his head. "The dragon wants it back when you're finished, and I promised him we would do so."

Gwyn paled as he realized who and what Illarion was. "How is this possible?"

Cadegan passed a grin to Josette. "It's amazing what a dragon whisperer can do." He handed the claw back to Illarion. "Now if you don't be minding, we're all a bit wanged out from our adventure, and we wouldn't mind seeing those rooms you promised us."

"Very well." Gwyn snapped his fingers.

A servant peeled itself off the stone wall. Without a word, it showed them to rooms. But Cadegan refused his.

"I'll sleep on the floor outside your room, lass. Just to make sure no one bothers you."

Jo smiled. "You could just sleep in the room with me. Be easier to protect me that way."

His cheeks mottled with color in a way that seriously amused Illarion. The two of them must not have been together for very long. "Are you sure about that?"

Nodding, she pulled him into the room with her.

Cadegan paused to look back at Illarion with an arched brow.

Well, Illarion didn't know what that expression meant or what kinky things they were into—but he wanted *no* part of it. *Uh, yeah, I'll be back in the morning. Not sure I want to be sleeping in this place, anyway.*

"I feel your sentiments, brother. Had I a choice, I'd go with you. And be bringing Jo behind me."

I'll see you two in the morning.

Cadegan held his arm out to Illarion. "Thank you."

Illarion hesitated, not quite sure if this was sincere.

Or a trick.

In this place, the latter was far more likely. But so far, they'd given him no reason to doubt them and they seemed to have been as innocently sucked in here as he and Edilyn. So for now, he'd do what he hadn't done in a long time.

He'd trust them.

And if they stabbed him in the back . . .

What the hell? Wasn't like he had much to live for at this point anyway. At least it was a break in the monotony of his life. If they did manage to kill him, he'd be with Edilyn again.

He hoped. The fear that he wouldn't was the only reason he hadn't killed himself or allowed the others to do him that favor. Honestly, he didn't know why he kept on living at this point.

But in the end, he shook Cadegan's arm, then turned to leave them.

16

Biting her thumbnail, Jo—who'd been transformed by fey magick into Cadegan's male body—paced the giant cave Illarion had called home since the night he'd been damned to this shadow hell realm by Gale and Morgen.

In dragon form, he crouched a few feet away, while he watched her through hooded eyes. *It'll be all right, Jo.*

She shook her blond head in denial. It was really messing with Illarion to watch her while he knew she was Josette in that very Cadegan body. To see *his* form and features, and *her* movements and mannerisms. "We don't know where Cadegan is or what happened. . . . Who has him?"

The fact that Cadegan was in her body and lacked his normal strength was no doubt adding to her stress. Illarion knew the exact horror of being trapped inside a foreign body and not understanding its weaknesses. Of looking in a mirror and not recognizing yourself.

It was an unimaginable nightmare he'd wish on no one.

I know, child. Would you like to go look for him again?

"Please." She smiled at him. "And thank you, Illarion. For everything."

Still in his massive dragon form, he gave her a slight bow of his head before he lowered himself enough so that she could climb onto his back. The moment she touched his flesh, he winced as agony pierced his heart.

"Are you all right? Am I too heavy for you in this body?"

He laughed bitterly. *No, lass. While I know you're currently trapped in Cadegan's body, I'm painfully aware of the fact that you're not really a man. And I was only remembering my precious Edilyn who once rode to battle in the saddle where you sit now. She was the last and only female I ever allowed to ride me.*

"What?" she breathed.

His heart aching and heavy, Illarion gave her a sad nod as he fought against his tears. *It's where the legends of the virgin sacrifices to dragons come from. They weren't really our sacrifices. Rather, they were offered to us as hopeful spouses.*

Centuries ago, my kind were used as weapons in war. To entice us to fight for them, humans would offer up their sons and daughters to us, to make sure that we had a vested interest in battling in human armies, and for their causes. Many of my kind mated with the strongest of your people and we would fight together in battle as a single unit.

"Was Edilyn your wife?"

In a simple word, yes, but she was a lot more to me than that. She was my best friend and the very air I breathed.

"What happened?"

I failed to protect her. She was ripped from my back during battle and slain before I could stop it.

Her heart wrenched at the agony he betrayed. "I'm sorry, Illarion."

Thank you, lass . . . it's the only reason I'm willing to help the two of you, when normally I'd have left you to rot. I know what it's like to live without my better half. It's a painful bit I'd wish on no one. Your courage and resilience remind me much of my Edilyn. And I want to see you back with your Cadegan.

She leaned forward and hugged him in a way that was all too much like his Addie-Rose. "Were you there when she died?"

He nodded. *It was both a curse and a blessing. I'd promised her that I would never leave her in this life or the next. That we would always be together, and that no other would ever claim my heart the way she had.*

When my kind bonds, we're supposed to die with our beloved. But her people had a sorcerer who'd found the magick here that undid ours, so that they didn't lose the entire battle team. When we crossed over, our bond was broken. In the end, my body lived on, but my heart and soul went with Edilyn into eternity. I hated her people after that.

The only part of my oath to her I was able to keep was that I was there, holding her hand, when death claimed her. I have never loved anyone save her.

And I never will.

With her head on his neck, she stroked his scales. "I am so incredibly sorry."

Thank you.

Jo took the reins, wishing there was something, anything, she could do to make things better for him. Unfortunately, grief like his wasn't easy to come back from. It could destroy the person who felt it. She'd seen firsthand what it'd done to her family when her cousin Tiyana Devereaux had died. Even now, her heart was broken at the loss. Not a day went by that she didn't think of Tiyana at least a dozen times.

Almost a decade later, they still mourned her.

They always would.

Just like Illarion mourned his wife. Poor dragon. Life wasn't fair and she knew that as well as anyone. But it was now clear why Illarion had fought so hard for her when there was no reason for him to do so. Why he'd been determined to get her free of Morgen's vicious mandrakes and gargoyles.

Once she gave Illarion the signal that she was secure, he left the cave and took flight.

Jo continued to worry her lip as she scanned the nasty gray scenery for any sign of her Cadegan, and where he might have been taken. Reaching down, she stroked Illarion's scales. He reminded her a lot of Cadegan. It was a pity the two of them hadn't found each other before now. They could have been great friends who watched over each other in this vicious realm.

Or committed murder.

Perhaps they were too much alike. The two of them might get on each other's nerves like her cousins Amanda and Tabitha did. The twin sisters swore they were absolutely nothing alike and yet they were so similar, it was more than obvious they'd come from the same egg.

Laughing at the thought as they flew, Jo still couldn't believe Illarion had returned just minutes after Cadegan had been sucked out of the castle. His psychic powers had warned him something was wrong and he'd been desperate to check on them.

But for the dragon's return, there was no telling what would have become of her. She'd owed the dragon a debt she couldn't repay.

Illarion slowed and rose up like a falcon to hover over the ground so far below. *Something's amiss.*

Latching on to him with all her strength, Jo scanned the countryside. "I don't see anything."

It's not my eyes that sense it. I feel it. A change in the air. Morgen is launching her army again. Gargoyles and mandrakes are taking flight. They're headed this way.

"What do you think it is?"

Dangerous. In a word. I have no idea why she'd do such. But it doesn't bode well for any of us.

Jo frowned as she caught sight of something off in the distance. "Is that part of her army?"

Illarion turned to look. *Not sure. Those creatures were once servants of King Arthur, but have been enslaved by others since his death.*

"Others, like . . . ?"

Our friend the fey king Gwyn.

"Should we attack them and see if they can help get my body back?"

Are you up to a battle?

"I am Cadegan, right? I have his powers. No idea really how to use them, but I'm willing to give it a go, *if* you are."

He snorted. *Hold tight and pray.*

Illarion headed straight for them.

Jo hung tight and stayed low to his neck as they flew. She felt something rumbling in his stomach. "Hungry, sweetie?"

Getting ready to breathe fire if I need to.

"So it comes from your stomach?"

No. I have anatomy you don't. Let's leave it at that.

Okay then. She wasn't sure she wanted a dragon biology lesson.

As they neared the giant muscular gryphon birds, Jo saw the two riders on their backs. This couldn't be good.

Preparing for attack, Illarion dove for them.

But as they drew closer, she realized one of the riders was extremely familiar.

"Wait! It's Cadegan!"

Illarion pulled up. *Are you sure?*

"Pretty much. I think I'd know *my* body anywhere."

Laughing in her head, Illarion projected his thoughts to the riders.

The moment he did, the one in her body headed for them.

"Josette?" Cadegan called.

"It's us, Cade!"

Not sure about all this or how it had come into being, Illarion led the way to the meadow below. The huge gryphon birds landed not far away, while Jo jumped down from his back, and then ran to meet them.

With a happiness that made Illarion long for Edilyn, Jo ran to Cadegan. She buried her face in his neck and held him for everything she was worth. "I thought you were gone forever."

He was actually trembling in relief. "I thought Morgen had you. We were on our way to assault Camelot."

Illarion snorted. As if that would have worked. . .

But he understood the stupidity better than he wanted to.

Jo laughed as she glanced at his massive army of two. "Assault how, honey? You wouldn't have stood a chance without your body and powers."

He winked at her. "I hadn't quite mastered the plan in me mind. Was hoping for a bit of inspiration once I arrived."

"You are so nuts!" She kissed him.

Until her gaze fell to the man with him. All humor fled her face.

"Hi." He held his hand out to her. "I'm—"

Before he could say another word, she punched his jaw as hard as she could. Then cursed. "Oh my God, I think I broke my hand." She cradled it to her chest.

With an arched brow, Cadegan moved to inspect it. "Not broken, love, but remind me, I need to teach you how to hit someone."

SHERRILYN KENYON

The man glared at her as he rubbed at his bruised jaw. "What the hell was that for?"

Illarion exchanged a bemused gape with the gryphons, who understood this as much as he did.

"You bastard!" she snarled at the man nursing his bruised jaw. "It's for what you did to Cadegan. How could you!"

"You don't know what happened."

"No, Leucious. *You're* the one who doesn't know what happened! I have Cade's memories. You worthless son of a bitch!"

He didn't speak as his gaze dropped to the scars on her arms. Scowling, he moved to her back.

Jo pulled the T-shirt off so that he could see the full range of damage done to Cadegan's body. "Proud of yourself, you shit!"

His face pale, he met Cadegan's gaze. "What did they do to you?"

Cadegan put the shirt back over her. "It matters naught."

Jo reached to slap Leucious, but Cadegan stopped her. "Let it go, lass."

"Why are you with him?"

"He's a friend of your cousins'. He's here to take you home."

She stepped past Cadegan to poke Leucious in the chest with her index finger. "No. You're taking *us* home. I won't leave here without Cadegan."

"Lass . . ."

"I mean it, Cade. Unlike your worthless family, I will *never* leave you. Especially not alone in this hell."

Illarion flinched. Damn, she was so much like his Addie.

Cadegan pulled her into his arms and kissed her cheek. "We'll worry about that later. First, we have to switch ourselves back."

Leucious screwed his face up. "This is disturbing, isn't it? Hearing your words coming out of her body? Yeah. I think I'm getting a migraine."

"Could be a tumor," one of the birds said. "Or aneurysm. I was watching a show on that just—"

"Would you shut it, already, Talfryn!" the other bird snapped at him. "Can't you ever learn to read the room?"

"There's no room here." Talfryn glanced around "Are you daft?"

Jo scowled at them before she looked back at Cadegan. "Should I ask?"

"Nay, lass." Cadegan quickly introduced everyone.

Apparently Talfryn and Ioan were two Adar Llwch Gwin or gryphons, for lack of a better term, Cadegan had taken from Gwyn to come rescue Jo. Like the demon hellchaser with them Leucious, they were snotty little bastards.

Which meant Illarion liked them.

Leucious sighed as he met Illarion's gaze. "Call me Thorn." He held his hand out to him.

Illarion shook it without comment.

With a fierce grimace, Jo tapped the bracelet on her arm. "Do you think *this* has anything to do with our *Invasion of the Body Snatchers* where I woke up a man and Cadegan as a woman?"

Cadegan nodded. "Aye, and I say we go back to the castle and beat the shite out of Gwyn until he fixes this."

Thorn snorted. "Now there's the brother I remember. When all else fails, beat them with a stick."

Works for me. Illarion grinned in total agreement.

Cadegan inclined his head to Illarion. "I have a suspicion that you and I shall be good friends."

Thorn snorted at his brother. "Why don't we just pull the bracelet off and see what happens? Shall we?"

Ioan moved forward to stop him. "That might not be wise. Who put it on her and why?"

"Gwyn, to ensure that we returned to Galar by fey vespers." Cadegan sighed. "I agree with Ioan. It's possible that it could hurt her. I trust Gwyn even less than I trust *you*."

Thorn glared at him. "Like you wouldn't cut my throat."

"Aye, I would. If ever given the right and proper chance." Cadegan took Jo's hand.

Just as he started for Ioan, the sky above them darkened.

Jo looked up and gasped. Morgen's dragons and gargoyles filled the sky.

And they were headed straight for them.

17

Without thinking twice, Cadegan grabbed his sword from Josette's hip and prepared to fight the approaching army. Even though she was in his male body, he pulled her behind him as the dragons and gargoyles descended to attack them. Illarion moved to shield them both.

The moment he did, a strange red haze rose up from the ground and formed a dome over their small group. A dome that Morgen's soldiers slammed into, and recoiled off. If not for the fact that this could be an even bigger threat to them, it'd be comical.

Scowling, Cadegan looked at his brother. "That you with a shield?"

Thorn shook his head. "Definitely not me." He glanced to the Adar Llwch Gwin. "Frick? Frack? Can you explain?"

Slack-jawed, they shook their heads in unison.

Illarion pulled back. *It feels fey, but not as dark as Morgen's magick.*

No sooner had he pushed that thought to their heads than the ground below their feet opened up and swallowed them.

Cursing, Cadegan wrapped himself around Josette to cushion her fall as they tumbled into a deep, dark cavern.

For a minute, Illarion feared it to be a bottomless pit.

Until they struck a hard, black floor. Though it was dark, the walls around them glistened with glowing vines.

Josette landed on top of Cadegan, a few feet from him.

Cadegan let out a harsh groan. "I'm the one what needs to lose weight, me lady. Oof! I weigh a mighty ton. How do you stand me weight atop of you?"

Her face turned red before she shifted to speak in his ear. "I love your weight on me. But not like this." Josette slid from his body. He pushed himself to his feet while the others followed suit.

"Well, well, what have we here?" a woman asked from inside the dark.

Retrieving his sword, Cadegan took Josette's hand to hold her near him, while Illarion moved to stand at his back.

"Why have you trespassed upon my lands?" There was a shrill note to the woman's irritated tone.

"We meant no disrespect." Thorn spoke up first.

"Actions are far more important to me than words that profess intent, as those actions, more oft than not, betray your real heart. Case in point . . ." A red mist appeared before Cadegan and Josette. "You two protect each other, without a single word. Does this mean that you don't care for one another?"

When Josette started to speak, Cadegan squeezed her hand to warn her not to. At least not until they knew more about what they were facing.

The mist went to Thorn. "Who do you protect?"

"None of your business."

The mist solidified into the body of a beautiful woman. With long black hair, she had an oval face, and large, dark eyes.

Ah, shit, this was a bitch Illarion knew all too well. They were so screwed.

"You like your words, don't you?" she asked them.

"They've been known to serve me well."

She scoffed at Thorn before she came over to Cadegan and Jo. A slow smile curved her lips as she danced her gaze over Cadegan's handsome body. Until she cocked her head and studied their locked hands. "Now you, *you* must have significant value for your lady to covet and protect you so."

Before either of them could speak, Jo was ripped away from Cadegan. Cadegan, still in her body, rushed for her.

As Jo tried to reach him, a twisted golden cage came out of the ground to surround and hold her in a tiny room. Similar cages sprang up to imprison Illarion, Ioan, Talfryn, and Thorn.

The woman moved to confront Cadegan. "Do you know who I am?"

"Queen Cordelia."

She inclined her head in approval. "So you know of me?"

"Everyone in Glastonbury knows the tale of Gwyn and his wife, Creiddylad."

She wagged her finger before his face. "Nay, not until All Hallow's Eve. For now, I belong to Gwythyr ap Greidawl, who won me again last May Day." Sighing heavily, she cast her gaze back toward Cadegan's caged body. "And I grow weary of my place as trophy. There was a time when I would have given up my very soul for Gwythyr. But those days have long passed, and now I long for another to hold. A man worthy of the title, who will always win my hand above the others."

The queen's speculative gaze went back to Cadegan's body before she returned to face *Josette's* body. "What say we fight for your man and the best lady keeps him?"

Illarion scowled at her question. Did she not know they'd been exchanged?

Was this a trick of some kind?

"Fight how?" Cadegan asked.

"A joust. You against my champion. If your love and heart are true, you will win back your man. But be warned . . . if you've spoken falsely of your feelings, all will know you have lied, and you will surely lose."

Cadegan arched a brow. "Majesty, do you know who I am?"

She gave him an insidious smile. "Do *you*?"

"I know me heart."

"Then a joust it shall be."

"No!" Josette shouted in denial as she fought against the gold bars that held her. "I won't have it! What if you're hurt?"

Cadegan took her hand into his and pulled it to his cheek. "I will heal." He turned back to the queen. "But there is one thing I want for this."

Cordelia arched a brow. "And that is?"

"Win, lose, or draw, Josette returns to her true home, intact. Body and soul."

She took a moment to think the offer over. "Only if you agree that should you lose, I shall own Cadegan forever. Body and soul."

It was a steep price, but apparently he was willing. And that, too, Illarion understood. "Done."

"No!" Josette screamed. "No! I won't agree to this. I refuse it!"

Cordelia snorted. "Not your bargain to make. The deal is done." She stepped back and clapped her hands.

A whirlwind swept through the cavern, blowing all of them around. It plastered their clothes to their bodies and forced a severe chill into the room. Suddenly, a golden stallion appeared. It had red eyes and a shimmering mane as it stamped at the ground and eyed Cadegan with malice.

In the blink of an eye, gold armor encased his body, complete with a basinet helm, red plumage, and a war lance.

The horse glared at Cadegan as he pulled himself into the saddle to fight whatever opponent Cordelia demanded.

Borne by fey magick, the lance rose from the ground to hover by his side until he took it into his grasp. As soon as he gripped it, his opponent appeared at the opposite side of the glowing list. Wrapped in silver armor with blue plumage and riding a silver horse, the rider glared through his helm at Cadegan with red, demonic eyes.

Illarion cringed at the sight. This was bad. . . .

For all of them.

Cordelia manifested a huge, thorny throne at the same time a pixie with wings appeared near the field, holding a flag.

Cadegan waited for the pixie to drop the banner. The moment she did, he kicked his horse forward. He held the lance at the ready for a fair strike and braced himself for the blow.

Just as he should have struck, his opponent vanished into thin air. His horse galloped past and as it did so, Cadegan was no longer on the field.

Nor was he in Josette's body.

Illarion cursed as he realized the game Cordelia played and the test that she'd fashioned for Cadegan.

One that if he failed, would screw them all . . .

The warrior was now in the distant past. A frightened boy among his king's soldiers.

Cadegan froze as he heard them speaking those words that had no meaning to him. As they cast scornful glances in his direction as if he were a mongrel dog about to shite their shoes.

One of the knights threw a basket of rusted chain-mail at him, and a sword that appeared to have been scraped from the bottom of the Thames. . . .

And smelted back together as a child's learning project.

Confused, he'd looked up at the man who'd sneered words at him he couldn't understand, but the tone said that it was all the likes of Cadegan deserved.

The others had laughed at his new armor the king had instructed them to find for him since he hadn't any of his own.

Still, they laughed at him.

Alone and homesick, Cadegan had dug through the basket, only to realize the other knights had soaked all the contents with their urine. And they laughed even harder while they watched him curl his lip in repugnance.

Worse, it still bore the blood of the last knight who'd worn it, or rather, given the size of the hole in the side, had died in it.

Unwilling to let the others know how much their words and actions cut him, Cadegan had washed the armor as best he could, and patched it with leather straps he'd cut from the tops of his shoes.

On their first day of battle, he'd donned the armor and ignored their ridicule and disdain, and was grateful he could only ascertain their biting tones and not their actual words. One was bad enough, he definitely didn't need the other.

Since he had no horse, they'd left him to fight on foot, with only the damaged sword and no shield.

None of them had allowed him to be part of the army group. One by one, they'd pushed and jostled him until he'd been relegated to the side of their forces, to fight alone. No one at his side.

No one at his back.

It was the worst moment of his life. Because all the soldiers had refused to train him, he'd known nothing of war. He'd barely known how to properly hold his sword. But the moment the Mercians had

attacked and blood had flowed thick on the field at their feet, Cadegan had held his own with everything he had. Determined only
not to die that day.

However, his opponents had mercilessly sought to lop his head
off and knock him to the ground.

He'd refused to give them their desire. He had no intention of
going down. Not this day or any other.

As he fought, he'd seen one of the Powys knights fall from his
mount. The Mercians had set upon him like a pack of starving
wolves. Ferocious. Merciless. They had hacked until they knocked
his helm free.

It was the same man who had cast the soiled armor at Cadegan
and laughed while he did so.

For the merest heartbeat, Cadegan had gloated at seeing the
man's fate.

Until his mind flashed on Brother Eurig, who'd used his hands
to lovingly and patiently instruct him on decency and mercy. *Honor
is what separates man from beast. The greatest way to live with
honor in this world is to actually be what we pretend to be. Let
others laugh and mock those of us they perceive beneath them,
but remember, good Cadegan, honor lies inside our hearts and it is
that which makes us act with mercy and compassion against those
who have most wronged us. Even if the jackal wounds your pride, do
not reward such knavery by surrendering your honor to him. Only
then have you truly lost all. Never let anyone take your soul, for they
are not worth your eternity or your heart.*

Instead of walking away and leaving the knight to die as cruelly as he'd lived, Cadegan had charged forward and bravely sought to protect him from their enemies.

Though the knight had survived that encounter and Cadegan—wounded himself—had carried him to the physicians to be tended, the knight's injuries had been such that he'd died the next day. But an hour before his death, he'd summoned Cadegan to his bed.

His gaze warm, he'd offered his hand to Cadegan and had given him his own sword, armor, and helm, and told the soldiers with him that he wanted his horse to be Cadegan's as well.

It was that knight's sword that Cadegan carried to this day. A reminder to himself that even those who appeared the cruelest and most evil in the world were never above salvation. That, by the right actions, anyone's heart could be changed. And a reminder to Cadegan that *all* people deserved the utmost respect. To remind himself that he never wanted to be the one who brought such pain to another living creature's misery.

As Brother Eurig so often said . . . *No one ever gets over great pain, of any sort. It merely carves the soul into a stronger, better person.*

He would never dishonor Brother Eurig or his teachings.

"Would you give your honor for your love?"

Cadegan froze at the queen's disembodied voice. "Pardon?"

"What do you value most?" she asked him.

"Me lady. Always."

"Then prove it. Remove your clothes."

Cadegan shook his head. "I am in her body, and I will not dishonor her. You asked if I would sacrifice me honor, and so I would.

But what you ask of me now is to sacrifice hers, and that I will not do."

"Not even to save your life?"

"Nay. Me life holds no value to me. I will never dishonor me lady."

Cordelia grabbed him by the throat and slammed him against the wall. "I will rip out your heart!"

"You promised me that you would not harm Josette. Win, lose, or draw, me lady goes home alive and intact. Your word to me." A strange fissure went through his body.

The queen narrowed her gaze on him with rancor. "And now?"

"Now what?"

"You have your body back, Lord Cadegan. Will you give me your honor for your lady?"

Cadegan looked down to see that she was correct. He was himself again. "I will give anything for her freedom."

She inclined her head to him. "You will have three passes at my champion. If you are unhorsed, you will surrender yourself to Morgen. No questions asked. No escape. If you lose, you belong to me as my slave. Forever."

Cadegan would rather they kill him. But he had no doubt that he would win. He'd never once lost in a joust. "Done. But are we going to actually complete the match this time?"

She clapped her hands.

Cadegan was again on his horse. It was the moment right before they would have crossed lances, when his opponent had vanished. This time, his opponent's lance slammed into his shoulder.

He fell back on the horse, and almost came free of the saddle.

Illarion grimaced as he felt the pain of that blow as if he was the one who received it.

Gah, that had to hurt. The pain of that single blow had to be searing, and while her champion's lance had been snapped in twain, Cadegan's remained perfectly intact.

The urge to cry foul overwhelmed him. Yet he knew better than to utter those words.

Cordelia wouldn't care. This wasn't about fairness. It was about winning.

Unlike her and the dark forces she served, there was no victory Cadegan wanted badly enough that he'd cheat for it. He rolled his shoulder, trying to ignore the pain of it, as he turned his destrier back toward the list.

The pixie appeared again with her flag.

She looked at the giant he'd tilted against, then him. With a quick nod to the queen, she lowered her banner.

Cadegan spurred his mount forward. This time, he took aim for the giant's heart, and again leaned into the blow. He struck his opponent straight and true. The giant reeled back, but caught himself before he fell from the horse.

Thorn and Josette cried out in happiness of Cadegan's clear victory. Illarion raised his fists in solidarity.

Cordelia's eyes darkened, warning that she wasn't through with them, nor would she take loss lightly.

Cadegan tossed the remains of his broken lance to the ground.

Jo bit her lip as she watched Cadegan take another magical lance from the air and prepare for their final pass.

He lifted his helm's visor to smile and wink at her.

Illarion glanced toward Cordelia as a bad feeling went through him. Something about this wasn't right. This was too easy.

Something that proved to be all too true as the giant rose up during the last pass, to kill Cadegan. As it did so, Cadegan's armor went flying in all directions. He emerged out of it like a demonic butterfly from a cocoon. His eyes glowing yellow, he now had long blond hair, and claws. Huge fangs. His skin turned an unholy mixture of yellow and orange. Large, black wings sprang out of his back.

Thorn cursed as he saw him.

"What is it?" Jo asked breathlessly.

But Illarion already knew exactly what that beast was, even before Thorn explained it.

"We're in deep, serious shit. They've just awakened the Addanc."

"The what?"

Thorn met her gaze through the bars. "It's why I trapped Cadegan here in this realm." He jerked his chin toward the monster. "It was to keep *that* from being unleashed on the world. Each demonkyn holds in his heart his true form. The soulless bloodthirsty beast that is virtually invincible. One that cannot be stopped." Wincing, he cursed again as deep sadness marred his handsome features. "The Addanc has swallowed him whole and we're next on the menu."

18

They might be next on Cadegan's menu, but Illarion intended to fight.

With a string of profanity that left Jo blushing, Thorn stepped back from the bars of his cell. "Jo? Look at me. I'm about to do something really fucking stupid. When I do this, I need you to remember three words for me. *Omni rosae spina.*"

She scowled at him. "Every rose has its thorn?"

"Good, you understand Latin. Yes. Commit them to memory in the event I lose control. Okay?"

"Lose control of what?"

Yeah . . . Illarion would like to know that answer, too.

He had it a moment later when Thorn's eyes turned a vibrant green, laced with red, and his face became that of a demon's. Then his body followed suit, complete with wings and gold armor.

Talfryn went wild in his cage. "Help us! Someone! Rambo! We've got to get out of here!"

"Why?" Jo asked.

Before he could answer, Thorn channeled his powers and blasted them from their cages. Illarion rushed to her side to protect her as Thorn and Cadegan attempted to murder each other.

Laughing, Cordelia turned on Jo's group with a smug smile. "Thank you for allowing me to own the one weapon neither Morgen nor Merlin can stop. He's mine now!"

One moment they were in the cavern and the next, all of them, including Thorn—who was still a demon—were thrown into some house in another dimension, on the other side of a mirrored door.

What the hell was this?

Stunned, Illarion gaped as he glanced around at the unfamiliar place he'd never seen before and a group of people he'd never met. How Thorn had managed to get him through the portal without shifting into his dragon form . . . he had no idea. And that said it all about Thorn's incredible powers. Still in his demon's body, Thorn turned on them all and let out a fierce howl. He moved in to attack them.

Say the words! Illarion warned her.

"*Omni rosae spina!*"

The moment she spoke them, Thorn threw his head back and

cried out in agony. He froze as if he were fighting himself even harder than he'd fought Cadegan.

His demonic body slowly melted back to his human one. Tears streamed down his face. He visibly shook and gasped for breath.

Damn . . .

Without a word to them, Thorn wiped the back of his hand over his face and left through a side door.

One of the unknown women followed after him.

Another one, with long curly brown hair, grabbed Jo up into a fierce hug. "This is you? Right?"

"Yeah. Why?"

"After that crazy guy who was here in your body, I just wanted to make sure."

"Cadegan," Jo said, irritated at the way the woman talked about him.

But Illarion didn't really hear them. His gaze had locked onto the one person in the room he did know.

Intimately.

Unable to believe his eyes, he stared at his brother. Maxis. Tears filled his eyes.

"Illarion? Is it really you, little brother?"

Nodding, he rushed to gather Max into a tight hug. With his blond hair cut short, he barely resembled the fierce beast Illarion was used to, but it didn't matter.

This was his beloved brother he hadn't seen in centuries.

He clutched at him, so grateful to finally have family again. To be safe and away from that hell realm.

I can't believe it's you! Max's voice filled his head.

Nor I you! I've missed you so. He clenched his hand in Max's hair, then stepped back to meet Jo's curious gaze. *Josette, this is my brother Maxis.*

She inclined her head to him. "Nice to meet you."

"And you. Thank you for helping my brother." He gaped at Illarion. "I still can't believe you're here. I thought you'd died with the others."

Jo returned to the other woman. "I have to go back for Cadegan."

When she started toward the mirror, three Thorns appeared to block her way. "You cannot release him now. It's too late to save him."

Jo glared at them. "I will not leave him in there. Alone. If I have to go back by myself, I will."

Thorn returned to the room with the woman who'd gone after him as the three images blocking Jo's way vanished. He cast his glance around the people gathered there. "For the love of God, will someone *please* talk sense into Queen Hard Head?" He glared at Jo. "You can't go into Terre Derrière le Voile and release a banished demon into the world of man."

To Illarion's complete shock, Jo rushed Thorn and shoved him back. "You should never have banished him there! This is all your fault!"

"I had no choice," Thorn growled at her. "He was slipping from us every day, turning slowly more bitter and angrier. I saw it in his eyes. I did everything I could to keep him grounded and anchored, and then when he came to me that night to tell me that he'd killed innocent people, I saw that he was just about to blossom into the Addanc you saw earlier."

"So you abandoned him to it?"

He winced before he met her gaze again. "We have to leave him where he is."

She shook her head in denial of his solution. It wasn't that simple and she knew it. "We can't. We've awakened the Addanc within him. He is the very weapon you once feared unleashing. What if your enemies find him now? Are you any more able to kill him today?"

Thorn looked away.

"That's what I thought. Before all this started, Cadegan was dormant in his cave. Alone and safe. You and I have awakened his demon side, and it's up to us to do what you should have done a thousand years ago."

"Kill him?"

"No, Thorn. *Save* him."

19

"I agree with Jo. I think the most irresponsible thing we can do is leave Cadegan in Terre Derrière le Voile without supervision or protection. We've awakened the demon inside him. It's our duty to watch over and guard him."

Every head in the room stared at the Dark-Hunter Acheron as those words left his lips. Some were happy about it.

Some, not so much.

Illarion fell into the latter category. Last thing

he wanted was to return to the hell realm that had been his home and cost Edilyn her life. He wasn't into saving mankind.

Personally, he'd like to help Cadegan end them.

By the expression on her face, Jo wanted to kiss the ancient Dark-Hunter for backing her wishes to save her lover. The expression on Thorn's face said he wanted to choke him. Karma Devereaux, who'd been lobbying to banish Cadegan to an even bleaker realm, was furious.

Fang Kattalakis, a handsome, dark-haired wolfwere who worked as a Hellchaser for Thorn, exchanged a gaping stare of disbelief with his blonde werebear wife, Aimee. Their group was currently meeting in the back room of the bar and grill called Sanctuary, which the two shapeshifters owned in conjunction with Aimee's Were Hunter family.

The room they were in was a bit cramped with Karma and her sisters Selena, Tabitha, and Amanda, along with Tabitha's husband Valerius, who'd once been a Roman general, and Amanda's husband, Kyrian, an ancient Greek general who'd been killed by Valerius's grandfather Yeah, they had awkward family get-together. Then there was Talon, an ancient Celt who'd once worked with Valerius and Kyrian—all as Dark-Hunters under Acheron's command, who sat between them.

Just in case.

While Kyrian and Valerius had learned for the sake of their twin wives and five children to let bygones be bygones, they still had a tenuous relationship at times. One Illarion was beginning to learn was quite complicated.

And some of the more interesting glances he'd noted between

Karma and Thorn said there was much more to them than just mere friendship.

While they discussed Cadegan's future, Acheron's demon daughter Simi sat beside him, eating from a plate loaded with barbecue chicken, while Acheron's twin brother, Styxx, kept adding french fries and coleslaw to her meal whenever she ran out.

Styxx and Acheron were an odd duo, indeed. They were identical in absolutely every way, except hair color and style. Acheron's black curly hair was cut just below his ears and fell around his face. Styxx was blond and brushed his short curls back, out of his eyes. Acheron's clothes were black on black and as Goth as a *45 Grave* audience . . . including his black titanium wedding band that had skulls and crossbones on it.

On the flip side, Styxx had a preppy style and wore a dark blue shirt and jeans. His yellow gold wedding band appeared to be engraved with Egyptian hieroglyphics.

Also in black, Thorn sat beside Jo, while Illarion and Max leaned against a wall next to Ioan and Talfryn. The Hellchaser Zeke had stepped out only a few minutes ago to take a call, while they discussed what to do about Cadegan.

Illarion was really too tired to deal with this shit, but if his brother was in for their fight to save Cadegon, he was in.

Thorn sighed heavily. "You didn't see him, Ash. He is the Addanc. Fully morphed. Are you really willing to unleash him into this world, where we might not be able to stop him?"

Ash met his brother's gaze. "I've learned to reserve judgment on people for their actions, especially when they've been wronged by family." He turned back to Jo. "What do you honestly think?

You've spent the most time with him out of all of us. And remember, if you guess poorly, you'll probably end the world as we know it."

She snorted at Acheron's words. "No pressure, there, right, buddy? Wow, Ash. I know why you don't have your own self-help show . . . *Lifestyles of the Morbid and Terrifying*. Stay tuned, folks. This week we learn how to end the world with a flourish and get rid of those pesky dog flea problems, all in ten minutes."

Talon and Styxx burst out laughing.

"Hey!" Simi said. "No picking on the akri! He not the one who gots us into this . . . for once."

Offended, Acheron snorted. "Thanks, Sim."

"Anytime, akri. That's what the Simi's here for. Make sure you don't get one of them big heads."

Ignoring their segue, Illarion stepped forward. *I haven't known him long, but he seemed decent enough. For a demon. And I've known many of them over the centuries. I think we can trust Jo. She is his anchor, from what I've seen. There's nothing he won't do for her. He even spared my life at her command. So long as she lives, I think he's safe.*

Ash put his hand on Simi's shoulder. "That's the one truth of demons. They are all enslaved to their hearts. So long as it remains flesh and not stone or ice, we can control them."

Karma shook her head in denial. "But you're talking about someone who's been locked away for a thousand years. How will he acclimate to the modern world? You can't just let him loose and say, 'Hey, dude, welcome to the Electronic Age. Make sure you don't put your finger in an outlet.' "

Styxx waved his hand at her in a gesture that said to take it down a notch. "Lower the disgust in your tone a bit. As one who was locked away in solitary confinement for eleven thousand years, I can say that no, it won't be easy. You people are effing nuts in this day and age. You make as much sense as a blind rat in a shifting maze. But with a guiding hand, we're not psychotic. I think Julian, Seth, and I have proven that. We have yet to run screaming naked through the streets."

Selena grinned. "Your sessions with Grace must be going well."

Styxx nodded. "She's helped a lot, and we can get Cadegan the same counseling. Plus . . ." He glanced over to his brother. "We could set him up in one of our temples to live. There are still plenty that sit vacant on the hill."

Ash arched a brow at Styxx's suggestion. "You want him that close to your wife and toddler?"

A slow smile spread across Styxx's face. "I'm pretty sure Bethany can handle it. I have no fear for them. From this, anyway." He glanced over to Jo. "If we can save him, I think we should try. I stand with Acheron and Jo on this matter. We unleashed him. We police him."

Talon nodded in agreement. "If he really is the grandson of the Mórrígan and the Dagda, that makes him the first cousin to my wife. Family is family. We protect that always."

Karma sighed. "Normally, I'd agree with you all. But do we protect him at the expense of the rest of the world? Is there not any way to bind his powers?"

"Duct tape?"

They all cast a droll stare to Fang.

"Oh, don't give me that look. Like none of you have never wondered why a witch doesn't use that in a binding spell. Nothing gets away from duct tape without losing half their skin and all their hair."

Thorn snorted. "Really don't want to know about your kinky sex life, wolf. Your wife handles my food, and now I'm grossed out."

They laughed.

Acheron turned back toward Talon. "So, Celt, does anyone in your camp know Cordelia personally?"

"My mother-in-law probably does. She's a member of the Tuath Dé. Technically so am I, and my wife. But Starla lived among them in her youth. She knows everyone who's still living in their pantheon."

"Tuath Dé . . . " Acheron repeated that under his breath as he narrowed his gaze on Jo.

"Does that ring a bell?" Kyrian asked.

Acheron pulled out his cell phone and dialed it. "Yeah, it does, and not for the obvious reasons." He held his hand up to let them know the person he was calling had picked up. "Hey baby, how's my girl?" He paused to listen before he laughed. "Give them both a big kiss from Grandpa and tell them that I'll be by later to tuck them in." With his inhuman, swirling silver eyes, he stared at Jo in a way that was really making her uncomfortable. "Yeah, actually I could use you for a minute. Can you pop over for just a few minutes?" He nodded. "I'm at Sanctuary. Back room. You can ask Dev when you get here and he'll show you in. Thanks, precious. Love you." He hung up.

"Kat?" Styxx asked.

Acheron nodded again. "She'll be . . ." The door opened to

show an insanely tall, gorgeous blonde woman who appeared even older than Acheron. "Walking in the door, right now."

Wide-eyed at the number of people inside, Kat cast her gaze around the room. "Hi, Daddy." She moved to kiss Acheron on the cheek before she hugged Simi and Styxx. When she went to steal one of Simi's french fries, the demon gasped in horror.

"You won't share fries with your sissy?" Kat asked the demon.

Simi eyed her with mock ire. "Good thing I love my baby sissy. But . . . Daddy Akri, Akra-Kat stealing your Simi's fries! Make her stop!"

Laughing, Acheron shook his head. "Don't make me put you two in separate corners. Play nice."

"Yes, sir." Kat stepped to the side.

Simi handed Kat another fry before she laughed and returned to her barbecue.

Acheron jerked his chin toward Jo. "Does she remind you of someone?"

Screwing her face up, Kat licked the ketchup from her fingers. Suddenly, recognition lit her green eyes and she gasped. "Are you thinking Brit?"

"Yeah."

Kat nodded. "Spitting image of her. But I haven't seen her in centuries. It's why it took me a while to realize it."

Jo frowned at their discussion. "Who's Brit?"

"Britomartis," Acheron answered. "She was a cousin of the goddess Artemis. They played together when they were girls on Olympus."

Kat nodded. "She's the one who gave my mother her famous nets that no one can escape from. As a thank-you for them, my mother gave her an enchanted mirror that had once belonged to Apollo. The mirror could show events of the past, present, and future. But most of all, it showed Britomartis the true heart of those around her."

Acheron nodded. "She was gazing in that same mirror one day when she fell in love with a Welsh prince and demigod named Arthegall ap Tyr, whose face she saw while he was jousting against another knight."

Jo gaped. "I saw Cadegan in the mirror before we met. It was how I ended up falling through it and into Glastonbury Tor."

Thorn rose slowly to his feet. "That's one hell of a coincidence, isn't it?"

Acheron nodded. "And I don't believe in them."

Kat moved closer to Jo. "Brit had a son and daughter and both she and Arthegall gave up their godhoods so that they could live out their lives in peace with their children."

Karma folded her arms over her chest as she jerked her chin toward her cousin. "Jo could always see things in mirrors. She used to accuse us of planting it in her mind, but she's a born scryer."

"I have no powers."

"Would you let us test your blood?" Kat asked.

Jo hesitated. "Test it how, Draculina?"

"A little prick?"

Talfryn snorted. "Little prick's what got her into trouble."

Ioan shoved at him. "Shut it."

"It's true. Just saying."

Kat ignored them. "Can we?"

Jo held her hand out toward the woman. "Sure."

Kat pulled out a small knife and lightly pricked the edge of Jo's finger. She pooled the blood on the knife's blade before she took it to her father and handed it to him.

Acheron dipped his finger into the blood then tasted it.

Jo screwed her face up in absolute repugnance. Nasty!

After a second, he nodded. "It's the same bloodline as Artemis."

"You sure?" Thorn asked.

He gave Thorn a droll stare. "Yeah. Pretty sure. I've tasted it before. Jo is from Zeus's bloodline."

Jo scowled at all of them. "What does that mean?"

Kat winked at her. "We're very distant cousins."

"For another," Acheron continued, "there's something much larger at play here. Your ancestor was pulled into Terre Derrière le Voile by a mirror to meet her future husband, who was a Welsh prince and demigod."

"You think the two of them are reincarnated?" Selena asked.

Talon passed a knowing look to Acheron. "It happens, and you don't want to get in the way when it does. Two lovers will not be denied."

Except for him and Edilyn. Illarion choked on that thought as he forced down his own pain.

"Then how do we get him out?" Jo asked.

Talon stood. "I'm part of the Tuath Dé, so I'll lead us in."

Styxx nodded in agreement. "Since we're trespassing into another pantheon's realm, I think we should keep the group small. Jo has to go, because we'll need her to deal with Cadegan. Thorn's Frick and Frack, since they'll follow us in, anyway." He grinned at Talfryn's disapproving growl over their nickname. "Thorn and me."

Simi looked up from her food. "No Simi?"

Styxx kissed her on the forehead. "Not this time. I don't want to risk you and I know your father agrees with me. We need you here to protect our small sons and Kat's son and daughter."

That placated her. "Okies. But you have to let me put hornays on Baby Ari."

"Sure, as long as they're detachable."

She blew him a raspberry.

Their stupid solidarity pissed Illarion off. But more than that, it touched him.

Damn him for it. And before he could stop himself, he made a decision he'd sworn he never would.

I will come, too.

For Edilyn. If she were here, she'd be among the first to volunteer to help them. The romantic in her wouldn't rest until the two lovers were reunited. So for her, he would act against his own nature.

If he couldn't have her, he could at least do this in remembrance of her.

Max sighed. "Then I will go, too."

Illarion glared at him for volunteering for such a suicidal task.

But Max refused to back down. "You've been too long alone. I won't let you do this without a *wing*man."

Styxx nodded. "That actually works. It leaves a mount for each of us."

Jo stepped forward. "Then we're going after Cadegan?"

Thorn inclined his head to her. "May the gods have mercy on us all. The last thing we need is to face an even stronger creature."

20

Cadegan dove beneath the blackened waves as he sought some sort of refuge from the hell that had become his world. Hatred and bloodlust pounded through him without letup. He wanted to taste the entrails of every creature dumb enough to approach him. While he'd never been friendly, this was completely different.

He had lost all ability to feel for anyone or anything.

Opening his eyes, he breathed in the water and scent of blood that still clung to him. The giant had been his first victim.

Too bad Cordelia had run screaming before he had a chance to finish the giant off and add her to his menu. Since then, he'd flown over the countryside, looking for more food. How he loved the musical cadence of screams echoing in his ears.

Truly, there was no better sound.

Drunk on the panic he'd induced, he dove deeper into the water. This was what he'd needed. The water's caress. The sound of his heartbeat echoing in his ears.

He froze his muscles as his instincts picked up on the sound of creatures approaching.

Curious, he tucked his legs and floated to the surface. With only his eyes out of the water, he scanned the banks until he saw Morgen's men. Fey Adoni armor glistened in the grim, gray light. Armed with crossbows and spears, they sent out lures to flush him to the top.

Did they think him as mindless as he was soulless?

Hah! They were about to learn the truth of his kind.

"Cadegan?" Morgen called. "We are here to free you."

Her gown was the only color in the dreary landscape. Bright bloodred, it clung to the voluptuous curves of her body. Something that brought out a new hunger inside him as she stirred his lust.

"Come to us, love. We will care for you in ways you cannot imagine."

Tempted, he moved his gaze to the MOD on Morgen's left-hand side.

Bracken. His uncle, who'd once tortured him at Morgen's behest. He wanted to spear the bastard through his missing heart. But he refused to give them his location.

Especially since half her army carried nets he knew were there to capture him.

"Cadegan? Come, child. Let me care for you."

He went perfectly still at the sound of a voice that was identical to his mother's. For the merest instant, he was a boy again, sitting on the edge of the tower window as he counted down to the bell toll. As he looked out upon the endless land and wondered if his mother was out there, somewhere.

If she ever gave a passing thought to the child she'd left behind.

Furious, he started forward, wanting more blood.

But as he moved, the water caressed his demonkyn skin like the hand of a lover.

It caressed him like . . .

He struggled to remember. It was important that he recall the sensation.

'Tis nothing. Devour them!

He pulled back. Placing his hand upon his cheek, he heard the faint memory of laughter.

Gentle teasing.

Like a wombat in a cornfield.

"Josette," he breathed as he remembered feeling something other than burning hatred and the stinging hunger for death and blood.

I will never leave you.

But she had left him. Just like everyone else.

His rage built even higher. It was true. She'd betrayed him. Abandoned him the first chance she'd had to go home.

And here he stayed. With no one and nothing.

Morgen wants you.

Nay, she did not. He was not so stupid as to be that easily fooled. She wanted to use him.

No one ever wanted to keep him.

"Cade?"

At first, he thought himself dreaming. Imagining the sound of a voice that was forever gone.

"Sweetie? Where are you?"

It was Josette. His heart pounded as a hope he despised filled his entire being.

'Tis a dodge from the Queen Bitchtress herself.

Suddenly, two dragons and two Adar Llwch Gwin swooped down to attack Morgen and her army. Exploding into action, Morgen's forces flew to engage them.

But the moment he was alone, a slight movement on his right caught his attention. Crouched low in the shrubs was the last person he'd ever expected to see.

Josette.

She stretched her hand out toward him. "I'm here to take you home with me. Come, my lord. I won't let anyone harm you."

Cadegan started forward instinctively. Until he saw that she wasn't alone. Two men were with her. His bastard brother and one he knew was related to him. He wasn't sure how he knew, but he'd always been able to feel any member of the Tuath Dé what came near.

Josette glared at them. "Do you mind? He doesn't trust any of you."

"Why should I trust you?" he growled low in his demonic voice.

Josette met his gaze without flinching. "Because I love you. I promised I wouldn't let them have you and I meant it. Come home with me, Cade. Let me give you the love you deserve."

She's lying. 'Tis the worst sort of dodge ever handed you, lad. Don't be an imbecile.

But he saw no deceit in her eyes. Heard no tremble in her voice.

Before he could stop himself, he was on his way to her. He expected her to scream when she saw what he looked like. Horned, winged, and foul. Even he'd glimpsed himself and thought, *That can't be right.*

Yet it was. His outside now betrayed the truth of his blood. It telegraphed to the world exactly what a monster he'd been born.

Like the warrior she was, Josette didn't flinch at his approach. He saw no condemnation in her dark eyes. Only a warmth he'd never known anywhere, other than her arms.

She again reached for him. "I'm here for you, baby."

He pulled back. "Don't look at me. I'm hideous."

"There is nothing about you I find repellent." She leaned so far forward to reach him that she almost crashed into the water.

Cadegan rushed to catch her and push her back to safety.

And the moment he felt her hand on his skin, he calmed down to that quiet serenity that eased him deep inside his soul.

She wrapped her tiny hand around his miscolored, clawed one. "Ever my hero. Thank you."

Cadegan stared at their laced fingers. As always, her skin was the perfect porcelain blend. Soft beyond imagining. "Aren't you afraid of me?"

She shook her head. "I will never fear you."

Before he realized what she intended, she bent down and kissed his scarred lips.

Jo tried not to think about the fact that he could tear her apart as he lifted his hand to cup her face while he kissed her. Her body went from cold to hot faster than she was prepared for. More than that, he kissed her with an untasted passion.

When he pulled back, she expected to look into reptilian eyes again.

They were again his vibrant blue. She smiled at him as she danced her gaze over his perfect, male body. He looked just as he had before.

Slowly, his eyes locked on hers, he lifted himself out of the water and neared her. Like an exhausted cat, he laid his head down in her lap and pressed her hand to his cheek.

"Me precious Josette."

She brushed her hand through his hair. "My beautiful Cadegan."

"I still cannot leave this place, me lady. I am forever damned here."

"No, sweetie. I've come to get you. I can take you through the portal, the same way we took Illarion."

Lifting his head, he met her gaze. "Do you swear to me?"

"Every effing day." She rose and held her hand out to him. "Come home, Cadegan."

He glanced to his brother, who watched them with a worried expression. "Are you here to stop us?"

Thorn shook his head. "I'm here to help."

"And you are?" he asked the blond man beside his brother.

"I'm Styxx. They brought me along because I have Asshole Brother issues, too. Mine, as well as his goddess girlfriend, locked me in a hole for eleven thousand years. I know *exactly* how hard it is to trust again. And I know the hunger you have to be free of this place. Come with us, and we'll take you to a place where you'll never be alone again."

"Will you be there?" he asked Josette.

"I promise I will never leave you."

"Take me home with you, Josette. 'Tis the only place I wish to be."

Thorn stepped back as he watched his brother, now in human form, lay his head down on her shoulder. It was the damnedest thing he'd ever seen.

One minute, Cadegan had been a full-fledged, blood-crazed demon.

The next, he was perfectly calm again. Serene, even. Acheron was right. So long as they had Jo, they had a leash for Cadegan.

But as he opened the portal and allowed them to walk through it, he knew it wasn't this easy.

Something bad was going to happen.

21

Cadegan hesitated at the portal as the others went through. Styxx stayed behind with him and Josette.

On the other side, Thorn turned to face them. His expression seemed sincere enough. But Cadegan wasn't accustomed to trusting him.

Not for anything.

"I am here for you, little brother."

That only made Cadegan more apprehensive. Thorn killed or banished creatures like him. He didn't suffer them to live among the world of man, and he damn sure didn't help them to reach it.

Unsure, Cadegan met Josette's dark gaze, and tightened his grip on her delicate hand.

"I trust him, Cade. He won't betray you. And if he does, I promise to serve up a part of his anatomy that he'll definitely miss."

He smiled at that.

"I am here for you, Cade. Always."

Those words touched a part of him he'd never met before and they choked him. In that moment, he craved her with a madness that made the demon inside him tremble in fear. Cupping her cheek, he kissed her and wished they were alone so that he could ease the other ache inside him that begged for her touch.

With a breath for courage and her hand in his, he stepped through and waited for the wall to slam shut in his face. For him to walk into a solid wall that kept him where he belonged.

In hell.

But it didn't.

Holding his breath, he stepped through, into a horrifically bright room. Unused to actual daylight, he flinched and held his hand up to shield his squinting eyes. Even so, he reveled in the pain of it.

Sunlight. Real and true. He could even feel the warmth of it on his skin.

Amazed, he held his hand out and let the rays dance over his flesh.

"Dang it, Karma! Close your curtains. Fast!"

A woman who looked similar to Josette ran to obey.

Jo bit her lip as she watched the awe and marvel play across Cadegan's handsome face. He was like an infant discovering his feet for the first time.

And he looked so out of place here with his black monk's robe and chain mail and spurs.

Karma raked a sneer over him, but he didn't pay a bit of attention to her. Not while unbelievable joy spread across his face, as he turned a small circle and glanced around the brightly painted room and decorated bookshelves.

He met Jo's gaze. "Where am I?"

"Karma's house."

Cadegan digested that news slowly as he continued to look about. Scowling, he paused and cocked his head at the sight of a familiar stranger. In the far corner was a man who appeared identical to Styxx, except his hair was black and his eyes a swirling silver, instead of Styxx's deep blue.

"Severe Asshole Brother issues," Styxx repeated in Cadegan's ear. His voice was filled with humor as he cracked a wide grin. "Every time you think you have it bad, just remember, you don't see Thorn's face every single time you stumble in front of a mirror."

Cadegan snorted at something that wasn't really funny. "I concede this issue to you, me lord. By far, yours is the greatest indignity."

He clapped Cadegan on the shoulder. "If only you knew, my brother. If only you knew." Rubbing his arm affectionately, Styxx went to his brother's side. For all of Styxx's protestations, he and Acheron seemed to get along well.

In fact, Acheron embraced him. "Glad you're back. I was starting to worry."

Patting him on the shoulder, Styxx indicated them with his chin. "Acheron, I present to you, Cadegan."

Acheron inclined his head respectfully. "Welcome back, my lord."

He seemed sincere and decent enough. But Cadegan was suspicious of the demon blood he sensed inside Acheron. Blood Styxx didn't share.

What was he? Why would one twin be demonic while the other wasn't?

"We have clothes for you," Acheron said graciously. "Whenever you're ready, Styxx or I can show you to your new home."

Cadegan arched a brow. "My new home?"

"In a realm called Katateros."

His stomach wrenched as his anger grew. So he wasn't free after all. He'd only gone from one prison to the next. That was what he got for trusting them. He should have known better. "Then I'm not to stay in this realm?"

The men stepped back in trepidation.

Jo placed her arm on his and calmed him as she saw the demon rising to the forefront. She placed her hand on his face and forced him to meet her loving gaze.

His eyes went from yellow back to blue as quickly as they'd switched before. "Shh, Cade. That's not what they meant. You'll have the freedom to come and go as you wish. And I'll be with you the whole time. If that's what you want."

"You will?"

She nodded. "I will be with you so long as you want me. Just promise that if you want to get rid of me, you'll tell me and not cut my head off or something equally mean."

"I would never do such, lass." He pressed his cheek to hers before he stepped back to eye Thorn. But at least this time, he remained fully human.

Jo wrinkled her nose playfully at him as he held her hand. "Your eyes are like an old-fashioned mood ring. The moment you get angry, bang . . . the demon rears its ugly head and stares at me. Kind of scary."

"I would never cause you harm, Josette."

"You mean you hope you'd never harm her."

They all turned to Thorn, who'd spoken. Unrepentant, he explained his point. "The demon in our blood isn't always under our control. For that reason, Jo, you need to learn when to run from it. Lest you be harmed, and he be devastated by his own inability to control himself."

"Really?" she asked, suddenly apprehensive of Cadegan.

Acheron nodded. "I almost killed my wife once in the throes of it. And I'd sooner cut out my own heart than make my Tory frown."

Cadegan hesitated at those words. Since he was so seldom around others, and never someone he loved, he hadn't even considered that. "Is this true?" he asked Thorn.

"Sadly, yes, brother. But you know that. It's what led me to banish you. You unleashed the demon within and killed without reason."

Aye, he had. But, unlike Josette, they had meant nothing to him. Suddenly, fear rose up inside him. He tightened his grip on her hand. "Then I should be apart from you."

"Not on your life, bucko. Call me Velcro. You go, I go. I promised you that and I never break my word, either." Her eyes darkened as she passed a knowing smile to Styxx. "Would you mind showing us to our new home now? I should like to introduce Cadegan to my three children."

He choked and coughed at that. Was she serious? "Pardon, lass?"

Jo blinked innocently as she heard the panic in his voice. "Didn't you know, sweetie? You're a father."

The expression on his face was priceless.

"Only you could make stark cold terror look sexy, Cade." She kissed his cheek. "Relax, sweetie. It's just my three dogs. You'll love them."

Finally relaxing, he shook his head at her.

Laughing, Styxx returned to their sides. "If you're ready?"

Cadegan nodded.

One second they were at Karma's with all the group that had rescued Cadegan. The next, they were gone.

Max clapped his hand over Illarion's back. "You ready to leave?"

Illarion nodded, even though he wasn't sure if that was the truth. In all honesty, he didn't feel like he belonged here any more than Cadegan did.

And unlike Cade, he didn't have the love of his life to help him adjust. Strange how as bad as it'd all seemed at the time, in retrospect, being damned to the Shadow Tor hadn't been that awful.

At least Edilyn had been with him.

Now . . .

He felt adrift and without purpose.

While he still had the Halter and the Spartoi, they were meaningless to him. So he allowed Max to take him to his home in Sanctuary.

A huge loft apartment that was modified to accommodate a dragon's weight.

Max kept looking at him with a state of utter disbelief. "I just can't believe you're here and alive."

Neither could he, honestly.

Aimless, he wandered around Max's apartment that held some of his sacred items Max had guarded over the centuries. *Why do we do this again, brother?*

Max frowned at him. "What do you mean?"

He met Max's gaze that was so different from his. *Not the human forms that were forced on us. The original curse placed on our mother by Azura that damned the lilitu to only birth dragon children . . . monsters to be solitary. To live immortal lives of isolation and misery. Is it any wonder why the Daimons eat human souls to elongate their lives? I actually understand their motivation. It's not fair that we be cursed by the gods for actions none of us took.*

Max had that look on his face that he'd always gotten, whether dragon or human, that said he never bothered with such philosophy.

Curse of his Arel father.

Duty. Honor. Protect.

Illarion's curse was more—kill. Maim. Screw them all.

It was a wonder they ever got along or saw eye to eye on any matter.

Never mind. I'm just tired.

"Then rest. I have to work in the bar next door. If you need anything, just call."

Illarion nodded. Shifting into his dragon form, he lumbered to the straw to lie down.

But as he did so, his past played through his mind. The horrors of those who'd mocked. Those who'd tortured and tormented him.

And his soul screamed out for the only balm it'd ever known.

A single crystalline tear fled down his cheek with the knowledge that for him there would never be anything more than duty. Nothing more than misery.

Nothing more than mere existence.

Forevermore.

And while he'd once been content with that, Edilyn had taught him to want more. To need more. Now he hated and resented his birthright with every shitty breath he drew.

22

The hardest part about living a life not bound by linear years was gauging length. But then, even those bound to finite life spans in sequential order occasionally suffered from a form of temporal displacement where sometimes a single year could seem like a blink or a week could last an eternity.

With Illarion, he kept drifting back to his days in Greek captivity when they'd forced him to become a man against his will.

To those escape attempts with Max when he'd been reliant on his brother.

Probably because he felt that way now. Only this wasn't a physical need for protection. It was emotional, and he hated that even more. He wasn't physically weak and unable to fight. In fact, he'd never been stronger in that regard.

It was his spirit and soul that were sick. The need inside him to feel connected again.

He'd never craved that. Not until Edilyn. Her absence left such a vacuous hole inside him that it was as if a part of him had been carried away into the grave with her.

It didn't help that he was here with the Peltier bears and Kattalakis wolves and their mates. Daily reminders of what bonded mates were like.

What they *should* be like.

Max was his brother, not just in blood, but in misery. A mated dragon whose partner had abused him to such extent that Max had left her in the Stone Age and sought refuge thousands of years out of her reach.

Yet he would sometimes mumble Seraphina's name in his sleep. Illarion never mentioned it to him, and if Max remembered doing it, he never spoke a word about it. Nor did he ever talk about Sera at all.

In fact, no one here other than Illarion even knew Sera existed.

Max kept that as his personal hell.

So on the night when she and her Amazon tribe made a thunderous appearance in the Sanctuary bar and grill, Max turned more than a few Were-Hunter heads.

But the bomb she laid on them all was the one none of them, especially Max, have ever suspected. . . .

Blaise shoved at Maxis as Illarion joined them in the private room inside Sanctuary that was reserved to isolate rowdy patrons. He'd been awakened by their shouting. The last thing he'd expected was to find his two brothers embroiled in a heated argument in front of Seraphina.

"Max is planning to leave us behind and go fight demons on his own for his dragonswan. Go on and tell him how stupid he is, Illarion. I tried and he's too stupid to listen."

Illarion arched a brow at that. His sharp, steely gaze went to the titian-haired bitch who'd all but destroyed his brother and narrowed with a bloodlust that visibly scared her. And well it should, since he meant it.

Shaking his head, he let out a frustrated sigh as he returned a furious glower to Maxis. *So can I kill her now?*

Eyes wide, Seraphina stepped back. "Excuse me?"

"No!" Maxis snapped. "And stop asking me that."

Illarion looked up at the ceiling. *It's so not fair. I lost my Edilyn and yet* this *bitch lives and returns? Why, gods? Why?* His jaw ticcing, he looked to Blaise. *Is there not some transmutation of souls we can do? Place my mate's soul in her body?*

"Maybe."

Max growled at them. "Stop it! Both of you! You're not going to swap out her soul."

I don't understand why you continue to protect her. She's never brought anything save utter hell and misery to your door. You told me yourself that she could barely look at you when you lived to-

gether. So why are you so eager now to die at her command? Let her rot in whatever mess she's woven. It serves her right.

Seraphina winced.

"Enough, Illarion! She's the mother of my young and I will not have you say another word against her."

That news cold-cocked him. *You spawned with her? Are you infinitely stupid?* The answer to that was obvious.

Instead of saving their race, Max, you should have cut that ungrateful whore's throat and devoured her unborn young when you had the chance. Saved us all the misery and heartache they've caused us since then. Not to mention indigestion and ulcers.

Illarion raked another cold sneer over Seraphina. *Be grateful you're his mate. That alone stays my hand from ripping out your heart and feasting on it . . .* Arcadian.

But Max wasn't in the mood to give him any reprieve. "If not for them, Illarion, you'd have never met your Edilyn."

Illarion winced at his brother's cruel reminder, and looked away. *You're not helping your cause, brother. You're only reminding me why I hate them all and what they've viciously taken from me. . . . Now, what's this infernal madness you're on about?*

Max glared at him. "You're the only being alive who can talk to me like that and not be gutted on the floor."

"Um, yeah," Blaise said in an irritated tone. "Why does he get that favoritism? You'd lay me out cold for it."

Illarion cut another malicious glare at Seraphina before he answered Blaise's question. *Before you were born, Blaise, I was the one who found Max after her tribe all but gelded and skinned him alive. They had him muzzled with a metriazo collar that restricted his ability to use his magick in any way. He couldn't even transform to heal himself. Had I not found him when I did, he would have died. I doubt he'd have made it through another three hours in the condition he was in.*

Blaise sucked his breath in sharply at what that meant as Seraphina closed her eyes in sympathetic pain and horror.

Giving her no reprieve from his wrath and hatred, Illarion circled her. *Had an enemy found him, he'd have been gutted and tortured even more. I don't say worse, because no one could have done him worse harm.*

"Enough," she breathed.

But he refused to take mercy on her. *They'd even clipped his wings to ground him.*

"Stop!" Max snarled.

Now even Blaise glared at her.

Maxis broke between his brothers to approach her. True to his damnable Arel blood, he gently lifted her chin until she met his haunted gaze. "My wings grew back together."

After two hundred years, Illarion reminded him. *Leaving you at the mercy of enemies you couldn't escape until you could fly again.*

He glanced over his shoulder toward Illarion. "It taught me to be a stronger fighter. Now leave it. This isn't about me or the past. It's about my dragonets and their survival today."

Illarion moved to stand at Maxis's back. He placed his hand on his brother's shoulder. *You are the only parent I've ever known. And you're my best friend. I will not let you fight alone.*

Blaise nodded. "Three dragons are better than one."

Scoffing, Max dropped his hand from Seraphina's face. "Two dragons and a mandrake."

"How exactly are you a mandrake and related to them?" she asked.

Blaise sighed wearily. "My father was the leader of the mandrakes under King Uther Pendragon. When I was born looking like this—" He held his hands out to show off his features that clearly betrayed his albinism. "—our demonic mother decided she had no use for her *special* mandrake son. She handed me over to my father, who then took me out to the woods and left me to die."

"I'm sorry."

He shrugged at Sera's sympathy. "Don't be. Got over it. And given my mother's wonderful personality, and my father's oh-so-*kind* temperament, prefer it to having been kept by either of them. Normally, I just tell folks I know nothing of my parents and leave it at that. It's easier than dealing with their pity over something that really doesn't affect me."

Like him and Maxis. It'd never bothered them, either, that their mother had abandoned her nests and left them to either die, or survive on their own. It was the way of their species.

Tears gathered in Sera's eyes as she stared up at Max. "Gods, I thought this would be easier to do."

"What?"

"Consign you to death. Again." Seraphina bit her lip as she glanced between them. "I don't know what to do, Maxis. Even though they can't use the hearts of our children for the spell they have, Nala will gut them if I fail to deliver the Dragonbane's heart to her."

Why him? Illarion asked.

She shrugged. "The spell they have requires the heart of the father of our race. The firstborn Apollite-dragon who drew first blood."

The Dragonbane.

Max met Illarion's gaze and knew the secret the two of them had shared for five thousand years. They weren't just bound by their mother's blood. They'd been bound by one prince's and pantheon's savage cruelty.

Blaise cleared his throat. "You know . . . having been raised around the queen bitch of the fey folk and watching the nasty shit she's pulled on everyone . . . The backstabbing. The lies. Half-truths, et cetera, I just have to ask one simple question. . . . Has anyone bothered to find out what this spell will actually do once it's cast?"

Max laughed bitterly. "I have a really good idea since they have Hadyn's Emerald Tablet."

Blaise's eyes bugged at the mention of that. "Combine that with what you guard—"

And your heart, Illarion finished.

"Bishhhh!" Blaise made the sound of an explosion as he flung his hands out.

Seraphina scowled. "I don't quite understand what you're saying."

Max locked gazes with her. "They're not just planning on destroying this Daimon leader, Stryker. They're planning on releasing the Atlantean Destroyer, reuniting the gods of Chaos, and reestablishing the old order."

Blaise nodded. "If they succeed in this, honey, it ain't just your kids they'll kill. It's every creature who has an ounce of light energy in them."

Illarion let out a silent sigh. *Which means all of us and everyone we love, and a few we're not that fond of, either.*

23

Off to the side while they stood in a group in the main room of Sanctuary, Maxis locked gazes with Seraphina. "I might be able to find the kids. But it will require my mate to trust me and do something that's repugnant to her."

Her eyes widened at that. "What?"

Knowing the exact stupidity his brother had in mind, Illarion took his arm and vigorously shook his head no.

Maxis ignored him. "It'll be fine."

Illarion rolled his eyes and mouthed a silent curse.

Blaise burst out laughing, then stopped as he realized the rest of them weren't in on their private conversation. Clearing his throat, he slinked off to a corner to examine a spot on the wall, even though he was blind.

Seraphina scowled. "What's going on?"

Max hesitated as he swept his gaze around everyone gathered there. This motley hodgepodge was his family and he didn't want to risk losing any of them. "I can track the children."

Illarion growled, knowing just how stupid it would be.

"There's no way," Sera said affirmatively. "They have them shielded. If it was possible, I would have done it already."

"I can find them." His tone held absolute resolve.

Her doubting expression was comical. But then she'd always underestimated his brother's abilities. Most creatures, to their detriment, did. "How?"

"If you'll trust me. Completely. I can do it."

Fang cocked his head as if he now understood what was going on. "You're part Oneroi?"

Illarion snorted at the assumption that Max was one of the gods who raided human dreams so that they could siphon off emotions.

"Don't insult me. I'm not Greek. I was captured and dragged to Arcadia. It was never my homeland."

Fang's jaw dropped. "Seriously?"

Illarion nodded. *While I'm a son of Ares, we're related only through our mother. Max is a lot older. His powers much stronger and more akin to those of the gods than a typical Were-Hunter.*

Even the Arcadian bear Dev Peltier was awed. "So what are you, then?"

"Xarunese."

"Bless you," Dev said drily. "You need a Kleenex? Benadryl?"

Max sighed heavily at the bear's fucked-up sense of humor. "Land of Xarun. Much like Atlantis, the gods took issue with it. What little remains sits at the bottom of the Black Sea. I'm one of the very few who survived the sinking."

"Ouch."

Max inclined his head to Kyle Peltier for his verbalizing the pain of *that* particular nightmare.

"So wait a minute." Dev cocked his head as if he just realized what Max was telling them. "You're not Greek or Apollite . . . how exactly are you Katagari?"

Carson Whitethunder, the hawk who was also their resident vet and doctor, passed a smirk to Dev. He and Aimee were the only two creatures here who had ever seen the mark that was branded on Max's thigh. And only because they had treated his injuries. Aimee when Max had first arrived one heartbeat from death, and Carson decades later after a couple of their grittier confrontations with enemies who'd tried over the years to destroy the Peltier family. "Haven't you ever wondered why, in over a hundred years of living here, Max has never stepped a single foot outside of this building?"

Dev snorted. "We're all freaks here. I don't judge."

Max glanced to Seraphina as he remembered the less than pleasant way she'd handled the news when she'd first learned what that mark was. Why he bore it.

He'd never intended for anyone here to learn about it. But it was time to come clean.

"Remember that you're all bound by the Omegrion laws. None of you can attack me on Sanctuary grounds."

"Sheez, boy," Dev groused. "What are you? The Dragonbane, or something?"

Max inclined his head to him, and as soon as he did, it sucked every bit of oxygen from the room. Half the shapeshifters around him took a step back, as if terrified being near him would taint them.

All humor and friendliness evaporated from Dev's eyes as he gaped. "Are you shitting me? *You're* the sole reason for the war between the Katagaria and the Arcadians?"

Illarion stepped between them. *It's not that simple, Dev. Calm down.*

Dev curled his lip. "Not that simple, my ass. You murdered Lycaon's heir in cold blood and started this bloodbath between our people, and you're telling me it's not that simple?"

Max had that same sick look on his face he got any time someone saw his mark and recognized it.

He was the most hated among his people.

No, not *his* people.

They were Greeks and Apollites.

He wasn't. He'd never really been one of them. Forever a hated outsider. An interloper who'd been mistaken for them since the day Dagon had captured them and mixed them in with their ancestors.

"Enough!" Fang shouted, holding his hands up to get the others to settle down. "We'll deal with the Dragonbane issue after this is over. Right now, we need to focus on getting Max's kids away from the gallu demons before they convert them into zombies. Regardless of anything else, they're innocent in this."

His eyes haunted, Max held his hand out toward Seraphina.

"I trust you, Lord Dragon. Lead me to your lair."

Illarion and Blaise followed Max and Seraphina to the huge attic where Maxis made his home. His brother used his powers to light four huge iron candle stands. The light flickered and merged with the rays of the dawning sun to cast their shadows against the wall.

Blaise closed the door.

Sighing, Sera met Blaise's blank stare. "Illarion doesn't think much of me, does he?"

"I'm trying to remain impartial, but if one-quarter of what Illy is saying right now to Max about you is true . . . Do your people really make jewelry from the tusks, scales, and bones of dragons?"

Heat crept over her face. "We don't hunt mandrakes."

"From what I'm hearing, you don't know. Your people don't exactly bother to find out if they're hunting Katagaria or not. You basically kill indiscriminately and go after any large serpent that isn't Arcadian."

"Stop, Blaise," Maxis said in a gentle tone. "She's not to blame in this."

No. We are, you and I. I curse the day I ever let you talk me into saving their kind. Illarion raked her with a chilling stare. *We should have let the gods have them all.*

"Enough, Illarion. I have to focus."

Illarion threw his hands up. *Fine. Let's see how she handles this.*

After all, she never bothered to ask you anything about what you really are. Where you came from. How you were dragged into her world to become part of it. The three years you lived with her, she never once cared enough to learn.

Maxis growled at his brother. "Stay out of my head and thoughts. . . . I swear, I should have eaten your egg instead of nesting it."

Seraphina arched her brow at that. "You nested him?"

"Sadly, yes, and I did a piss-poor job of it, too. As you can see."

Illarion rolled his eyes.

Blaise laughed. "Max attempted to nest all of his siblings. At least those of us he could find. Once a year while she lived, he'd journey to where our mother placed her eggs and collect them so that they wouldn't have to hatch alone, and flounder for survival."

Max taught us the Bane-Cry to clear our lungs and so that no matter how far apart we were, we could always call out to each other for help, should we need it. And while the rest of our siblings might not respond, Max would always come to us if he was physically able to do so.

"Neither here nor there," Max said, passing an annoyed grimace at each brother in turn. He led her toward a large area of the attic that was curtained off.

Illarion shook his head as he caught the look of reservation on Sera's face. *This is a bad idea.*

Sighing heavily, Maxis passed an aggravated stare at his brother before he took her hand and pulled her inside the curtained-off area. "I know that you've never seen me as anything more than an animal, and I'm well aware of what you think of my species. Just remember this is for your children and hold that thought tight. Don't worry. We both know the grisly truth. I am an animal. Hatched and spawned." He stepped back. "Blaise? Can you hold her for a minute? I'm not sure how she'll react to this."

When Max shifted, she all but screamed. Not that Illarion blamed her.

Even as spacious as the attic was, Maxis had to crouch low and could barely move about. He completely filled the area. For that matter, he couldn't turn around. Rather, he had to back himself against the wall where she assumed he slept.

Like him, his brother was a huge bastard.

"You okay?" Blaise rubbed her arm for comfort.

Swallowing hard, she nodded. "It's just been a long time since I was this close to a living dragon. And never one that wasn't trying to kill me."

Maxis's iridescent scales glimmered like jewels in the dim light. And as he moved, Illarion saw on his wings the vicious scarring Nala and her Amazon tribe had left behind. How he could still love Sera, he had no idea.

But that wasn't any of his business.

Max rolled slightly so that she could settle comfortably in the shelter of his arms. One talon was almost the size of her entire body.

"How did you ever get captured by Dagon?"

Max came to help me, when Dagon had me trapped. Fury darkened Illarion's eyes. *My powers bound so that I couldn't fight or protect myself.*

It wasn't your fault I flew in blindly, Illy.

Because I called in a panic and you were too worried to be cautious.

Max sighed. *It doesn't matter. I don't really need a reason to be stupid. Can find plenty of reasons to partake of that particular vice on my own.*

Illarion snorted as he and Blaise moved forward to help settle Sera against him.

Blaise stepped back. "I'll keep guard at the door to make sure no one disturbs you."

"Thank you." Sera was rigid in his arms.

Illarion moved to the curtains. *I'll wait to join you.*

"What do you mean, join us?"

He smiled, but didn't answer before he closed the curtains and left them alone.

She turned her face toward Max. "What did he mean?"

Nothing. Close your eyes and think of our little ones. Imagine being with them and let your thoughts stay with them. Whatever happens, don't let anything or anyone distract you.

"Maxis?"

Illarion froze at the strange sound of Sera's voice. Rushing back toward Max's sleeping area, a bad feeling went through him. He flung the curtain wide to see his brother gone and Sera scowling. *What happened?*

"I don't know." Looking sick and weak, she wiped at her neck to find the smallest trace of blood there. "He drank from me?"

Illarion felt the color drain from his features. *What?*

She showed him her bloodstained hand. "He bit me . . . *bit me!*"

she emphasized, gesturing toward her neck, "and then I woke up here. Why?"

Blaise came rushing up behind Illarion. "What's going on?"

Disgusted and pissed, Illarion let out a deep, guttural growl. *Max just took her blood so that he could track their dragonets on his own, then sent her back here without him.*

Cursing, Blaise ground his teeth. "Why would he do that? We had a plan! A fairly, almost decent one . . . That could have almost worked. Maybe, in the right light and with good timing. Why would he alter it?"

Because this was his *plan, all along. To face them without putting any of us in danger. The stupid bastard plans to battle them alone. 'Cause he's an effing idiot! I knew better than to trust him. I knew it!* He shook his head. *Why did I ever trust him?*

Horrified, Seraphina pushed herself to her feet. "We can't let him do that! One bite. One scratch and he'll become a gallu!"

Illarion laughed bitterly at her concern. *That's not our worst fear.*

"How in the name of the gods is that not our worst fear? Barring his death, that is."

Illarion sobered as he faced her with a dry, cutting glare. *You really, truly don't know* anything *about my brother, do you?*

24

Illarion turned at the bright flash, expecting to find Maxis there. Instead, it was two dragonets.

Shrieking in relief, Seraphina ran to them and grabbed them into a tight embrace. The boy immediately let out a verbal protest that she was hurting him.

"It's all right, Mama," he breathed as he rested his chin against the top of her head. Like Max, he towered over her. "We're fine. It's all good."

Illarion wasn't sure about that. The boy was covered in blood and bruises. His homespun clothes torn and filthy.

Her breathing ragged, Seraphina pulled back to examine the girl. Like her brother's, her tunic and breeches were torn and covered with filth and blood.

"Hadyn kept them from me," the girl assured her quickly, as if she could read her mother's thoughts.

"Barely." He staggered back and collapsed to sit cross-legged on the floor. Hard. Raking a hand through his short auburn hair, he let out an exhausted breath, then winced as he grazed his knuckles against his bruised cheek. He glanced up at her with an adorable frown that was identical to one Max had used. "Where are we?"

Seraphina didn't answer his raspy question as she stepped over his legs and glanced around, looking for Maxis to join them. He should have been here by now. "Where's your father?"

"I knew that was him!" The girl smacked at her brother, who grimaced and shoved lightly at her so that she wouldn't hit his shoulder again. "Told you!"

"No you didn't."

Ignoring his ire, she met Seraphina's gaze with sadness in her eyes. "They attacked him and he sent us here while he fought them. I don't think he was able to follow."

Blaise cursed and so did Illarion.

I'm going to kill him!

It was only then that her children realized there were others in the room with them. The girl pulled back as Hadyn rose to his feet to put himself between them and his uncles.

Though to be honest, there wasn't much the poor boy could do right now in his wounded condition, except fall down and trip them on their way to attack her, had that been their intent.

Sera let go of Edena to gently take Hadyn by the waist and scoot his teen body aside. Rubbing his back, she smiled proudly at him to let him know how much she appreciated his thoughtfulness. "Edena, Hadyn . . . meet your uncles. Blaise and Illarion."

"Hi." Blaise gestured toward the wall.

Bemused by that, Hadyn scowled at her and Edena.

Illarion ignored them all. *Screw the pleasantries. We need to get to Max. Where is he?*

Hadyn's frown melted to a mask of shock. "Anyone else think it odd that one uncle can't see and the other can't speak? Is there a reason for that?"

Blaise shot a jolt at him that left him yelping. "Careful, whelp. I don't need my sight in this form to spank your ass. As for the voice, Illarion had his vocal cords cut by moronic humans trying to stop him from breathing fire when he was a kid. Be glad they didn't get their hands on you."

He immediately hung his head. "Sorry. I didn't mean to offend either of you. I'm an insensitive idiot who doesn't always check with my brain before I engage my mouth, especially when I'm hurting. If it makes you feel any better, in the last twenty-four hours, I had three demons try to eat me for dinner, a dozen Arcadians kick the crap out of me, and my sister scream my eardrums to bleeding. Pretty sure I lost some testosterone along the way. Definitely a shit-ton of pride and dignity."

"Hadyn! Watch your mouth!"

"Sorry, Ma."

Shaking her head, Seraphina went and grabbed Maxis's battle sword from the hanger that secured it to his wall near the door.

As she started to leave, Illarion caught her. *What are* you *doing?*

"You and Blaise watch the kids. I'm headed after Maxis."

"That would be a profoundly *bad* idea."

Seraphina glanced over her shoulder to see Fang standing in the now open doorway. "Excuse me?"

He stepped aside to show her the tall, dark-haired Arcadian Sentinel behind him. One Illarion hadn't seen in an exceptionally long time.

Dressed in medieval chainmail and a yellow surcoat, and with his hair pulled back in a ponytail, he had an aura of regal refinement and fierce, arrogant warrior that made Illarion want to punch him. While most Sentinels chose to hide their facial markings with their magick, his were more than apparent.

Fang gestured between them. "Seraphina Drago, meet Sebastian Kattalakis, Prince of Arcadia."

Illarion snorted disdainfully. *So fucking what, Fang? You're a Kattalakis, too.* For that matter, Illarion qualified as an official Kattalakis. More so, in fact, than either of them.

Sebastian arched an arrogant brow at his rude dismissal. "Yes, but my grandfather was the king's son. The original Apollite heir born from his queen, Mysene."

Well la-di-da, Mr. Fancy Pants. Aren't you special? You want a hero cookie to go with that title?

Blaise feigned a coughing fit. "Excuse me. I'm having a weird Kerrigan flashback. Should I leave now before lethal things start flying?"

No, I'm the one leaving. My brother needs me and the air in here is suddenly stale.

"Wait!" Sebastian ordered in a tone that left Illarion with a soured expression on his handsome face. One that said Sebastian was about to be in serious pain. Or in a burn ward. "I came here to warn Fang about what was happening. A few minutes ago, I received a summons from my cousin to attend a harrowing for the Dragonbane he's captured."

Seraphina gasped at his words.

Why did you come here?

Sebastian shrugged at Illarion's belligerent question. "I thought you might want to get word to Savitar to stop it. As a limani, Fang has the ability to contact him. I don't. And having been harrowed, myself, I don't condone this against another. Ever. I find the whole practice of it distasteful and beneath both our species."

Illarion glared at each of them in turn. *What did you people do? Take out ads? For thousands of years, Max stayed hidden and safe.* He pinned that hostile glare on her. *You come back into his life for five minutes and it starts falling apart again. Everyone now knows who he is and they're all attacking him. Why do you have to ruin his life every time you come near it?*

"That's not fair!"

No, it isn't! He never did anything to you, except try to protect you. I wish you'd do him a favor and get out of his life before you kill him.

Blaise gasped. "Illarion . . ."

Don't, brother. It's the truth I speak. We're all thinking it. I just said it. I'm sick to death of watching my brother bleed for her.

Seraphina took a step toward him, intending to make him eat those words, but before she could, a loud thump sounded on the other side of the curtains.

All of them froze.

In unison, they turned toward the unexpected rustling. An exasperated sigh was punctuated by the curtains parting only enough to launch a round object from between them. It shot across the room and landed with another wet, squishy thump on the floor before it rolled a few feet.

Edena shrieked and danced toward her brother as the object came to rest near her and turned out to be a disembodied human head.

An instant later, a huge, spiny dragon poked his head out from between the curtains to offer a lopsided grin. "Sorry, love. Didn't realize anyone was here." He arched one dragon brow at Sebastian. "Hope that's not a friend of yours. And if it is, tough shit. He was an asshole. Anyone got some extra-large dental floss on them? I've got a chunk of Arcadian dragonslayer stuck in my teeth. Nasty-tasting stuff, that. And Illarion, you're wrong. It does *not* taste like chicken. More like three-day-old rotten ass."

Blaise and Fang burst out laughing. Sebastian looked offended. Hadyn and Edena gaped.

"If I said that, I'd be on restriction forever," Hadyn mumbled to his sister.

"Yes, you would. And don't forget it." Shaking her head, Seraphina closed the distance between them so she could check on Max and make sure he was all right.

She was so upset she couldn't speak. Instead, she rose up on her knees and wrapped her body around his, and held him in a tight embrace with her cheek pressed against his heart. She had one arm draped around his neck and the other beneath his arm, and clutched her hands behind his back so tight, he wasn't sure she'd ever let go.

Completely baffled, he met Illarion's gaze over her shoulder. *Help?*

For the first time, Illarion looked at her with something other than unreasoning hatred.

Just hold her, Max. She needs to know that you're really alive and whole. It's how women are sometimes.

Max nodded. "Fang, it won't take the Arcadians long to track me here and demand you turn me over to them." Since he was the Dragonbane, the laws of Sanctuary didn't apply to him. He was the one creature they could legally deny shelter to. It was entirely up to the owners if they wanted the heat of it.

"If you'll protect my family for me—they're innocent in all this—I'll make sure I lead the others away from your door. I just need a minute to catch my breath, and collect a couple of things. I promise I won't draw Sanctuary into the cross fire of my mess."

Snorting, Fang tucked his hands into his back pockets. "Boy, don't you dare insult me with that shit. They can kiss my furry wolf ass, which is exactly what Aimee would skin alive if I dared let them have you. I don't give up family." He paused. "Well, they could have Fury. I'm not *that* attached to *him*. But they'd only keep him till he opened his mouth, then launch his ass back to me with a catapult. He's like a bad boomerang that way."

Illarion laughed at his surly tone, knowing it for the bluster it was. Fang would kill for his brother.

"You really don't want this kind of heat. Trust me."

Fang glanced around at the other dragons in the room. "You were one of the first residents the Peltiers took in when they moved here. When Eli and his pack used their witch to set fire to the first bar, you're the one who saved Aimee, Dev, and Cherif from burning alive in it. And you're the only reason that fire didn't spread to Peltier House and trap the others who were sleeping there, including a Dark-Hunter who would have been trapped inside by the day light. I know the stories, too. Brother, there ain't a shifter in this place who wouldn't fight for you. Now I don't know what happened to cause you to get marked and I don't really care. . . . The one thing I do know is *you*. And if you killed him, he had it coming. So you're free to stay. If they're dumb enough to attack, I know a bar full of hungry Charonte over in the Warehouse District who would love to chomp dragon meat." He glanced over to the head on the floor. "And unlike you, they don't care if it tastes like chicken or not." Then he scratched his chin. "You are picking that up, right? 'Cause I don't want to have to explain it."

Rubbing his forehead, Sebastian let out a slow breath. "I hope you know what you're doing, wolf."

Fang arched a brow. "Have you met me? Of course I have no idea what I'm doing."

Ignoring Fang's surly comment, Max rose to confront Sebastian. "Go to your Regis and tell him that I'm calling hazard on the ones who took and held my dragonets. They want the Dragonbane? I want their throats. Fair combat. In the circle."

"No!" Seraphina gasped.

"No?" Max arched a brow at her.

"I want to kill them."

He smiled at her. That was his dragonswan. Ferocious to the end. "Too late. I called challenge first."

"I birthed them. I should have the honor of avenging them."

"And in the event this goes badly, I'd rather they lose the parent they don't know than the one they're attached to."

"I'd rather not lose either," Edena said. "No offense."

Hadyn nodded his agreement.

"I'm concurring with the kids." Blaise smiled.

Ignoring the comment, Sebastian met Fang's gaze. "If you want me to issue the challenge, I will do so. But watch your back. I have a bad feeling about all this."

Fang sighed. "We will. Give Channon my best."

Sebastian inclined his head to them before he vanished.

Max sighed. "The gallu aren't going to stop and neither will the two packs coming for me. This is a blood feud that is centuries old. I need my children where they can't reach them."

Blaise nodded as he understood what Max wasn't saying. "You want me to take them to Avalon?"

"Please. It's the one place I know is beyond their reach."

Hadyn and Edena immediately protested.

"Your father's right. It's just for a few days. I promise. Go with your uncle and we'll get you soon."

As Blaise started to leave, Max stopped him. "Tell Merlin not to worry. I have not forgotten my oath or my duties. Should I fall, guardianship will go to Illarion and then to you."

He arched a brow. "Not to Hadyn?"

Max shook his head. "I would never do that to him. The curse of it's too strong."

"So you give it to us. Thanks, brother."

Max laughed. "Getting you both back for all the years of hell you've given me."

Blaise sobered. "I'll tell her. You be careful."

"And you." He kissed Edena's cheek and hugged Hadyn one more time.

It took Seraphina longer to say good-bye. "I will come for you very soon. I love you both. Guard your sister."

"I will." And then they were gone.

Alone with Maxis and Illarion, Seraphina felt so strangely empty. She'd been a mother for so long that she'd forgotten what it was like to be by herself. To not have to look over her shoulder to make sure her children were keeping up with her and not falling behind.

Now . . .

"We have to prepare for war."

Maxis nodded.

Illarion went to the grisly head. *I'll take care of this.* He wrapped it up in a T-shirt. His eyes sad, he locked gazes with Maxis. *I'm so sorry I dragged you into this.* Then he looked at Seraphina. *And I'm sorry I've been so rude to you the entire time you've been here. You're not really the one who fucked my brother's life over and ruined it, my lady. I am. And I swear to you both that I won't take my hatred for myself out on you anymore. Please forgive me.*

Max grabbed Illarion's arm as he started to leave. "You have nothing to apologize for where I'm concerned." He cracked a chiding grin. "That being said, you could have been a little kinder to my dragonswan."

The tormented agony in Illarion's gaze was searing. *How can you not hate me? At the very least, blame me or curse me for what I've done to you?*

Max buried his hand in Illarion's long hair and locked gazes with him so that his brother could see the sincerity in his heart. "Would my life without you have really been better? Really? Let's say that none of this had happened. That I remained a fully blooded drakomas. Where would I be now? In a cave somewhere alone like you were, enduring in Glastonbury? You're right, Illy. You're a rank, effing bastard to spare me *that* god-awful fate. I should take you outside right now and beat the shit out of you for doing this to me."

Illarion snorted. *I hate you.*

Smiling, he tightened his grip in his brother's hair before he released him. "I hate you, too."

Then Illarion pulled Max into a tight hug and held him there.

When he finally stepped back, he refused to look him in the eye. *I'll check on the others. I'm sure the two of you could use a moment to yourselves to catch your breath, and decide what to do about her tribe and the demons out to claim you.*

"Thanks."

Illarion inclined his head to him, then left.

A few hours later, Illarion stood with Dev, Fang, Vane, and the wolves and bears in the bar, ready to war against every member of

Seraphina's tribe. Thankfully, the bar was still closed to humans or this would have been an even worse situation.

"I demand you hand over the Dragonbane! He attacked our patria, killed our members, and—"

"Cry to your mama, bitch, I don't care." Fang flipped the Arcadian wolf off.

"Fang!" Vane put himself between his brother and the other wolf. "Not helping!"

Dev laughed. "Maybe not, but he's highly entertaining and helping lift my mood immensely."

Samia smacked her husband in the stomach. "Stay out of this. If we wanted to blow the bar up, again, we'd have brought Rémi out here."

Sera brushed past Max to address the group. "This isn't about the Dragonbane. It's about Nala's pact with a demon."

"Hold your tongue." Nala glared at her.

"No. Not in this. I won't watch you destroy my mate again."

"Seraphina . . ."

But Sera wasn't having any part of this. "I will renounce my allegiance to the tribe before I allow you to take him." She pulled her sword from its sheath. "You want Maxis . . . you have to come through me."

Shocked, but determined to protect his sister-in-law for his brother, Illarion moved to stand at her side.

Fang took up the position on the left-hand side of Sera's body. "As you can see, we like our Dragonbane. He goes really well with the furniture."

Sarcastic applause sounded, breaking the tension. "Nice." From the rear of the Arcadians, a demon stepped forward. He wasn't Kessar, but there was something remotely familiar about him. Illarion tried to remember where he'd seen him before.

Definitely gallu. The stench was unmistakable.

The demon stopped in front of Fang and raked him with a sneer. "However, you're all forgetting something. While you are bound by the laws of your Omegrion, we are not. Do you really want me to unleash my warriors here? How long do you think you and your animals will stand?"

Fang didn't miss a beat. "Long enough to mount your head to my wall."

The demon opened his mouth to speak, then began a strange gurgling noise.

Illarion stepped back. As did Nala. Max closed the distance between them to protect his family.

Quicker than he could blink, Dev grabbed a mop bucket and had it in front of the demon in time to catch him as he unloaded the contents of his stomach. Grimacing and cursing, he glanced over to Sam. "Yeah, you raise as many nieces and nephews as I have and run a bar, you learn that attractive I-ate-too-much sound, so-grab-a-bucket-uncle-I-gotta-hurl." Making an even worse face, he turned back toward the demon. "You through? 'Cause dude, this is some nasty stuff you got going on. And I really hope this shit ain't contagious."

Instead, the demon fell to his knees in agony. He was in so much pain, he couldn't talk.

Dev set the bucket aside as they all stared at the demon in stunned silence. "Anyone know a demon doctor?"

"What's wrong with him?" Nala asked.

Fury shrugged. "I'm thinking his last victim didn't go down right. Who'd you eat?"

Dev snorted sarcastically. "Judging by the contents of the bucket, I'd say a Muppet. Looks like Kermit."

Sam let out a sound of extreme pain. "Y'all are all so gross."

With an exaggerated gesture, Fury's mate Lia nodded her complete agreement.

And still the demon convulsed and gagged. Wheezed and sputtered.

Then burst apart.

In unison, everyone stepped back from the spot where he'd been as if afraid that, too, was contagious.

"Holy shit," Dev breathed.

Fury took Lia's hand. "My freakin' giddy aunt."

Fang and Vane toed the smoking remains of the demon before they swept their gaze around the room.

"Savitar?" Vane called.

Fang scowled. "Thorn?"

No one answered. His features pale, Fang met Max's gaze. "Have you ever seen or heard of anything like this?"

Before he could answer, Nala gasped in alarm. Then she cried out in pain.

Sera stepped toward her. "Basilinna?"

She held her hand up to show that it was slowly turning gray. "I think I'm returning to stone . . . you?"

Horrified, Seraphina examined her own body. "I don't think so."

Her breathing ragged, Nala shook her head. "What is this?" Shrieking, she vanished, and took her Amazons with her.

Fang and Vane turned to the Arcadians, but without their demon and Amazon warriors, their bluster faded.

"This isn't over," the wolf leader promised. "I, too, am a Kattalakis Lykos and I demand the satisfaction of seeing the one who cursed our race pay for his crimes. I'll be back!"

And with that, they were gone.

Max noticed that Sera was paler than she'd been. "Seramia?"

"I don't feel right, either." She pressed her hand to her forehead. "It's so strange." Her legs buckled.

Max swept her up in his arms and teleported her from the bar, back to Peltier House and into the infirmary. "Carson!"

The Gerakian appeared instantly. "What's wrong?"

"I don't know. She's sick or something."

Max stepped back so that Carson could examine her.

"This is weird. It's like the spell that Kessar unlocked is reversing itself." Kessar was the gallu demon who'd rescued Sera and her amazon tribe from being stone. He'd undone the curse and made them live again.

Max's breath caught in his throat as fear went through him. "What?"

"She's slowly turning back into stone."

In that moment, he felt as if all the wind had been violently knocked out of his body. "Bullshit! Don't fuck with me, Carson."

Illarion felt sick for his brother. He knew that pain and he hated for Max to feel it.

He pulled the stethoscope from his neck. "I'm not." Patting Sera gently on the shoulder, he offered her a sad, sympathetic smile. "I'm sorry. I have no idea how to fix or treat this."

Her eyes glistened as she met Max's gaze, but she managed to blink her tears back. "I should have known the gods wouldn't allow us to go free. We were meant to be punished for riding against them. Let's face it, they're not exactly known for their mercy."

She was right and Illarion knew it. It was why Edilyn had been taken from him.

Max sank down on his knees in front of her. "I can't lose you again."

She brushed her hand through his hair. "I'm sorry. I should never have followed Nala in her war against the gods. She was so sure the Sumerians would take over Greece." Laughing bitterly, she winced. "Stupid bitch never backed a winning side in any conflict."

Unable to witness this, Illarion left them. Max's pain was too close to home. Too bitter for him to relive.

And in that moment, he hated his silence more than he ever had, because inside, he was screaming.

Yet only he could hear it.

Max hesitated as he did something he knew was all kinds of stupid. The kind of stupid that if one of his brothers had done it, he'd have beaten them senseless. Thrown water on them to revive them.

Then beaten them more.

But he couldn't think of any other way to spare his dragonswan from her fate. And if he didn't move fast, it would be too late.

With a deep breath, he closed his eyes and ignored the pain of his wounds. He summoned every ounce of dragon's breath inside him and teleported from Sanctuary to the Gates of Samothraki. While the humans in this time and place saw nothing but the jagged remains of a bygone era, he knew where the opening to a most sacred place lay. Much like the gateways to Avalon and Kalosis, it shimmered only in the faintest heartbeats right at dusk and dawn. So quickly that it was easily missed or dismissed as a trick of the eye.

But this was one of the last places where his brethren slept in the modern world.

And this was one of his last remaining siblings.

"Falcyn?"

Nothing but the evening sea breeze answered him. Max picked his way through the ruins of the ancient temple complex where mankind had once paid tribute to the gods of old. Where they'd once made offerings to his kind, hoping to win their cooperation and affection.

Things today were so different.

"Damn it, Falcyn! If you can hear me, answer!"

"I don't answer to humans. If you want to speak to me, pick the right language."

Max laughed bitterly as he switched over to Drakyn. "I don't have time for you to be an asshole. I need you, brother."

Something struck him hard across his chest and knocked him flying. By the pain of it, and the distance he flew before he slammed into the ground, he'd say it must have been Falcyn's barbed tail.

With a pain-filled groan, he pushed himself up. "Feel better?"

"Not really. When I slit you from asshole to appetite, then I should rally emotionally."

This time when he attacked, Max caught the blow. Using his force field, he blocked and sent it back at his older brother. "Please, Falcyn . . . please."

The pressure against him lessened.

Then it vanished. Max relaxed, only to realize too late that it was a trick. Falcyn materialized at his back and caught him in a vicious headlock. He choked him hard as he held Max against his body.

"Behold what is left of my island because of you, *brother*. You brought those Greek bastards here and I hate you for it!"

Yeah, okay, this might have been a massive mistake. He'd hoped a few thousand years would have mellowed his brother's wrath.

Apparently, Falcyn needed a few thousand more.

"I'm sorry. I had nowhere else to go."

"And I have nothing more to say to you."

With no choice, Max turned on him and flipped him. "Listen to me! I don't want to fight you."

But a fight it was. Falcyn came after him like a starving dog in a buffet line that was after the last pork chop. Damn, he'd forgotten how hard his brother could hit. With no choice, he transformed to a dragon. It was the only way to survive and he didn't really want to kill his brother.

Well . . .

Theoretically. However, if Falcyn didn't come to his senses soon, Max might change his mind. He didn't need his brother alive to claim what he needed. Only his conscience required a breathing Falcyn.

Oh dear gods, really? Suddenly, Illarion was between them in his dragon body, pushing them apart. *Stop it! Both of you!*

Falcyn spun around, trying to sting Max one more time with his tail.

Max caught it with his talons and bit it so hard, Falcyn yelped.

Illarion glared at him. *Was that necessary?*

Max released his tail. "Little bit."

With an irritable growl, Falcyn shot fire at him.

Illarion froze it with his powers. He glared at Falcyn. *We are down to the last four of our house. Can you please not cull our lineage any more?*

"Then you'd best get him out of my sight."

Falcyn . . .

"I mean it, Illy. I'm not in the mood." He lumbered off toward his gate.

"I need a dragonstone, Falcyn. My children and swan will die without it."

Falcyn froze. "You dare to ask me for that?"

"You're the only one left who has one."

Illarion cringed as he remembered why he no longer had his. Max should be throwing that in his face, since he was the one who'd lost Max's.

Yet his brother didn't say a word to pin that blame where it fully belonged. He didn't even mention it.

Falcyn was not so kind. The centuries had left him very bitter and even harsher than before. He turned to pin each of them with a fierce, stern glower. "And I really don't give a fuck. Go home. Both of you. I never want to see you again."

With those cold words spoken, he vanished between the gates.

Stunned, Max stared after him. "Are you serious?"

I'm sorry, Max.

Unable to believe this, he laughed bitterly. "I knew you were selfish and cold, Fal, but this . . . Mom would be proud to know how much you take after her. I wish I'd killed you when I had the chance, you bastard!"

Stop, Max. You know why he feels this way.

Yeah, sure. Like everyone else, he blamed Max for things Max hadn't wanted. For things he couldn't help. That he'd done everything to avoid.

Now Sera and his children would pay for it.

His heart broken that he'd failed, he led Illarion back to Sanctuary so that he could spend whatever time he had left with his wife before the gods returned her to a cold, dead statue.

And Illarion was left to grapple with the guilt of what he'd done to his own brother.

25

Illarion waited outside of Max's room for his brother to answer his knock. His brother had sent him to Avalon to retrieve the children so that they could say good-bye to their mother. But the moment he'd started to contact Blaise, he'd remembered something important.

The lesson about his mating mark and magick between the two realms.

Given what had happened with him and Edilyn,

he didn't dare bring the children back through the Veil. It could be catastrophic.

"Come in!"

Holding one of Merlin's magical spheres, Illarion opened the door.

Max scowled at him. "Where are the kids?"

They're fine and still in Avalon. Since they're not in the process of reconverting to stone, Merlin kept them there. We spoke about it and she thinks whatever is affecting Sera and her tribe here can't break through the barrier to reach them on her side of things. We were afraid that if she sent them back, they'd begin to turn, too.

Sera let out a sound of happiness as she sat up. "They're not changing back?"

Illarion held the crystal ball for her to see into it.

Both of the children were there, in Merlin's castle. Happy, but concerned about their parents.

Edena bit her lip as she moved her head about like a little bird, trying to focus on her mother's face. "Mom?"

Sera smiled at her as she took the ball into her hands. "Edena? Hadyn? Are you all right?"

Hadyn nodded. "We're fine. You?"

"Wonderful, now that I know you're both okay."

Edena's lips quivered. "Is it true? Are you changing back?"

She nodded. "I want you two to listen to your father and let him take care of you for me. Can you do that?"

They both nodded.

"I love you, Mom," Hadyn said, placing his hand on the orb. "I wish I was there to say it to your face."

"As do I. Just remember that no matter what, I will be close. And Edena, I need you to be kinder to your brother in my absence. Stop trying to clip his wings all the time. Let him learn to fly or crash on his own."

"I shall try. For you."

"I love you both. Please take care of each other and your father and uncles for me."

Edena started crying as Hadyn pulled her into his arms to comfort her.

Max swallowed hard. "Merlin? Are you there with the children?"

The beautiful white-blonde enchantress moved to stand next to them. "I'm here. What do you need?"

"If I brought Seraphina to you in Avalon, do you think you could stop her from turning? That whatever is saving the children could save her, too?"

Merlin hesitated. "It might, but it could also kill her, since she's in the process of changing already. I don't know what type of spell Zeus has her under. You know as well as I do how unreasonable magick can be, and the unforeseen consequences." She glanced to his children. "Plus, she's not your bloodline. While she carried your young and has mixed her blood with yours, it's not the same as being born of the drakomai. There's just no telling what might happen. I'm sorry, Max. I don't want to try something and lose her."

Illarion agreed with that. No one could ever predict what magick would do when it crossed pantheon borders.

Damn the gods for that. Because she was part Apollite and not drakomai, she couldn't even go into a torpor.

"Thanks, Merlin."

She inclined her head to Max before the mist in the orb swallowed them.

Sera cocked her head to stare up at him. "What's with that look? What are you planning?"

Yeah, you're scaring me, too.

He stood up. "I'm going after Kessar and the Tablet."

"Are you out of your mind?"

For once, Illarion agreed with Sera.

Max shook his head. "It's the only way. He used it to free you. Then I can use it to keep you here, too." He looked at Illarion. "Right?"

Illarion hesitated. *Yeah . . . no, this is a really bad, bad idea. Like trying to blow-dry your hair while showering, or piss into a high wind. Are you out of your mind?* He repeated Sera's words.

"No. I'm desperate."

Same thing.

He gave his brother an irritated smirk.

Well, it is.

Sera stood up beside him. "I agree with Illarion. Don't even think about doing this. Are you insane? You can't walk into a colony of demons and Amazons who want you dead, and take the Tablet the head demon covets most. They tend to react badly to such things. Believe me. I've seen it. I do believe Nala wears the claw of the last dragon possessed of such arrogance."

Illarion nodded vigorously. *How many more challenges are you planning to issue? Sheez, Max. There are far less painful ways to die. Drowning in acid comes to mind.*

Suddenly, a light flashed in the room with them. Max started toward it, but something kept him in place. A strong, unseen force he couldn't break.

Furious, he manifested a fire blast to attack. Until he recognized the source of the power.

Falcyn.

Only this time, he wasn't in dragon form. Dressed in their ancient black war garb, he wore the skins and furs of the slayers who'd made the mistake of coming after him, as trophies and testament to his unsurpassed martial skills. His black hair was short except for one long braid that was wrapped around his throat and adorned with a silver dragon pendant that matched his pale eyes. They flashed like mercury in the dim light.

And they missed no detail at all.

Illarion's eyes widened as he saw him there. He inclined his head in acknowledgment of his older brother's birth order and out of respect.

Returning the gesture to Illarion, Falcyn closed the distance between them with that fierce predatorial walk that was uniquely his.

Without a word, he stopped in front of Seraphina and met Max's gaze. "May I?" It was forbidden for a drakomas to touch another's mate without permission. To do so was a killing offense in their culture.

Max nodded.

Sera frowned at him as she looked back and forth between them. "Max?"

"It's all right, Sera. This is my brother Falcyn. I trust him . . . most days."

Ignoring his teasing barb, Falcyn touched her icy forehead, then her hand. "Who curses her?"

"Zeus."

He scoffed disdainfully. "Then I hope this seriously pisses that bastard byblow off. You should have told me that originally. I wouldn't have had to soul-search nearly as long before helping you."

With one claw, Falcyn made a small incision on his wrist until he could gather three drops of blood. From his satchel, he pulled a small oblong ball that resembled an egg, then coated it with his blood. He placed it in her hands and cupped them around it while he chanted in their mother's tongue. He used her hands to turn the egg round and round.

After a few seconds, Sera sucked her breath in sharply, but Falcyn held her hands in place around the egg. She hissed. "It's burning."

Max tightened his arms around her. "It'll be all right. He's drawing the poison from you. Give him time to work."

Only then did she relax a degree.

By the time Falcyn finished the ritual, she was even paler, but her breathing was more solid.

Falcyn wiped the stone off on his sleeve, and returned it to his satchel. He glanced about the loft expectantly. "You said you have dragonets?"

"A son and daughter. They're with Blaise. In Avalon."

For the first time, Falcyn's stern features softened. One thing about their brother, he had a soft spot for dragonets and for Blaise. "I'll see them protected and shielded, too."

As he started to leave, Max stopped him. "Thank you, brother. Can I ask why you changed your mind?"

Falcyn turned at the curtains to look back first at Max, then to Sera. "I still think you're an idiot. I still hate and begrudge every breath that fills your lungs. But you are my brother and we are drakomai. It's not my place to take from you your heart. . . . If there is any way to help her, then I am honor bound to do so. You know the code we live and die by. Regardless of my feelings for you, it is my responsibility to protect what you love and preserve our bloodline."

"Again, thank you."

Falcyn didn't respond to that. It was as if a part of him was embarrassed by the gratitude. Instead, he turned toward Illarion. "You still have your dragon's claw I gave you?"

Always.

"Yeah, not what I heard." Falcyn clapped him on the arm. "I heard you loaned it out to an Addanc. What the hell's wrong with you? Did I teach you nothing?" He shook his head at Illarion. "An Addanc? Really?"

Falcyn made a sound of supreme disgust. "All my brothers are morons. I swear. Now take me to the dragonets before Blaise sucks what little intelligence they have out and leaves them lacking, too."

Illarion rolled his eyes and followed Falcyn from the room.

Outside, Falcyn turned toward him. "I'm sorry."

For what?

"About Edilyn."

Illarion swallowed hard as he pushed the pain away. He wanted to say something, but there was nothing to say. Words would be insincere.

And Falcyn hated insincerity even more than he did.

I've lost my way, brother.

Falcyn snorted. "What makes you think anyone has a road-map? You think I know where I'm going? That I ever have? We're all mice stumbling in our mazes, trying to find our cheese. Hoping the levers we're pulling are the right ones and not the ones designed to shock us."

The problem was, Illarion was a warrior. He needed a target and in this, there wasn't one. How could he defeat death? It was the one bastard who gave mercy to none and spared no creature its eternal bite.

26

Illarion was aghast at the gathering in the parlor of Peltier House. For the life and sake of his brother, basically every adult resident under the roof, as well as every Dark-Hunter in New Orleans, former and current, along with Acheron, Sin, Zakar, and Styxx, had come together to keep Max safe.

It was incredible.

"This is utter bullshit!" Dev snarled, unaware of Max's and Sera's presence behind him. "I say we tell Savitar where to shove it!"

Acheron laughed as he glanced past Dev to meet Max's gaze. "I dare you. Double bear dare you."

Snorting, Max stopped next to Dev and put his hand on his shoulder. "It's all right, bear. I'm not afraid."

Seraphina laced her fingers with his. "For the record, I am."

With a stern frown, Aimee caressed her distended belly. "Can't we do something? Max is here under our protection. I thought our laws protected him, so long as he doesn't leave."

Styxx sighed heavily. "They did. But the other dragons are calling for his ass. He attacked and they have the right to demand a hearing for his new crime . . . and the old when he appears for it."

Vane nodded. "That's why we're all going. As Kattalakises, we're character witnesses. Our family started this against you and we're going to do our damnedest to finish it."

Hadyn's scowl matched Aimee's. "And if you can't?"

Dev cracked a wicked grin. "I'm tossing the dragon over my shoulder and running for the door. You gonna cover my retreat, kid?"

Sighing heavily, Samia pressed her gloved hands to her nose. "I wish he was joking with that threat. Instead, I have this awful vision in my head and an ulcer in my stomach."

Dev kissed her cheek. "I promised you that living with me would never be boring."

She let out a tired breath. "That you did. You are definitely a bear of your word."

As they started to leave, Illarion stepped forward to go with them to the Omegrion.

"No!" Max roared, pushing him back toward his brothers. "Blaise, keep him here."

Illarion was aghast. *You can't leave me out of this. I'm part of it.*
"I can and I will."

Illarion shook his head in denial. He tried to step around Max, but Max wasn't having any of that.

Max pushed him back again. "I mean it. You go and I'll run." He looked to Falcyn, then Blaise. "He's not allowed to go. You have to keep him here. No matter what."

Seraphina gaped at Illarion. "You killed the prince, didn't you? It wasn't Maxis. It was *you*."

"Sera," Max growled. "Stay out of this."

Releasing Max, she went to Illarion. "Tell me what happened."

"It doesn't matter." Max swallowed hard. "I'm the Dragonbane, not Illarion. Leave him alone." He glared at his brothers. "Do not let him leave here."

Before she could say anything more, Max vanished.

"No!" Terrified and shaking, she turned on Illarion. "Tell me the truth. What happened?"

It was an accident.

She met Acheron's gaze. "We've got to get the others to listen. Somehow."

Vane agreed. "Don't worry, Sera. They can't start the council yet. Four of the members are still here."

She arched a brow at the number. "Four?"

"Me, Fury, Alain's mate—Tanya, and Wren Tigarian, who's behind you."

Like Illarion, Wren held that same disturbing aura of quiet predator that said he was eyeing everyone around him like prey. Sizing up their every movement to detect the weakness he was about to use to bring them down for a kill. The most disturbing thing was the way his eyes changed color depending on the way the light hit them. They went from a light gray to a vibrant turquoise.

Highly disturbing.

Until he unleashed a friendly grin that made him appear boyish and shy, and around the same age as Hadyn. "Sorry. My wife Maggie is always getting on to me for making people uncomfortable. Although she seems to enjoy my doing it at her father's cocktail parties. Sometimes she even puts me up to it, but it's a bitch at the playground. I've sent three of my daughter's playmate's nannies into therapy."

Illarion laughed. He could just imagine. The tigard was indeed a rare breed.

Tanya moved closer and rubbed Seraphina's arms comfortingly. "Don't worry. We won't let them take your Max, any more than we let them hurt Wren a few years ago when they called for his head. We always watch after our own."

But as they arrived in the Omegrion council room on the mysterious Neratiti island home of Savitar, Illarion wasn't so sure she could keep that promise.

The large circular chamber was decorated in burgundy and gold. Through the open windows that spanned from the black marble floor to the gilded ceiling, he could see and hear the ocean. Oddly enough, the entire room reminded him of an ancient sultan's tent. Lavishly decorated, it had an enormous round table in the center that was presided over by Savitar, who wore an angry, pissed-off grimace.

Still dressed in a black wetsuit, Savitar sat on his throne with damp hair and his arms crossed over his chest. So silent you could hear the wood drying on the walls around him.

Yeah, that wasn't creepy or disturbing at all.

Composed of one representative from each individual breed of Arcadian and Katagaria Were-Hunter, the Omegrion council made the laws that governed their races.

It should have had twenty-four members.

But one chair at the table remained conspicuously empty. An eerie warning and eternal reminder that back in the day, it'd belonged to the Arcadian Balios, or jaguar patria. Legend had it that centuries ago, the Regis of that group had run so afoul of Savitar's temper that he'd single-handedly destroyed every member of their species.

Total annihilation.

Which said it all about the power and temperament of the disgruntled Chthonian sitting in judgment of them all. And today, Savitar glared at the group with a particular air of *I've had it, folks*. "How nice of you to join us. I trust all of you had a nice nap after I summoned you?"

Acheron had the audacity to laugh. "Miss a gnarly, awesome wave, Big Kahuna?"

"Don't start, Grom. Not in the mood." Savitar sat back on his throne. But it was the collection of Arcadian and Katagaria dragons and the Arcadian Kattalakis wolves on his right-hand side that set his jaw ticcing.

Savitar let out a long, exasperated breath. "Hear ye, hear ye . . . ah, fuck it. We're here today for bullshit and we all know it. So let's dispense with the usual formality and get on with this witch hunt before I lose what little grip I still have on my patience." He ran his thumb along his goatee. "So, Dare Kattalakis, state your case and demands to the council. And do it fast, with as few words as possible."

As a littermate to Vane and Fang, he bore a remarkable resemblance to his brothers.

Too bad they all hated each other. Passionately.

Clearing his throat, he moved to stand in the center of the open round table to plead his case. "First, I want to restate what a travesty it is that my family's seat is taken by—"

"Wah, wah, wah . . . quit crying at the tit," Savitar snarled. "Your brother Vane is the head of the Arcadians and Fury leads the Katagaria. Seek a therapist who gives a shit, or if you'd like to challenge either of them for their position, we can do with some entertainment. Hell, I'll make popcorn for the show. Otherwise, bitch, get on with it."

Illarion passed an amused arch of his brow to Blaise. Damn, Savitar was in rare form, even for Savitar.

Dare lifted his chin, but wisely kept his gaze away from the surly ancient. "Fine. We all know why we're here. Maxis Drago as the Dragonbane is the cause of the war between the Arcadians and the Katagaria. Because of his actions alone, all of us have lost family and been scarred and cursed into perpetual war. Now he's unleashed the gallu and Apollo on us! He's—"

"That's not true!"

Illarion was shocked that Seraphina finally rose to his brother's defense. It was about time she did so.

Savitar's features finally softened, as if he approved. "The dragonswan speaks."

"She's his whore!"

Savitar slung his hand out and caught the Kattalakis dragon who'd insulted her with an unseen force that lifted him up and pinned him to the wall between two of the open windows. "Only I'm allowed to be an insulting asshole in this room. Understood?"

The dragon nodded.

Savitar dropped him straight to the floor, where he landed with a pain-filled groan and in an unceremonious lump. Then he returned his attention to Sera and spoke to her in a kind, fatherly tone. "You were saying, dear?"

Yeah, his kindness was even scarier than his nastiness.

"It's okay, Sera," Max said, reaching out to touch her hand. "You don't have to speak up for me."

"No, but someone does. I don't know who released the gallu—"

"That would be us," Zakar said, raising his hand. "Oops. Sorry about that."

Illarion snorted at the Sumerian god's effed-up humor. They'd unleashed them centuries ago. Not for this particular misadventure.

Savitar rolled his eyes. "Sit your punk ass down and shut up. You and I will talk later."

Zakar laughed good-naturedly. "Hope you take your Abilify first, old man."

Yeah, only a god could get away with that.

Or Acheron.

Savitar started to wag his finger at Zakar, then gave up and waved him away. "Shut up." He returned his attention to Sera. "You were saying?"

"Just that my mate is innocent. The gallu came after him first.

And neither of us have a clue about Apollo. We don't even know what you're talking about." She tucked her marked hand into Max's.

He winced before he laced his fingers with hers and clutched her hand tightly in his.

Savitar watched that single gesture closely for several heartbeats without comment.

"I demand he pay for his crimes!" Ermon Kattalakis—one of the Arcadian dragons—demanded. "It was the blood of my grandfather he spilled!"

Like hell—Illarion barely kept that explosion to himself as he met Savitar's gaze through the crowded room.

Without a word, Savitar stood and closed the distance between him and Max. "It occurs to me, Maxis, that with our historian, Nicolette Peltier, gone, there's no one here who knows the history of this council. She died before she could pass the origins along to her only daughter, Aimee." He turned toward Tanya. "I suppose you should inherit that part of her job as well, no?"

Tanya looked as frightened to be under that fierce scrutiny as Sera had been. "It would be my honor to record it, my lord."

Savitar glanced back to Max. "What do you say, drakomas? Have I your permission to break our pact?"

Illarion saw the indecision in Max's golden eyes as he debated. He glanced to Illarion, then to his mate and their children.

It's time. Illarion inclined his head to him. *Tell the truth, brother. Let them decide for themselves.*

With an audible gulp, Max nodded. "Although, I would remind you both that when the truth was told last time, it didn't help. No one cared."

Ignoring that, Savitar stepped back then so that he could walk a circle around the table. "Some of you have been coming here for centuries. You occupy seats you inherited from your family or won through combat. All of you know what an honor it is to sit here and represent your independent species. Both those who hold human-Apollite hearts and those born with animal hearts. Two halves of a single whole. Both sentient, and forever condemned by the gods to war against each other for no real reason, other than the fact that the gods are assholes. Everyone knows that part of the story. What none of you know is why you answer to me. Why you answer to this council specifically . . ."

Savitar gestured to Max. "You blame the Dragonbane for the war that divides your two branches of the same species, but he didn't do this to you. That belongs to the three bitches who cursed your race in the beginning. To Zeus and Apollo and their childish tantrums that made them cry to the Fates to do something because they felt cheated that you were spared the Apollite curse that would have required all of you to die horribly at age twenty-seven over an event you had no part in. But as with all history, that is only one tiny, bit part that you've been told, which was colored by those seeking to sway your opinion and make you hate for no real reason. To keep you divided when you should be whole and focused on the real tragedies you have in common. The ones that unite you as a single, sentient species. Follow me, children, and let me show you what you've never seen, but what you need to know."

With that he threw his hands out. The doors crashed closed and darkness fell into the room so completely that for a moment, Illarion felt as blind as Blaise.

When the light finally came up, he winced at the sight of a much younger Max.

Of a much younger him. It brought back forgotten memories and emotions that he'd intentionally buried. Now, those old wounds bled anew.

The two of them were locked in a cage, starved and ragged. Filthy. Damned to remain in human form by the collars Dagon had fastened around their necks. Collars that were humiliating and choking. And as they sat starving and freezing in their misery, another man stared in at them. Unlike them, he was impeccably groomed and wore royal princely garb.

An identical copy of Illarion.

It was the face he despised most. A face he wore only to please Edilyn, because of how much he hated it and because of the bitter, hated memories like this that it stirred within him.

Half the room turned to stare agape at him as they realized that Illarion was the prince and not Max, as they'd all assumed before this.

Max had been created from the son of the prince's bastard half brother. A slave.

And beside that despised prince stood an elegant dark-haired lady. While they'd seen the prince numerous times since they'd been caged here, the woman was a new addition to their drab, dingy home.

"Eumon?" she whined, trying to pull the prince away by his arm. "Why did you bring me here? Don't you grow weary of looking at them all the time? It's so creepy!"

They were creepy? Really? Personally, he'd much rather be an immortal dragon than one of those disgusting creatures who'd been cursed by Apollo to die painfully on their twenty-seventh birthday. There was nothing *creepy* about being a dragon.

Human-Apollite bodies?

That was the stuff of nightmares. They were weak and pathetic. And smelled to the highest level of Olympus.

The prince smiled at his beautiful, petite wife, but his gaze never wavered from the two inside the cage. "Look at them, Helena. But for the fact that he doesn't speak, you'd never know he wasn't me. And the other . . . he is the very image of Pherus. It's as if I'm still looking my brother in the eye."

She wrinkled her nose in distaste. "Pherus was never your brother. He was the son of a slave."

"Slave or not, he was my brother through my father. And I loved him as such." And he'd died as soon as they'd tied his life force to Max's. Eumon licked his lips. "Do you think they can understand us?"

"No. They're animals and you're lucky you survived the merging your uncle did to you. Now, can we go? I don't like it here. It smells." She pressed her dainty hand to her nose to illustrate her point.

Only thing that smells, bitch, is you.

Instead of leaving, Eumon knelt down and held his hand out to Illarion. "Here, boy . . . come to me."

Tempted to bite him, Illarion scooted closer to Max before he gave in to that urge.

Eumon lowered his hand and sighed. "It seems like we should be able to train them. Doesn't it?"

Illarion slid a snide grimace to Max. He'd like to learn the prince a few things himself.

"Maybe so as not to wet the rugs or their beds, but I wouldn't hold out hope for any more than that. As I said, they're stupid animals, incapable of thought or civilization."

Oh yeah, *they* were the problem in this equation. . . .

"You are terrible, Helena!" he teased.

All of a sudden, a large number of guards stormed into the dungeon. Illarion narrowed his gaze on them. *That* never boded well for those kept in cages.

Anytime that many came in like that . . .

One of the prisoners got seriously hurt.

Or seriously dead.

Prince Eumon shot to his feet to confront the stone-faced soldiers. "What's the meaning of this?"

"Orders from the king, Highness. We're to destroy all the experiments to placate the gods."

Oh like hell . . .

The prince's face went white. "What?"

The guard nodded. "The dictate came from the head priest this afternoon. The gods are demanding that all the abominations be put down. Otherwise, they'll kill your father and you, and your brother."

Illarion exchanged a furious glower with Max.

Never fear, brother. I won't let them take you, Max promised.

But that wasn't Illarion's fear. No, he wasn't going out without a fight.

By the gods, he'd take them with him. As many as he could.

With a mighty roar, Max rushed at the bars.

The prince stumbled back with a fierce gasp, dragging his wife with him.

Screaming, she fell to the floor. "I told you! He's an animal! Kill him! Kill him now!"

Fury tore through Max with such ferocity that he lost complete control of his magick, even with the collar on to control it. The howls and screams of the others filled Illarion's ears as the soldiers set about carrying out their orders to murder them while they were helpless and caged.

This was utter bullshit! Illarion threw himself against the bars, over and over. When that wasn't enough, he and Max summoned every bit of magick they could and held their concentration. Then they sent it out into the air around them.

Like a thermal shock, it rolled and released a pulsating wave. One that shattered the cage and sent the guards, prince, and princess tumbling.

Weak, but determined, Max grabbed Illarion. "Free the others. Be damned if those bitches are going to take their lives for this!"

It's not our place! He had no interest in risking his life for them. Not after the way they'd treated them.

But Max misunderstood his protest. "I don't answer to the Greek gods. They can kiss my scaly ass." He grabbed the keys from the guard who was closest to him. Baring his fangs, he took the man's sword, then moved to free the Arcadians and Katagaria. "Illarion! Move! Save everyone you can!"

Disgusted by his brother's Arel ways, Illarion finally conceded. This would come to no good. He knew it.

Max always got them into trouble with shit like this.

Always!

As soon as they had the doors open and had started to leave, the guards moved to stop them.

"We have to talk to the king first. No one can leave here."

To his complete shock, Eumon stepped forward. "Let them pass."

"Highness—"

"Do it!"

Reluctantly, the guard stepped aside and ordered his men to stand down.

Max inclined his head to the prince. "Can you show us the way out, Highness?"

The prince narrowed an evil glare at him. "I knew you could speak! I need you to show that to my father."

"And we need a guide before your father learns of this and kills us. . . . Please. My brother and I have always been overtaken whenever we've tried to escape. I know there's a way to the forest, but we haven't been able to locate it."

Without hesitation, he nodded. "Follow me."

"Eumon!" his wife breathed. "You can't do this. If the gods have spoken—"

"They're sentient, Helena. Look at them." He gestured at Max and Illarion. "Half of them are Apollite. I can't condemn them to die, and especially not by execution in a cage after everything else we've done. It would be wrong. I'm their prince. It's my place to protect them."

"And what of your son I carry? Who will protect him when the gods kill you for this hubris?"

He kissed her lightly on the forehead. "Relax, precious wife. No one's going to kill me." Pulling away, he led Illarion and the others through the dark cavern. "Follow me and I'll see you to your freedom."

Illarion knew in his gut that this was going to be a disaster. He could feel it with every drakomas instinct he had.

Helena glared at Max as they started filing out of the dungeon. "I have a bad feeling about this."

As the last Apollite animal filed past them, Illarion began to breathe a little easier. They were almost out of here.

True to his word, Eumon helped them relocate to a small campground in the forest, where he and Max made sure everyone had a place to sleep and something to eat.

As Max started away, Eumon stopped him. "All these weeks and you've said nothing. You've pretended to be mute. Why?"

"There was nothing to say. Your uncle ripped us from our homes and lives for you. Both Apollite and animal. No regard for what we thought or wanted. And then we were turned into this?" He gestured angrily at his human body. "You may have desired the dragon in you, Highness, but I promise you, neither Illarion nor I wanted *this*. Nor did any of the others. Now that you have some of my brother's genetics inside you, you should know exactly how we think. What we feel."

"You have a fierce code of honor and kinship. That's where this comes from?"

Max inclined his head. "And now you tell me that your gods have decreed our death for *your* deeds. How do you think that makes me feel?"

"I will talk to my father. He's a reasonable man."

Illarion scoffed at his blind stupidity.

"He loves us."

"That just makes him highly unreasonable."

The prince nodded. "If you and your brother come with me . . . Let my father see that you're capable of rational thought and speech. It will change everything. I promise. Come and help me to set this right."

Illarion wended his way through the others to approach Max. *Surely you don't believe his lies.*

"We have to try."

Illarion wanted to beat him for that. The last thing he wanted to do was participate in this madness. But he loved his brother too much to let him go about his stupidity alone. Besides, he owed Max.

So together, they headed back toward the palace, with Eumon in the lead.

For the first time ever, they emerged out of the dungeon and into the palace grounds that led to the immaculate rooms the royal family called home.

They had just reached the gardens when a man who appeared eerily similar to Vane approached them.

"What is this?"

"We're going to see Father."

The newcomer scowled with fierce disapproval. "What have you done?"

The prince let out a tired sigh. "Linus, please. I have to speak to him and I don't have time."

"You heard what the priest told Father. We've angered the gods.

If you don't return them for execution right now, they'll demand our heads, too! Do you want to die?"

"And what's to stop them from doing that anyway after the others are gone? The gods are capricious. You know that. I don't trust them to kill us, anyway."

Linus gestured at Max and then Illarion. "But you would trust an animal?"

"They're not just animals. They can speak."

Linus scoffed. "Now you're being ridiculous. Did you perchance eat a bad lotus batch?"

"He's not wrong."

Linus's gaze had widened at the sound of Max's voice. "You can think and talk?"

"Of course."

Illarion cursed Max's trusting innocence as he saw the light in the prince's eyes. This was going to go badly for them.

His eyes darkened dangerously as he moved to confront Max. "Are *you* the reason Dagon did this to me?"

"Did what?"

In response to his brother's question, Linus turned on Eumon. "Or did *you* do it?"

"Do what?" Eumon repeated.

Linus raked him with a scathing glare. "You were always Father's favored son. Had your life not been threatened, I'm sure he'd have let me die, as he did our mother."

Eumon let out a tired sigh. "I don't have time for your insecurities. Move aside."

"Oh, right. You *never* have time, do you?" Linus sneered at Helena. "You took the bride that was meant for me and now you took my true animal form. *I* should have been the dragon. Not you!"

"What madness do you speak?"

"Helena was my bride!"

She lifted her chin defiantly. "I refused your hand after I met you. There's a cruelty in you, Linus, that scares me. Treaty or not, I would never have married into this family had I not met Eumon and seen for myself that, unlike you, he has a soul."

Shrieking in anger, he lunged at her, but Max caught him and forced him back. "Stop it. We have dire business to attend to here."

Linus roared in anger. "You could have convinced Dagon to give me the form I wanted, but instead you chose to remain silent? Did you kill your own to keep me from being like you, too? You did, didn't you?"

"What?"

Linus shoved Max away. "You all disgust me. You never let me have what I want."

He's mad, brother. We should leave.

Max nodded at Illarion, finally agreeing with him. *Protect the princess.*

As Illarion moved in to comply, Linus pulled out a knife and attacked. "Don't you turn your back on me, Eumon! I will not be disregarded!"

Eumon shoved him aside as he lunged for Illarion. "Are you stupid? He's the animal, you moron! I'm the prince. How can you not tell us apart?"

Those words were highly offensive. Especially since the only way to tell them apart was by the finery one wore and the filth that coated Illarion. In his opinion, it said more for Linus that he hadn't noticed their difference in dress.

Linus wrested his hand and weapon free from his brother. "I should have been heir! I'm far more worthy!"

Eumon had laughed in his face. "You were never worthy." With that, he disarmed him and kicked him back.

Horrified, Max had helped Illarion to his feet. Then placed his body between Illarion and the princes to protect him.

Rolling his eyes, Eumon threw the knife down. "Ignore him." He chucked Max on the arm and then Illarion. "Follow me and we'll settle this."

As they started away, Max caught the movement from the corner of his eye. He turned to disarm Linus, but he still hadn't mastered his human body. Before he could do anything to stop it, Linus stabbed him, then turned on the others.

Furious, Illarion attacked.

"Stop!" Eumon growled, trying to get between them.

Max knew the prince would be hurt if he didn't remove him from the conflict. "Highness?" He pulled him back at the same time Illarion and Linus staggered together, fighting for control of the knife.

They slammed hard into Max and Eumon, knocking them off balance and sending them reeling.

In a huge clump, the four of them fell to the ground.

As Max went to stand, Illarion realized they were covered in a lot more blood than they should have been. Stunned, it took him several seconds to realize it was Eumon whose artery had been sliced open in their fall.

Panting for air, the prince met Max's gaze. "Protect my wife."

His eyes haunted, Linus pushed himself to his feet and staggered back. Dropping the knife, he pressed his blood-soaked hand to his lips.

"Highness?"

Screaming in agony, Helena had rushed forward to weep by her husband's side. "Don't leave me, Eumon! Stay with me!" She applied pressure to his wound, but it was too late.

As his last act, Eumon reached up and removed Max's collar so that he could shapeshift freely. "Protect them all." And with that he expelled his final breath.

Helena had thrown her head back and shrieked like a harpy. "You beast! You killed my husband!"

"No . . ." Linus backed up in terror. "You saw for yourself. It was an accident."

Shaking her head, she sobbed and sobbed.

Max glanced to Illarion, who watched on with a sick feeling in his gut. They would take the fall for this. He knew it. *What do we do?*

I don't know.

But they both knew the truth. Linus was insane and he'd never tell the truth and implicate himself in this. His fear of being blamed for his brother's death wouldn't allow that. The gods had decreed them all to die. . . .

Max swallowed. *I have to get them to safety.*

Illarion cursed him for that thought. And before he could stop him, Max transformed and scooped him and the princess up in his talons. He took flight.

Her terrified shrieks filled his ears as she insulted his brother and tried to break free. Illarion fought against his grip. *Remove my collar so that I can fly, too!*

Not yet.

Illarion had a bad feeling about Max's destination.

One that turned out to be all too true when Max finally reached the southern beach. He laid Illarion and the princess down on the white sands, then landed. And before Illarion could protest it, Max summoned the Chthonian who'd been given domain over the demons. The one being who was given protection and charge over their kind.

Granted, no one had seen the bastard in centuries, and all kinds of speculations abounded. Some said Savitar had finally died of the wounds he'd sustained during the great Chthonian War. Others that the Greek god Mache had cursed him in retaliation for being bound and imprisoned.

Another said that the goddess Apollymi had drowned him when she sank Atlantis. There was even a rumor that Artemis had captured him and was keeping him as her pet on Olympus.

Throwing his head back, Max let out a summoning cry for the beast.

The princess shrank away from him as the waves rolled in and out on the beach.

"What is he doing?" she asked, throwing her hands over her ears to mute the sounds of his call.

Max ignored her as he continued to summon Savitar.

When he arrived, his lavender eyes glowed as he paused by Illarion's side and swept his gaze over the blood-soaked gown on the cringing princess. "Seems I missed an impressive party. Care to enlighten me, dragon?"

Max quickly told him what had been done to them, and what had happened to Eumon and Illarion. "I need your help, Chthonian."

Savitar had scoffed. "I'm done helping others. Last time I did that . . . it turned out badly for everyone. Especially me, and I rather like me, most days."

"They'll kill us."

"Everyone dies sometime."

"That's it, then? You're literally washing your hands of us?"

Savitar shrugged. "You have a new life. You should enjoy it."

"Until the Fates have us killed, you mean."

Savitar had gone stock-still. "Come again?"

"The Greek Fates? Because of Apollo and Zeus, they've ordered all of us to be put down."

"You should have led with that, little brother."

"Meaning?"

Savitar smiled. "Meaning there isn't much I wouldn't do to make those three bitches scream in agony. Take me to your camp."

By the time they returned, most of the Apollite-animal hybrids were dead. While Illarion and Max had been gone, the guards had found their camp and slaughtered them down to a meager handful.

Illarion had to force himself not to give his brother an I-told-you-so grimace. He just wished, just once, that Max would listen to him.

Disgusted by the cruel horror, Max had walked around the other newly made shapeshifters, assuring them as best he could. But Illarion didn't believe Max any more than they did.

This wasn't going to be all right. They'd all been screwed.

"What are we to do?" they asked in a unified voice.

Illarion met Savitar's gaze.

Savitar stepped forward. "As a new species, I offer you my protection. I will make it known that the Chthonians are aware of you and that no one, especially the gods, are to prey on you without repercussions."

While Savitar dealt with the new species, Max had finally removed Illarion's collar.

About time. Asshole.

"I know. I'm sorry."

Why did you wait?

"In case we were taken, you could have passed as the prince and escaped this cleansing. So long as you remained in a human body you were safe."

I'd rather be slaughtered. Illarion shook his head as he scanned the others. *We are an abomination. Are you sure we should have survived? Perhaps it would have been kinder to consign us to death.*

"Perhaps. But then, life isn't kind. All we have to get through it is each other. I couldn't stand by and watch them die."

Illarion let out a tired sigh. *Your Arel blood seriously screws you at times. What is this innate need you have to protect?*

"I don't know, but you should be glad I have it. A sane dragon would have left you behind."

To this day, Illarion wasn't sure if that wouldn't have been the better fate.

As they rounded them up, Lycaon and his army rode in to finish their slaughter.

Until the king saw Savitar. "What is the meaning of this?"

Savitar faced the king without fear. "I'm here to take them to their own lands to live."

"You can't do that."

Savitar arched a brow. "You want to cross me?"

"The gods have decreed—"

"And I, as a Chthonian sworn to protect mortal life from the gods, overturn that decree."

Lycaon shook his head. "You can't do that! They'll kill my children in retaliation."

"It's done."

While they argued, Helena grabbed Max's arm. "You can't let me return to the palace. Not after what's happened."

Confused, he scowled at her. "You want to travel with us, the animals?"

"Please. I'm afraid of what Linus will do to me and my children. While he might keep me alive and claim me as his, he will never suffer my children to live. Not so long as they are heirs to their father's throne. You saw him. His ambitions are ruthless and he will stop at nothing. Worse, we know he killed Eumon. So long as any of us are alive, he'll view us as a threat and want us removed. Understood?"

Illarion had shaken his head. *Max . . . I know that look on your face. You're the one who's always telling me to stay out of human affairs.*

Max had nudged the princess closer to Illarion. "Keep an eye on her for a minute."

Not quite sure what he was doing, Max closed the distance between Savitar and the king. The moment Linus saw him, he did just as his sister-in-law had predicted.

He ordered Max arrested for the murder of his brother, and demanded the return of Helena.

She was right. Linus would never suffer her to live and birth those children. He would kill them and remove them from the line of succession.

"He and his brother slaughtered mine, and I demand their heads for it!"

"Illarion is innocent. I, alone, am responsible."

Illarion started forward to protest, but Max wouldn't have it.

Savitar faced Max with a stern glower. "Do you understand what you're doing?"

Max met Savitar's furious stare. "I only understand what will happen if I don't."

Sighing in disgust, Savitar pressed his fingers to the bridge of his nose as if he had a brain tumor forming. As the guards came to retake Max, Savitar stopped them.

"No! The Arcadians you've created are a separate race and shouldn't be subjected to the laws of man." Savitar glared at Linus and his father. "They are a sentient group and should make their own laws to govern them. If Maxis is to face judgment, it will be by a jury of his own hybrid peers and not based on a decision handed down from a scheming brother and grieving father. If travesty is to be done, it should be impartial."

" 'Cause that makes it all so much better," Max muttered.

Savitar narrowed a threatening glower at him. "Don't lip me, dragon, or I'll turn you over to them."

"And what of this jury?" Lycaon demanded. "Who's to oversee it?"

"I will personally guarantee it," Savitar said. "You have my word."

Fury, and the promise that this wasn't over, glared out from the king's eyes. "Fine. I'll hold you to it. But I want that dragon's head mounted to my wall for what he's done! I will be expecting you to bring it to me when this is over. Otherwise, I'll be declaring war on this new breed." And with that, the king led his army away.

Illarion finally approached them. *I'm glad that's settled. Not even a little,*

Savitar laughed bitterly. "You're right. Nothing's over. This is just the beginning. Wait until Zeus and Apollo hear of it." He glanced around at the faces and animals. . . .

Apollites, lions, eagles, falcons, hawks, tigers, wolves, bears, panthers, jackals, leopards, snow leopards, jaguars, cheetahs, and dragons.

"What the hell was Dagon thinking?"

Max let out his own exhausted breath. "That his wife was grieving for her brother and that he had the magick to make it better and to save the lives of her nephews."

"You consider *this* better?"

Max shrugged at Savitar's question. "Better than death? Aye. Barely."

"And you, dragon, are an idiot."

"I've been called worse." He glanced to Illarion. "And that was just a few hours ago by my brother."

Illarion scoffed. *Seconds ago, actually.*

Savitar shook his head as he met the gaze of the princess. "Those are the first of their kind you're carrying, you know that, right?"

Her face had gone pale. "What?"

"You conceived them after your husband had been transformed. The good news is, they won't die of the Apollite curse that comes with Eumon's bloodline. The bad news is, the gods won't be happy that your prince thwarted said curse." Savitar growled in aggravation. "There's only so much mitigating I can do. Knowing the gods and those bitches in particular, I can tell you this isn't over. They will have something new in store for us all. And it won't be merciful."

And he'd been right. In spite of the evidence, and Helena's testimony over what had happened, Max had been found guilty during that first Omegrion meeting. When Illarion went to testify, Max had kept him out of it, lest he implicate himself and come under fire.

Better one should be marked than both. He'd pressed upon Illarion the necessity of keeping Helena safe and fulfilling their promise to Eumon. Something they couldn't do if they were both being hunted.

So he'd been marked while Illarion had been left as a Katagari guard for the first Arcadian princes born to a human mother.

But for Max and Illarion, there would have been no Were-Hunters spared the sword.

Only Linus and Eumon.

It was why Illarion hated all of them so.

Lycaon would have gladly slaughtered the rest to spare his two sons from the wrath of the Olympian gods.

One wolf and one dragon.

The worst irony was that neither he nor his brother even held a seat at the very council that had been started because of them. Rather Helena and another Drakos born from an earlier experiment between an Apollite slave and dragon had taken the first Regis positions. Helena as the Arcadian Regis, until her eldest son, Pharell, had been old enough to inherit it, and Cromus, who ceded his place to Helena's Katagari son, Portheus, when he'd come of age.

Linus had been left to found the same wolf bloodline that had led to Vane, Fang, and Fury. His ruthless need to put down all the others and rule them had forced Savitar to create the limanis such as Sanctuary so that the Were-Hunters would have some refuge from the gods and others out to slaughter them needlessly.

Now, Savitar pulled back and lightened the room. One by one, he met the gaze of those seated at the council table. "There you have it. Yes, Max technically drew first Were-Hunter blood, but he did so in protection of you all. Are you really going to be as the first council and condemn him again, knowing that?"

Damos Kattalakis, the direct descendent of Eumon and Helena who currently held the Arcadian Drakos seat, rose. Slowly, cautiously, he approached Max and Illarion.

His face unreadable, he removed the feathered mask that covered the Sentinel marks on his face. Running his hand over the scales and delicate workmanship, he studied the mask before he spoke. "It is the custom of my patria to make these out of the remains of the Katagaria we've slain. It's done to remind us that while they are animals, we are not. That we are civilized and descended from the blood of princes. In particular, Eumon Kattalakis."

He dropped the mask to the floor and met Max's gaze, then Illarion's. "I don't know why my great-grandmother failed to tell us of you, but I promise that if I should be fortunate enough to have dragonets one day, they will know the truth and what we owe our Katagaria cousins." Striking his shoulder with his fist, he saluted Max and Illarion. "Thank you for saving my family. As the head of the Kattalakis Drakos, I swear that should we ever hear the Bane-Cry of you, or your mates or children, every member of our patria will answer. On our honor."

Max inclined his head and saluted him back. "Thank you."

Smiling, Damos drew him in for a hug, then Illarion. "My father rolls in his grave." He turned back at Savitar and scowled. "Is this why you've always hated me?"

Savitar nodded. "Sins of the father, brother. Sins of the father. But today, you took the right step. And I saw it."

Snorting, Damos appeared less than amused as he turned toward Dare Kattalakis. "What of you, cousin?"

"They can kiss my furry ass. We're still at war."

"You should have eaten the wolves, little brother." Everyone in the room turned to look at Falcyn for his dry, emotionless, and very callous words.

He stared back, completely unrepentant. "Just saying. They're crispy when fried. Lean meat. Low gristle. It would have saved everyone the migraine of dealing with them now."

Fury choked. "Speaking as one of the wolves, I'm extremely offended by that."

"Good," Falcyn said without a hint of remorse or apology in his tone. "I've offended wolves and Were-Hunters alike. All I need to do now is feed on a cute, cuddly baby and my work for the day is done."

Blaise smacked Falcyn on the chest. "Don't worry, he's part Charonte. Hand him some barbecue sauce and he's happy."

Falcyn passed such an irritable scowl at Blaise that even though he was blind, Blaise felt it and shrank back—not in fear, but from common sense.

"He's not Charonte," Max said drily. "That would be too easy an excuse for him, and there really isn't one. He's just an irritable bastard. . . . Much like Savitar."

Savitar arched his brow. "I save your ass and you take a swipe at me? Really?"

"I'd apologize, but you hate insincerity more than you do insults."

"Yeah, I do." Savitar eyed the council members. "Well, we know where the dragons stand and where the wolves are officially. . . ." He looked at Vane for confirmation on their stance.

Vane cut a vicious glare at his litter mate, Dare. "Officially, the Kattalakis Lykos, both Arcadian and Katagaria, consider Max a brother. We have no issue with him and vote that the mark be stricken."

"I second that," Fury concurred. "And I hope you choke on it, Dare. It *and* my furry ass."

Dare took a step forward, but his sister caught him and kept him from doing something profoundly stupid. Like attacking his brothers in front of the Omegrion and Savitar.

Savitar turned his attention to the other Kattalakis Drakos, who was standing with Dare and Star. Tall and dark, the Katagari Regis favored Fang more than the others.

His ebony eyes flashed as he considered his response. After a few seconds, he pulled the silver dragon pendant from his neck and looked down at it resting in his palm. "I grew up with stories about the Dragonbane and how he killed the first Arcadian in cold, vicious blood, and started our war of species. My father impressed upon me that we were never to be such animals. That we should strive to find the human in us, even when it seemed buried and lost." He glanced to Dare and Star. "I'm thinking that my father was wrong. We should have embraced the Drakos more than that so-called humanity."

Darion came forward to lay his pendant in Illarion's hand. "I vote to remove the mark and I cede my seat at the council to the rightful heir. You are the one made from Prince Eumon's blood, not my family. It's only right that you should be the one making the laws for our people."

Illarion shook his head. *I can't take this.*

Darion held his hands up and stepped back. "You are Regis, Stra Drago. I refuse my seat. I have no right to it."

Savitar glanced around to the rest of the Omegrion members. "For the sake of brevity, I'm assuming the rest of you concur. Is there anyone who objects?"

Dante Pontis, the Katagaria panther Regis, held his hand up.

With long dark hair he wore in a ponytail, he was the epitome of a disgruntled predator. "I'm not protesting, but I have a question." He turned toward Maxis. "Why were you marked originally?"

Max shrugged nonchalantly. "I'm an asshole."

Dante grinned. "While, as a fellow asshole myself, I can respect that. Care to elaborate?"

"The council mood back then was a lot different. They were still raw and pissed off from being held in a cage and experimented on. They'd just been told about the curse the Fates had handed down, that we couldn't choose our mates. They'd be assigned to us, whether we wanted them or not—and that the Fates had decreed eternal war between our species."

And human rationale was new to the animals, Illarion inserted. *They were angry and lashing out at everyone, especially my brother and me.*

Max nodded. "When they started to attack me, I reacted as any drakomas would. I told them to fuck themselves and attacked back."

Savitar snorted disdainfully. "Talk about putting lipstick on a pig. . . . You are allowed to say that you reacted badly."

"All right, I reacted badly."

"Yeah, that's an exaggeration," Savitar said under his breath.

Max feigned indignation. "I don't know what you're talking about. It's been a million years since I last exaggerated about anything."

Savitar rolled his eyes.

"Anyway," Max continued. "I lost my temper over their accusations and . . ." He pointed up at the ceiling. "You can still see some of the marks where the fighting broke out and we almost burned down the building."

"That's where I reacted badly." Savitar flashed a fake smile. "As a result, Max was condemned and I was in no mood to refute or acquit their unanimous decision. We all had a very bad day."

"And I've had a few more," Max whispered loudly.

"Yeah. Sorry about that." Savitar crossed his arms over his chest.

"Wow," Dante said in a sarcastic tone. "Sounds like the mood I was in when I mounted my brother's hide to the wall of my club."

Savitar nodded. "Basically . . . So, we are all in accord?"

"Yes." Fury flashed a devilish grin. "Dare is an asshole and nobody likes him, at all."

Dare started for him.

Fury bared his teeth. "Bring it, you little punk bastard! Let's go! You and me. Here and now! I'm ready to pick your fur out of my teeth! C'mon!"

Vane caught Fury and pushed him back toward Max. "Did you by chance bring a leash? Or a muzzle?"

"No, but I'm thinking I should have."

Just as Dare broke loose to run at Fury, who was still taunting him and questioning his parentage, a bright flash lit the room, causing him to pull up short.

All movement stopped as Cadegan and Thorn appeared near Savitar. Both bleeding and in bad physical shape. Like near-death bad. They lay in a tangled heap at Savitar's feet.

Thorn had his arms around Cadegan as if he'd barely gotten them out of a nasty situation right before they'd been torn apart.

The paleness of his bruised features added further testimony to that assumption.

Stunned to see the two well-seasoned warriors like that, Illarion didn't move. Thorn had been born an ancient warlord, and had thousands of years of heavy combat experience against the damned and demented. Cadegan was a demon and Addanc of incredible power and skill.

One thing those two knew how to do . . .

Fight. Especially anything fanged, clawed, winged, and preternatural.

His breathing ragged, Thorn cupped Cadegan's face in a strangely tender gesture. "You still with me, little brother?"

"Ach, aye, boyo, but only because me Jo would kick me arse if I didn't come home to her."

Analise Romano, who was the Arcadian Regis for the snow leopards and a doctor, rushed from her seat to Cadegan to check on him.

Thorn carefully ceded his brother's care over to her before he stood and wiped the blood from his lips. He looked first to Fang, then Savitar. "Remember that situation I mentioned?"

"Blew up a bit?" Savitar asked sarcastically.

"Like your temper on Olympus during a full moon party. Needless to say, we have a massive problem. And our names are engraved all over that apple of fun." Thorn moved to drape one arm over Styxx's shoulder and the other over Acheron's. "Checked on Mom lately?"

Acheron visibly cringed. "Ah God, what's she done now?"

"Well," Thorn tightened his arm around both their necks, "I've just *got* to know . . . whose bright idea was it to surrender Apollo's custody to her?"

Styxx made the same grimace Acheron had worn a moment ago. "That idiot would be me. Why? What did I do?"

Thorn released Acheron to playfully slap Styxx on the face and squish his cheeks together. "Mama Apollymi found him a new playmate," he said in the same falsetto people used when talking to small children. "She fed his ass to Kessar, and aren't we happy he has a new friend to play with, boys and girls?" He shook his head. "No . . . no, we're not. In fact, I want to bitch-slap you."

"Oh dear gods." Zakar repeated Acheron's words and stumbled back. "Please tell me she didn't."

With a sarcastic, hysterical laugh, Thorn released Styxx, stepped back, and clapped his hands together. "No, wait! It gets so much better! You haven't even heard the good part yet. No! Yeah . . . she decided it would be a great idea to turn Apollo into a blood-bitch like you were, Z. Yes . . . yes, she did."

Groaning, Zakar covered his face.

Thorn nodded and clapped the Sumerian god on the back. "At least *you* see the train wreck coming. At least you can identify this nightmare as it's happening. Good for you!"

Acheron glared at him. "Enlighten those of us who can't."

Thorn stepped away to continue. "Long story short, Kessar fed from the god, and they made a pact to combine their fun-loving natures and kind spirits. Please note the sarcasm in my tone and don't miss the Alaska-sized ulcer. As a result, Apollo has attacked Olympus."

"No." Acheron shook his head. "I was there. That was Kessar who attacked Olympus."

"No, punkin.' *That* was Apollo leading those demons. It's how they got in. Three guesses what he wanted. And *world peace* is definitely not one of them."

"Revenge."

Thorn shook his head at Dante and made a sarcastic buzzer sound. "Too easy, and a given. Guess again."

Sick to his stomach, Max exchanged a panicked stare with Illarion.

Thorn applauded. "Oh look, I think the dragons got it. And why shouldn't they? Illarion, being the son of Ares, ought to know *exactly* what he wants."

He's after the Spartoi.

"Yes. Yes, he is."

Fury scowled. "What's the Spartoi? Is that like a plastic model of the *300* characters? God, someone, please tell me that it's an action figure and not what I fear it might be. . . ."

Seraphina grimaced. "No. It's your fear, I'm sure. They're a rather nasty and invincible branch of Ares's army. It's said that when a Drakone of Ares sows them into the earth, they sprout full grown, ready to battle and destroy at the command of whoever planted them."

"And guess who has custody of those little darlings right now?" Thorn pointed to Illarion. "How do *I* know this? Your father squealed like a thirteen-year-old girl at a Shawn Mendes sighting."

"Aye, he did indeed," Cadegan agreed as he rose on shaky legs, holding his ribs. "For a god of war, Ares is a bit of a wanker. He ain't no Aeron, that's for sure."

"And speaking of our favorite Celtic war god, he's still fighting them and I need to get back and help before they make a gallu of him and we all go down in a ball of sarcastic Aeron fire. They convert him, he'll convert his two best buddies, and I'm out. I don't want no part of that fight. Ever." Thorn glanced at Savitar. "Yes, I am that big a coward, for I have fought the evil that is Aeron and friends, had my ass handed to me on a platter with applesauce and garnishings, and yeah . . . no, thank you. Nothing is worth an ass-kicking that severe. Of which I got for nothing more than looking at his sister cock-eyed. Imagine what he'd do if I actually offended *him*."

Max stepped forward. "We'll settle this with you."

"We?"

"The drakomai."

Sera nodded. "And the Drakos."

Wide-eyed and furious, Max gaped. She passed a chiding smile at him. "Don't give me that look, Lord Dragon. I don't want you fighting, either."

Edena and Hadyn moved forward to join them.

"Oh hell no!" Max snapped. "I might not have a say in what Sera does, but you two I do!"

When they started to protest, Seraphina shook her head. "Your father's right. Neither of you is ready for this. And if you roll those eyes at me, young lady, I'll ground you till the sun explodes, and your brother, too, just because he taught you to do it when you were little."

Edena huffed and crossed her arms over her chest. "I liked it better when they didn't talk or get along."

Hadyn nodded his agreement, but wisely remained silent.

As Thorn moved back to leave, four Were-Hunters fell to the floor for no reason.

Dead.

Silence echoed as everyone knew exactly what it meant. Those were bonded mates whose spouses had been killed somewhere else. Three council members and one of the Arcadian wolves who'd come in with Star and Dare. For that to happen simultaneously, there was only one cause.

War.

"What the fuck?" Dante breathed.

Thorn and Savitar went pale.

As did Acheron. "They're dividing and attacking our families to thin our defenses and hit our morale."

"It's working," Fury said in a panicked tone.

Savitar motioned for Zakar, Sin, and Styxx. "We'll see to Apollymi in Kalosis and make sure she's secure."

Thorn jerked his chin at the Peltiers and the Kattalakis brothers. "We'll take Sanctuary. Sera, you better join us. Nala's with them. I can feel it."

Cadegan and Blaise exchanged a determined look. "We'll stay here to guard your young. No fears there for you."

Acheron looked to the drakomai. "We'll return to Olympus, and finish it. Once and for all."

Illarion and Max nodded.

"Remember, Maxis," Sera reminded him. "There is no *I* in *team*."

He winked at her. "True, but there is in *win*, *fight*, and *die*."

"And you'd best not do the latter."

Inclining his head, Max turned and joined Acheron and his brothers. It'd been centuries since he'd gone to real war with Falcyn and Illarion. Yet it seemed like no time at all as they changed forms and fell into formation.

As eldest, Falcyn took lead. The Katagaria Drakos came to fight with them on Olympus while the Arcadians went with Sera and the others to protect Sanctuary.

By the time they arrived, Apollo and Kessar had virtually torched every building, and most of the gods had withdrawn from the conflict. Only a brave handful remained to try and salvage what they could. The Greek god Demon and his twin, Phobos. Most of the Dream-Hunters.

Only Apollo's temple remained standing perfectly intact. But that wasn't their target or destination.

Ares's temple was what drew their attention. The iron structure had the front doors ripped open. And the perches that were usually manned by Insidia and Nefas stood empty. Bodies of demons smoldered on the steps.

Obviously, Kessar and Apollo had gone there looking for the Spartoi and found nothing.

It was easy to find where the Malachai demon—a natural enemy of the Greeks—was still embroiled in a bitter fight against Apollo and the gallu.

Illarion smiled at the sight. The Malachai had always been stubborn in a brawl. They never knew when to give up or surrender. It was one of the things he liked best about the man, Nick Gautier, and it was what had kept Nick from turning evil like the rest of his brethren.

So far, at least.

Even though Nick had been born cursed and destined to be one of the creatures who ultimately destroyed the earth, he battled an inner war every day to keep himself from crossing over and becoming what his father had been.

"Incoming!"

Max moved to engage the winged gallu demons first. Illarion and Falcyn stayed at his back, covering his flank.

Zakar had been right. The gallu were vicious in their skills.

"Don't let them scratch you!" Acheron warned, unaware of the fact that they were immune.

Illarion spewed fire and swept the ground, razing as much of it as he could. Fire would purify the gallu and keep their disease from spreading and infecting anyone else and turning them into mindless gallu slaves. He and his brothers fell in beside the former Dark-Hunter Zarek and the Dream-Hunter leader, Jericho while they tried to route a group of demons out of the Hall of the Gods.

It took a while, but they eventually had them on the run, headed up the hill toward Apollo's temple.

Winged himself and as a Titan god of war, Jericho shot up between the dragons. "Thanks for the assist."

Falcyn inclined his head to him. "What are they after?"

"Apollo showed up, telling Zeus to abdicate. You know how that went. Even though he's just a figurehead these days, Zeus tossed a few lightning bolts at him and it was on."

With a hand covered by sharpened silver claws he used as a weapon, Zarek grabbed a demon that tried to bite him, ripped out its throat, and slung it so hard, it flew up and almost hit Max.

"Hey!"

"Duck," Zarek said sarcastically, a little late.

Max flipped off the surly god.

For once, Zarek ignored the insult as he headed after another group. At least someone enjoyed the fighting.

Suddenly, Illarion caught an odd note over the sounds of battle. At first, he thought he was hearing things.

But it seemed to grow louder. . . .

He shook his head in denial. No.

It was a figment of his imagination. A vague memory caused by war and the memories it stirred. Nothing more.

Just something weird in the wind.

Yet it didn't abate.

Worse, it began to lure him like the call of a siren.

Without a word and unable to resist the musical summons, Illarion tucked his wings and landed near his father's temple.

Max landed beside him. "Is something wrong?"

Do you hear that?

"Hear what?"

Illarion cocked his head as he heard it even more clearly now, and it was definitely inside the temple. *It's Cercamon.*

"Who?"

A twelfth-century troubadour. Edilyn was forever making me take her to see him play.

Max heard it then. Light and subtle. Barely audible and yet distinct.

> *Bel m'es quant ilh m'enfolhetis*
> *E•m fai badar e•n vau muzan!*
> *De leis m'es bel si m'escarnis*
> *O•m gaba dereir'o denan,*
> *Qu'apres lo mal me venra bes*
> *Be leu, s'a lieys ven a plazer.*

What the hell? Why would that be playing in the background? It seemed a strange choice for a Greek god of war.

Metallica, Pantera . . . that would make sense. Death metal, definitely. But medieval love poetry?

Nah, it just didn't fit.

Illarion turned human so that he could sneak inside for a peek. Max followed suit only to find that it wasn't Ares who was playing and singing in the middle of battle.

It was Apollo. Which kind of made sense, he supposed, since Apollo was the god of music and poetry, and rather passive.

Sure, why not? Him and Nero. Fiddling while Rome, or in this case, Olympus burned.

The god probably needed the light from the fires to read with his old eyes.

As if sensing their presence, Apollo stopped playing and narrowed his gaze angrily on the shadows that concealed them. "Little dragons, all in a row. Tell the big Greek god, how deep does your sorrow flow?"

Illarion curled his lip.

Max grabbed Illarion's arm and tried to pull him back, but Illarion refused to obey.

He needed to wring Apollo's neck.

Apollo rose to his feet, while he continued to pluck at his lyre. "I know you're there, son of Ares. I can feel you. Come and give your uncle a hug . . . sing with me."

Illarion actually took a step forward.

Max sank his claws into his brother's arm, hoping the pain might get through to him since nothing else was working, and shook his head no. *It's a trick!*

Pressing his lips together, Illarion finally hesitated.

"Ahh," Apollo said in a petulant tone. He plucked a sour note. "Don't you trust me, Illy? You do know that's why Dagon chose you for his experiments all those centuries ago, don't you? Because you were my nephew, he thought to use you to spare the Apollites my curse. He knew my love for you, as your uncle, would sway my mercy. It's why I begged Zeus and the Fates to spare you from the slaughter."

Apollo tsked. "Your jealous half brother Max didn't tell you that, did he? That I never wanted *you* harmed. You and Lycaon's sons were to be excluded from the cleansing. Your brother lied to you, Illarion, to save his own ass, and to win you to his cause. It's what he's been doing since the very beginning. Why do you think he left you trapped all those centuries in Le Terre Derrière le Voile?"

Max gaped furiously at that accusation. *Bullshit! You know better, Illy. You were there. You heard them, same as I. That's not the way it happened!*

"Don't listen to him. You aren't born of Arel blood, little nephew. You have no loyalty to anyone save our pantheon. Join us and I'll give you what you want most."

"Illarion." Max spoke out loud, trying to reach his brother through whatever spell the god was weaving with his lyre and words. "Don't listen to Apollo. He's lying. You know he's lying!"

He was right. Illarion knew Apollo couldn't speak honestly if he had to. It just wasn't in the worthless bastard. Hell, even his instrument was pronounced as a liar.

Illarion took a step back and grabbed on to Max's arm to steady himself.

Relieved beyond belief that his brother had chosen wisely, Max wrapped his arms around him and held him close. He could feel Illarion trembling against him.

Until a light, musical voice called out with the cadence of a perfect angel.

"Illarion?"

In that moment, Illarion's world came crashing down.

For a full minute, he couldn't breathe.

Stunned. Shocked. Incredulous, he pulled back and looked up with wide eyes. No. It couldn't be.

Edilyn?

"I'm here, my precious dearling. I've missed you so much!"

Apollo laughed. "All you have to do is join me, nephew. Help me take back what was stolen and I'll see you reunited with your Edilyn."

Max shook his head and held on tight to Illarion's arm. "You can't do this! Illarion! It's a trick!"

Illarion looked from his brother to Edilyn. This was no trick. He would know that voluptuous body anywhere. Those blue eyes that laughed and shined more vibrantly than the sun . . .

That ebony hair that caressed his skin like the finest silk.

She had no equal in this world. No one could fake her beauty. He'd lain awake for centuries, tortured with the memories of every nuance of her.

His eyes haunted, Illarion met Max's gaze with a longing insanity. *And if it were Seraphina? What choice would you make, brother?*

The truth of that statement burned like fire in Max's golden eyes. He knew what choice he'd make.

The same one Illarion did as he shoved his brother back and ran to Apollo.

In that moment, Max knew he couldn't stay. If he did, he'd be forced to fight the last creature on this planet he'd ever harm.

The brother he'd spent a lifetime protecting.

Worse, he knew that wasn't Edilyn. It couldn't be. It was an illusion of some kind. But Illarion was so desperate to have her back that he didn't care. He was past listening to reason.

He was past caring about consequences and Max couldn't fault him for that. Not after he'd been there here himself.

Distracted, Max glanced back into the temple to check on Illarion as he embraced whatever demon or creature wore the skin of his brother's wife. His thoughts and emotions were so scattered and raw that for a moment, he forgot he was still in a human body.

Forgot he was in the middle of a war and a battle.

But he was reminded fast when a demon materialized in front of him and ran him completely through his heart with a sword, and kicked him to the ground, leaving him there to die.

27

Illarion was no longer on Olympus. He no longer heard the sounds of battle or Apollo's voice.

In one heartbeat, he was transported back in time. Back to the fateful day when Morgen had cornered him and Edilyn in the Tor.

He felt his wife on his back as she battled, giving him commands with her knees and feet. The pressure of her shifting weight and how she squeezed him with her thighs.

They'd fought together so many times by then

that they'd learned to become a single unit. A single beast, with one divine heartbeat between them. He knew Edilyn's skills and she knew his. They trusted one another implicitly.

But something had struck his chest at the same time Maddor had come at his back.

He still didn't know what the bastard had used to cut her from the saddle while Illarion had been too dazed to use his powers to teleport her to safety. To tear her from the magick harness he'd used to make sure that nothing could harm her.

"Illy!" Her anguished, fearful cry had splintered his soul that day.

Unable to catch his breath, he'd turned to save her. Only to find more mandrakes and gargoyles in his way. His powers wouldn't work.

Fighting desperately through them, he'd seen her plummeting toward the ground. Plummeting toward her death.

Edilyn!

He could never get that sight out of his mind. Any more than the last heartbeat of her dying. That last, single gasp that had forever haunted him.

Don't leave me! he'd begged through his tears.

But her grip had fallen loose on his hand.

His heart had shattered.

And then they'd torn her from his grasp. He'd relived that moment, over and over, until it'd driven him mad. Unable to forgive himself for failing her, he'd used his powers to sear the words of her favorite poem into the flesh of his arm so that he'd always have a piece of her with him.

At night, in his dreams, he'd imagined her with him again. Just the two of them . . .

In a world where their bond couldn't be undone. Where death could never take her from his arms. If only it were real. . . .

If only she were still alive.

"Did you break him?"

Apollo frowned at Kessar's question. How he hated the gallu demon. But sadly, the Sumerian bastard was a necessary evil for his plans to strike down his pantheon and Apollymi.

At least for now.

"Not sure. Never seen a dragon do this before. Did you or one of yours bite him and convert him to your slave?"

Kessar shook his blond head. "But now that you mention it . . ."

Apollo stopped him as he started to *fix* that oversight. "Convert the dragon, and he won't be able to access his island."

"Why not?"

"He will no longer be a true drakomai. He'll be a mindless gallu slave. Only one of his species can access the chest that holds what we need."

Kessar curled his lip. "Why do we need this army?"

Apollo strummed his lyre and did his best not to react to such a ridiculously dumb question. "In theory, we don't. Just makes our job easier. After all, this is not the only realm we have to take. And that little bastard there is a Dragonmark. Do you know what that is?"

The demon shook his head.

Of course not. Gallu were insanely stupid creatures.

Apollo sighed, but hid his aggravation. "They are a rare, rare beast. Only he and his sister, Xyn, bear that title anymore. Sadly, no one knows what has become of her. He's the last one we can find." He shot a god-bolt from his hand into Illarion.

The moment it hit him, it caused his human flesh to illuminate. And beneath it, an intricate pattern emerged. Like bony thorns, it spiraled over his skin. Lovely and at the same time terrifying.

Illarion's eyes glowed white.

Apollo passed a smug smile to the demon. "*That* is the Dragonmark. They absorb power from the gods and can use it to attack. It makes them stronger and harder to kill than their counterparts. There's a prophecy among my people that anyone who can command a Dragonmark in his army will never be defeated. Not by man. And never by the gods."

He jerked his chin to the demon. "You'd do well to collar him now while he's lost wherever it is he is. Once he comes out of that state . . . he'll probably kick our asses."

"I wouldn't chain him, if I were you."

Apollo arched his brow at the soft, feminine voice. "You dare question me?"

"You freed me to handle him, did you not?"

He turned his head to glare at Edilyn. "Yes. But not to contradict me."

"Not contradicting, my lord. Cautioning." She jerked her chin toward Illarion. "You chain him and he will react badly. I don't think you're prepared for what you will unleash."

Apollo glared at her. "Fine, then. You keep the beast under control. Otherwise, I will destroy you."

She inclined her head to him before she slowly approached Illarion.

Edilyn tried to ignore the wretched beasts around her and to not betray exactly how grateful she was to be here.

With Illarion.

This was a frightening game they were forcing her to play. But this was the only chance she had to save him.

And herself.

Terrified of how her dragon might react, she carefully touched his arm.

Illarion closed his eyes as if he savored that small bit of contact. *You're not real.*

She glanced to the others before she used her thoughts to answer his. *I am, my love. And I'm here. Come, Illy. Follow me.*

Trying not to betray them, she took his hand and led him from the temple to the hall where Apollo wanted them kept. It was basically a prison, surrounded by his faithful servants and demons.

But it afforded them a degree of privacy.

It wasn't until she'd shut the doors and started the torches that Illarion finally came out of his very mild torpor. Then, his anger was palatable. *You're not my Edilyn. You can't be.*

"Look inside your heart, Illy. Remember the day we met? You were in the guise of an old man. I had no interest in tying myself to a dragon lord. I wanted nothing to do with your world. Not until Morla snapped my bow that my father had made for me. And you, my precious heart, so kindly repaired it."

Illarion blinked as those words choked him. He stared down into those beautiful blue eyes that seemed so familiar. Into a face he'd loved for so long that he could no longer remember a time when he hadn't lived for her.

Dare he believe this was real? That she was somehow alive?

She held the same lush, full curves of his Addie-Rose. Her voice the same cadence and accent.

But . . .

I saw you die.

"You saw me shed my mortal skin. Remember that I told you my mother was a kikimora?"

He nodded.

Tears filled her eyes as she laid her palm to his cheek. "When Maddor killed me, I was pulled to her realm, to live among her people. But I had no key that would enable me to return to the Tor, or pierce the Veil to reach you. I've tried a thousand times, in a million ways. Ever wanting to be with you. But Merlin's magick was too strong. Not even in dreams could I find you."

Tears blurred his vision as indecision tortured him. Indecision that wasn't helped when she kissed him in a way only Edilyn ever had.

He knew the taste of these lips. The way her hands felt sliding over his body.

Closing his eyes, he inhaled her scent and let it take him back to the last time in his life when he'd felt whole. Intact.

And this time, she was the one who used powers she shouldn't have to remove their clothes.

Stunned, he pulled back to stare down at her. *Who are you?*

"I'm your Edilyn, but I have changed from the innocent girl who ran away with you. Time and longing have taken a toll on me."

And your sister?

Laughing, she nipped at his lips. "You're the one with a sister, love. Sarraxyn. Virag lives. Not happily, as I've made his life a living hell for what he did to us, and especially for his theft of your stone."

Tears gathered in her eyes as she drew a ragged breath. "Please believe in me, Illarion. I swear, I won't harm you. That is not why I'm here."

He sucked his breath in sharply as she reached down between their bodies to cup him in her palm. His blood raced through his veins. It'd been so long since he'd been touched by another. In honor of her, he'd never allowed any other lover access to his body.

I've missed you. Those words tore themselves from him before he could stop them.

"Missed you, too," she whispered against his lips. "Now come home, my lord, where you belong."

Pinning her against the wall behind her, he drove himself deep inside her. She cried out as he ground his teeth against the wave of excruciating pleasure that tore through him.

Edilyn fisted her hand in his long auburn hair while he made furious love to her. She screamed out in ecstasy at how good it felt to have him deep in her body again. It'd been far too long.

Now . . .

She never wanted to let him go.

Sinking her nails into the flesh of his back, she came in a blinding wave of pleasure.

Illarion hissed as he felt her climax. Kissing her, he quickened his thrusts so that he could join her. Even then, he didn't withdraw immediately. Rather, he stayed inside her for as long as his body would allow it.

But all too soon, they were forced to separate.

Taking his hand, Edilyn led him to a small bedroom that held a good-sized bed with furs for covers. She tucked him into it, then laid herself across him and savored his long, muscled body. This was all she'd wanted. For centuries, she'd craved this one homecoming.

Unable to believe this was real, he toyed with the wealth of ebony hair that fell over his chest in a beautiful cascade of waves.

In that moment, he wanted to die.

Because he knew that all too soon, Apollo would come to him with a price tag for this happiness.

And he knew that no matter what the god asked of him, he would pay it.

'Cause whatever the price, it would be worth it to keep her by his side.

Hell. High water. Blood. Bone.

Soul.

His or anyone else's.

I can't lose her again.

And no matter what, he wouldn't.

For a full week, Apollo left them alone. Every day that went by was worse than the one before.

And so much sweeter.

Illarion hated it because he felt himself drowning. He was so desperate to be with Edilyn that he spent most of his time in the body of a man. He all but abandoned his dragon form.

A dragon couldn't hold her. Couldn't bury his face in the crook of her neck and spoon up against her body to sleep. Nor could he lay his head between her breasts and sleep with her fingers tangled in his hair.

God help him, he didn't want to be a dragon ever again.

He just wanted to be with her. Curled up in her arms. Forever. This was all he needed.

All he wanted . . .

Edilyn kissed the top of Illarion's head as she cradled him against her. They'd been abed for days now. And while she was enjoying this thoroughly, she was concerned. "Illy?"

Mmm?

"I'm worried about you."

Why?

"You said in the beginning that you were afraid I wasn't me, but you're the one who isn't like himself. And it's starting to scare me."

He lifted his head to stare down at her with a fierce frown. *What do you mean?*

She brushed her fingers against his frown to smooth it. "You're like an addict, and you look dreadful. I don't think you're supposed to be in a human body this long."

Don't be ridiculous.

Biting her lip, she ran her fingers through his tangled hair. "I'm not, love. You need to look in a mirror. You're very pale. Your eyes are hollow and sunken. Gaunt, even. And you've lost weight. You need to eat and you've got to return to your true form."

Instead, he kissed her, then slid himself back inside her body. *I don't want to leave you.*

"Precious . . . you haven't even asked about your brother. Max was wounded badly in the fighting."

Max?

Edilyn went cold as she saw the confusion in his eyes. He truly had no recollection of his beloved brother. "Do you know where we are?"

My father's temple.

At least he remembered that much. But it wasn't like him to call Apollo father.

Bloody bastard.

Worthless . . .

Those were the normal epitaphs for the creature who'd sired him.

"What else do you recall?"

He kissed her blind before he began thrusting fiercely against her hips. *How much I love you.*

She groaned in pleasure as she struggled to remember herself why this was important. Yet she couldn't let him distract her. Not again. She had to stay focused. Had to make him remember himself. "And?"

I don't want to talk, Addie. I just want to feast on you. He pulled out of her then so that he could kiss his way down her body until he took her into his mouth and made her forget everything except how talented he was with his tongue.

Growling deep in her throat, she sank her hand in his hair and spread her thighs wider to give him all the access he wanted to her body.

At the rate he was going, she'd never walk again. He was

merciless and skillful in a way that should be illegal. And when she finally came, it was so intense that she screamed out from it.

Laughing, he rolled her over so that he could enter her again. This time, he positioned her on her stomach so that he could ride her furiously while his fingers kept time to his strokes.

And before she knew it, she came with him. His heart pounded against her shoulder while his ragged breath fell against her cheek.

I love you, Addie.

"Love you. But you've got to stop this, Illy. You are drakomai! You have to remember that."

He laid himself over her like a blanket, pressing her deep into the mattress with his weight. *Nay . . . I'm a man. For you.*

True fear cut through her at those words. This was serious. She needed to get him out of here and away from his uncle's clutches and schemes. There was something about this place that was damaging him. A spell or something . . .

But she would have to be careful. Apollo had them guarded and watched.

For that reason, she waited until Illarion fell asleep before she scooted away from him and dressed. Slipping off to the bathroom, she made sure that no guard or anyone else could hear her.

Then she used her powers to summon the last person she really wanted to converse with.

"Virag," she whispered. "Where are you?"

"Thought you weren't talking to me again, little sister?"

"Don't be a jerk. I'm not, but I need you."

"And *I'm* the jerk?"

She scoffed. "Of course you are. . . . Now can you come to me?"

"Where are you?"

"Olympus."

He let out a sarcastic laugh. "Seriously. Where are you?"

"Olympus. Seriously. Now haul your butt here."

He manifested as a shimmering shade next to her. "Wow, you weren't kidding. Why are you here?"

"Illarion. He's here, too."

His features paled. "Uh . . . then I don't need to be here."

She held him there with her powers. "Oh no you don't! Stay. I need you."

"For what? Target practice?"

"Illarion has forgotten himself."

He gaped. "How?"

"I don't know. Nor do I know how to repair it. Do you?"

"Of course not. I'm a kikimora, not a dragon."

She gave him a droll, irritated glare.

"Don't even. It's not like I've had a lot of experience with dragons."

Growling at him, she nudged him toward the bedroom. "Fine, then. I need you to do what you can."

His eyes widened. "And that is?"

"Pretend to be Illarion. They don't care if I'm here or not. But they watch him constantly. You can take on his form. Just pretend to sleep until we get back."

She expected him to protest.

But after an excruciating wait, he nodded. "Be careful."

"Thank you."

When she started away, Virag caught her hand. "I'm sorry, Eddie. For everything. You were never supposed to get hurt."

Tears filled her eyes as she remembered the day she'd died in battle. The way it'd felt to see the anguish on Illarion's face and know that she was the cause of it. She'd fought to stay with everything she had.

But the Fates had cruelly denied them.

Bitter anger had filled her as she was forced from his side and pain had torn her apart and left her heartbroken.

Virag had been the first one she'd seen when she'd crossed over to her mother's realm. Even now, she remembered the indignity on his face the moment he realized what had happened to her.

What Morgen had done.

"No! This was not the deal! Edilyn was to remain unharmed!"

Morgen's voice had cut through their realm. "You failed, demon. I warned you the cost of it! No one crosses me!"

Then, Morgen had unleashed her MODs—her death demons that existed only to hunt and kill—to go after Edilyn even in their realm.

Virag had grabbed her immediately.

Their gazes had met in the darkness and he'd given her that big-brother smile that had always promised her protection and safety. "Do you trust me, Eddie?"

In spite of it all, she'd nodded.

And when they'd come to kill her, she'd learned the true power of her mother's people. What made them so incredibly sought after by others who wanted to enslave them for their abilities.

As the MODs had closed in to deal her the last fatal blow that would have ended her existence in all realms, Virag had taken her form and received her death sentence from Morgen's minions without hesitation or reservation.

Or at least, that had been his plan.

It wasn't until after she'd seen them *kill* her body that Virag had appeared by her side, dazed and with tears in his eyes.

As befuddled and shocked as he appeared, she'd stared at him. "Virag?"

He'd sniffed back his tears as he took her hand and then run with her before Morgen and the others realized what'd happened. Without explaining why her *lifeless* body was lying on the ground on the other side of the meadow from where they had fled, he'd taken her to hide deep inside their realm so that no one could find them.

Only when they were safe and far away from Morgen's reach did he finally explain what had happened on her arrival to the fey realm.

"*I* was supposed to die for you, Eddie. To make up for what I'd done to you and Illarion." Sobs had racked him. "But she didn't give me a chance to make it right." A tear had slid down his cheek. When he spoke, his voice had broken on a sob. "That was our mother just then. She cast me out of your body at the last minute and took my place when they attacked. She's the one they killed in your body."

Edilyn had started after her, but he'd stopped her.

"It's too late. She's gone."

"Nay! I want to see her!"

Clearing his throat, he'd gathered her into his arms. "I know and I'm so sorry. All of this is my fault. But if you go back now, they'll kill you and undo her sacrifice."

She would have been angrier at him had he not been trying to make amends, but it was hard to fault him when his heart had been in the right place.

Instead, they'd reconnected after that day as he taught her the powers of their people.

Now . . .

She watched him assume Illarion's human body. "Virag?"

He arched a questioning brow.

"Stay safe, my brother."

A slow smile spread across his face. "And you." With a grand flourish, he took his cloak from his shoulders and wrapped it around hers.

She kissed his cheek, then went to her slumbering dragon. As gently as she could, she shook him awake. "Come, my lord. We should bathe." Glancing around to make sure the guards didn't stir, she pulled Illarion to the bathroom.

But the moment he saw Virag in his body, he hissed. *What treachery is this?*

Edilyn pushed Virag from the bathroom into the bed chambers, then turned to face Illarion. "No trick. I'm getting you out of here."

An even deeper rage darkened his steel eyes. *You're casting me out?*

Anguished pain sliced through her as she cupped his cheek in her palm. "Nay, my love! I'll be with you, but you can't stay here any longer. It's killing you and I can't watch you suffer another minute." She quickly conjured clothes for him, then took Virag's cloak from her body, and handed it to him, intending to help him dress. She placed his hands over the small stack and met his gaze. "We have to get you to a place where you thrive again."

But as she started to put the pants on him, Illarion stopped her. "Fetch your brother, Edilyn."

She froze at the deep, rich sound of a voice she'd never heard before. "You spoke?"

He didn't answer. At least not with words. Rather, his skin darkened to a rich, deep caramel as his eyes faded to white. Running across his body like a flowing river, a spiraling black tattoo appeared to form an intricate and beautiful thorny pattern. It even marked his face, bisecting each cheek and across his forehead.

"Illarion?"

He kissed her lips tenderly, then stepped back to pull his hair into a ponytail that he secured with a leather tie. "Get your brother, Addie. We must move quickly."

At the door, she glanced back and realized that the pattern over his flesh wasn't really random. It actually formed the image of a dragon that scaled the entire length of his body. And it was the beast's thorny tail that covered Illarion's face.

Unsure of what that meant or why it marked him, she went to get Virag.

At first, he protested.

"You need to come see something," she breathed insistently. "And stop arguing."

Finally, he obeyed.

The moment he entered the bathroom, he staggered back at the unholy sight of Illarion's new appearance.

Illarion stood there, not wearing the clothes she'd conjured, but dressed in black leather battle armor that looked as much like a dragon's body as his real form. The marks on his face were more pronounced now. His colorless eyes searing with their intensity.

"What did you do to your dragon, little sister?"

Illarion pulled something from the pocket of Virag's cloak. "Who is responsible for this?"

Edilyn had no idea what the small peach object was in his hand. Yet she wasn't willing to betray her brother, either. So she said nothing.

Virag, however, snorted. "Thought you might need it back to protect my sister."

She scowled at him. "What is it?"

Illarion's gaze softened. "My dragonstone that he stole on the day we met."

Her jaw went slack. "I don't understand . . . it healed your voice? How?"

With an incredibly handsome scowl, he nodded. "They're incredibly fickle things that heal from the heart of the one who carries them."

"I don't understand."

"My brothers' concerns were always for my life. So the stone healed my health alone." Illarion closed the distance between them so that he could cup her face in his hands. Tenderness creased his brow as he smiled down at her. "If I had any doubt that you are my Edilyn, this ended it. . . . While my brothers sought only to keep me alive, you wanted to make me whole again."

Tears blurred her vision. "Always."

The love in his eyes burned her to the depth of her soul, especially when he held up his palm and she saw the last thing she'd ever expected to see again.

His mating mark.

Gasping, she turned her palm over . . . and there it was. Back where Savitar had placed it.

Happiness flooded her and with it came a tidal wave of tears.

"You didn't just repair my voice, Edilyn. You unbound all the powers Dagon had blocked when he tampered with my bloodline. After all, I wasn't just a drakomai, I was a demigod first." With a precious smile, Illarion kissed her, then stepped back to clap Virag on the arm. "You ready to get out of here, old man?"

He snorted. "I don't think they're going to let us go."

Illarion winked at him. "Don't think they can stop us."

Virag cast a skeptical grimace to Edilyn. "He does know those are gallu demons out there, right?"

"Cast from the same lilitu demons that birthed and suckled me." Illarion winked at Virag. "Your mother may have been a kikimora . . . but my mother was the soul-sucking, blood-drinking badass bitch of the demon world—" He wrinkled his nose before he unfurled a set of black wings from his back—"Who got busy with a god of war. You really think that whiny sun boy and his band of B-grade horror movie rejects out there concern me?"

Virag leaned forward to whisper, "For the record, they *do* concern me."

"Then stay behind me and guard your sister's back."

When Illarion started for the door, Edilyn pulled him to a stop. "What are you doing?"

"Leaving."

"Shouldn't we—"

"I don't slink out back doors, my rose."

Virag gaped. "Uh, for the record? I do."

Illarion snorted at him before he threw open the temple doors and attempted to leave.

Only to discover they couldn't teleport out of this realm. They were stuck here on Olympus.

Now there was something Illarion hadn't planned on.

Damn you, Apollo. The worthless bastard had the whole of Olympus locked down.

Furious, Illarion left their hall to travel to Apollo's temple on the hill.

Edilyn exchanged a concerned frown with her brother as they struggled to keep up with his long, furious strides. "Not sure I should have woken him up."

"Yeah, you think?"

But there was no stopping Illarion. The dragon was out for blood and determined to leave.

As soon as he reached the steps of Apollo's sacred home, he used his powers to blast the huge golden doors from their hinges. He took the marble stairs two at a time and strode through the entrance to confront the god in the main hall.

Apollo came off his throne with a resounding curse.

"Knock, knock," Illarion said boldly.

Apollo glared at him as if he were the stupidest creature to ever live. "Have you lost your mind?"

"No. Just my temper." Illarion drew to a stop before Apollo's throne. "Let me go. Now!"

Arching a brow, Apollo stared aghast. "I think you've forgotten who it is you're talking to, little dragon. What I can do to you—" his gaze went to Edilyn as she came to rest behind Illarion "—and what you love."

Before she could blink, Apollo sent a blast for her.

One Illarion absorbed and returned to him before the god could think to dodge it. It landed a solid hit on Apollo's chest, and sent the god flying.

"Open a portal," Illarion demanded.

"No! We had a bargain!"

Illarion sighed and shook his head. "You're right. How foolish of me. We did have a bargain. But I can't fulfill it until you free me. Now open a fucking portal!"

Apollo pushed himself to his feet. "Fine, but your woman stays here."

"No," Illarion said in a firm tone.

Scoffing, Apollo arched his brow. "No?"

"Are you losing your hearing in your old age? Hell . . . no. I don't trust you. But I am a dragon of honor. I will return with what I promised you. You can trust in that."

From the shadows, Kessar came at Illarion's back.

Illarion caught the demon and flipped him to the ground. His serrated teeth emerged as he tried to bite him. Growling, Illarion flung him to land beside Apollo. "Just don't even . . ."

"You better return, dragon!" Apollo growled in warning.

Illarion gave Edilyn a grin over his shoulder that was absolutely chilling before he winked and the responded to his uncle's warning in the most nonchalant of tones. "As I said, dear uncle, you have my word."

With an irritated growl, Apollo opened a portal.

Taking her hand and kissing her knuckles, Illarion led them from Olympus back to Hybrasil.

In the main cavern of his home, he reluctantly let go of Edilyn's hand. "Watch your brother. He takes anything else, I'm going to eat him."

Virag held his hands up in surrender. "No worries. Though to be honest, I *was* expecting you to feed me to the demons on Olympus."

Illarion grinned. "Thought crossed my mind. Now if you'll excuse me, I have a promise to keep."

Gasping, Edilyn grabbed his arm to stop him. "You can't turn the Spartoi over to them. Have you any idea what they'll do with them?"

"If I don't, they'll take you from me again. And that I can *never* allow."

"Illarion—"

"You've already been ripped from my arms once, Addie. No one and nothing will ever do that again. Besides, don't you trust me?"

"Aye, but—"

"No *buts*." He kissed her cheek tenderly, then whispered in her ear, "Have faith."

Closing her eyes, she gave him one last hug and savored the way he felt in her arms. "You better stay safe."

"And you."

Edilyn watched as Illarion headed for the cavern where he kept his most valuable treasures. Her stomach cramped and heaved at the thought of his handing over something so dangerous to the likes of Apollo and Kessar.

"He's not *really* going to do this, is he?" Virag asked with the same grimace on his face that she felt in her heart.

But as Illarion came out with the Spartoi chest in his hands, she knew the answer. He fully intended to keep his word to the Greek god.

And there was nothing she could do.

Or was there?

28

The moment Illarion returned to Olympus, he cursed at his receiving line.

Acheron stood waiting, along with his twin brother Styxx, and Artemis, and of course Max, Blaise, and Falcyn.

Did the ancient Atlantean Dark-Hunter really think he could stop him? Never mind the rest of them.

There wasn't enough badass in existence to

come between him and his Edilyn. All this was doing was wasting his time and pissing him off.

Illarion shook his head at the group. "What are you doing, Acheron?"

"We can't allow you to surrender your father's army to Apollo."

Artemis nodded in agreement. "You've no idea how psychotic my brother is. Once the dog escapes the sack, there's no way back."

Illarion scowled at her nonsensical words while Acheron groaned out loud.

"Let the cat . . . out of the bag, Artie." He passed an irritated grimace at her.

Styxx scratched his chin. "I don't know, brother. Her metaphor actually worked this time."

"Please, don't encourage her."

"Anyway," Max said, stepping closer. "Edilyn told me what you have planned. We can't let you do this."

"You can't stop me. None of you can."

Falcyn scowled at him. "When did you get your voice back?"

Illarion sighed and attempted to move past them. "Completely irrelevant."

"And so are all of you." Apollo appeared behind Illarion.

Along with an army of demons.

Illarion's group tensed for battle, but he held his hand out to stay them from the fight. "We don't need for this to escalate to violence."

"Of course we do!" Artemis sneered.

Apollo glared at his sister. "You were always a traitorous whore."

"Taught it from you."

Acheron sighed. "Learned, Artie . . . learned."

"Whatever," she growled. "Can someone kill that bastard already and absorb his powers? Aren't you both Chthonians?" she sneered at Acheron and Styxx.

Falcyn snorted as he raked a disgusted sneer over Apollo's body. "Who needs or wants that indigestion?"

Ignoring them, Illarion pulled out a small red cloth that held the Spartoi.

Apollo's eyes widened with greed. "So you are a dragon of your word."

"Told you I was."

"Illarion!" Max started forward only to learn that Illarion had placed a force field around them to keep them from interfering.

Acheron blasted the shield, but not even he could break through it.

All his efforts did were strengthen the shield and Illarion's powers.

Apollo held his hand out. "Give me the Spartoi and you can go."

"No problem." Illarion closed the distance between them and held the cloth out to Apollo.

When the god reached for it, Illarion let go instantly, and the seeds fell to the ground.

Grimacing in disgust, Apollo bent to retrieve them. But before he could, two huge warriors sprang up in full armor, ready to battle.

They turned to face Illarion, who continued to eye Apollo. "I told you that you were to never threaten what I love. For I am drakomai. No one ever hurts what comes under my protection or takes from me with impunity. And you damn sure don't collar me without feeling my wrath." He dragged his gaze from Apollo to the Spartoi—who could only be commanded by the one who planted them and by a son of Ares. "Have fun, boys. Clean house."

And with that, Illarion turned his back on them and headed for his real friends and family.

As he drew near, Illarion smirked at the group. "You can stay and watch the show if you want, but I'd rather spend time with my dragonswan. Later."

And with those parting words, he vanished to return to Hybrasil.

Acheron stood in total stupefaction as Apollo screamed like a schoolgirl at a concert and ran from the Spartoi who set out after every demon on Olympus. "Well . . ." He glanced over to his brother.

Styxx laughed. "Have to say, I like it." He glanced over to the dragons.

Falcyn grinned proudly. "We raised our baby right . . . eh, Mom?"

Laughing, Max nodded. "So it seems . . . so it seems."

Blaise frowned. "You don't think he left a friend for Morgen to play with, too, do you?"

Falcyn let out an evil cackle. "Pretty sure that's a given." He clapped Max on the back. "Come on, brother, we have a bar to finish closing down."

Edilyn was waiting for Illarion as he returned to the cavern. She tsked at him. "You could have told me about your plan for Apollo, my lord dragon."

Unabashed, he shrugged. "What would have been the fun in that?"

Laughing, she drew him against her. "Did you really visit Morgen, too?"

"I owed the bitch a bill that was long overdue." He glanced around the cavern. "Where's your brother?"

"He returned home . . . empty-handed. I frisked him to make sure of it." Edilyn caught the shadow behind his eyes that dampened his happiness. "What's wrong?"

"You risked your life for me. I'm angry at you for it."

"Angry?" she asked as her own ire mounted.

He nodded. "Had Apollo caught you sneaking me out and my powers not returned, he would have killed you."

"It was worth the risk."

"Addie—"

She placed her fingers over his lips to silence his protest. "You were in danger, my dragon. And I protect what I love. So the only solution here is that you never do anything else dangerous again. For as you risk your life, you risk mine." She held up her palm to remind him of their bond.

The most amazing smile spread across his face as he took her palm in his hand and kissed it, then held it to his heart. "You're right. I will do as you say."

She laughed out loud at his ludicrous declaration. "I somehow doubt that."

But a deep, searing fire burned in his eyes. "Never doubt your dragon, my lady rose. For you alone have tamed the beast. And for you alone, I will heel and show caution."

Tears choked her. "And I love you enough, my dearest dragon, that I will never ask you to be anything but yourself. Wild and beastly. For I have seen you at your best and I've seen you at your worst, and I love all sides of you, whatever they are. And even when you're at your absolute worst, I would much rather suffer an eternity of those than spend one minute without you at all."

Illarion stared at her in complete and utter amazement. How strange life was. She'd never wanted to be bound to a dragon. Had fought against it with everything she had.

Now she gave him her entire life and heart.

And he who'd despised humanity, who'd never wanted to bear the skin of a man for even a microsecond, now would lay down his life to protect her without a single thought. More than that, he was more than content to stay in this body if it meant snuggling it against hers.

Forever.

Maybe that was the point of life. Not to get the things you wanted that you thought would make you happy. But to find the things you truly needed, those most wonderful people that you just couldn't live without.

EPILOGUE

Apollo growled as he surveyed the remains of his army. That little bastard dragon had taken a chunk of his demons.

And that pissed him off.

But it wasn't the end of him by a long shot. All the dragon had done was fuel his desire and determination to see this through.

Never underestimate me.

"Come in."

Apollo pushed open the door to the small council room where he'd set up a meeting with a petite and gorgeous blonde.

One who had as much of a reason to want the dragons put down as he did.

"Morgen."

She inclined her head to him. "Apollo. Last person I expected to see here."

"Indeed. But what is it they say?"

An insidious smile curved her lips. "My enemy's enemy is my best friend."

And while the two of them had failed alone . . .

Together, they'd be invincible.

And together, they would put down the dragons once and for all.